SLIPPAGE

TAMBO JONES

Cover Artist
JS DESIGNS

TAMBOWRITES

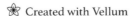

Praise for Tambo Jones:

Jones is not a familiar name in fantasy, but I don't think it will be too long before she is. ~ Science Fiction Chronicle

For a nice mid-West housewife, Jones is a sick lady. I mean that in the nicest way. ~ Sequential Tart

Praise for the Dubric Series:

A page-turning blend of fantasy and mystery, with touches of romance, action and the supernatural. A unique and compelling series. ~ Kelley Armstrong, author of *Rituals*

Ghosts in the Snow: *Refreshing medieval fantasy mystery... dour Dubric is the sort of detective who leaves you wanting more.* ~ Locus Magazine

Threads of Malice: *Keeps you guessing until the final pages... no one will be the same after this story—not the characters, and certainly not the reader.* ~ SFRevu

Valley of the Soul: *Sometimes there are no happy endings.* ~ SFRevu

Mixing fantasy and murder mystery is difficult to do well because magic suggests so many ways to cheat, but Jones has managed to find a kind of middle ground where the two sets of conflicting literary devices can work harmoniously, and she's developed her series character into one of the more interesting recent creations in fantasy. ~ CriticalMass

Praise for *SPORE*:

Jones uses the zombie and pandemic ideas of horror to create something unique, a novel of pure horror that stays away from

cliché and never lets up on the suspense until the end. In focusing the story on the micro instead of the macro, SPORE elevates itself to the level of a superior novel.~ Cemetery Dance

Praise for *Morgan's Run*:

If you like thrillers, romance, or redemption tales, Jones has you covered. ~ Catherine Schaff-Stump, author of *Pawn of Isis*

The Stone Spies Series:

The Well Digger's Son

Gods, Monsters, and Spies

Mirror/Mirror (coming April 27, 2021)

ALTERNATE VISION DUBRIC

Pieces of the Valley Series (Alternate Vision of Valley of the Soul)

A Tale of Two Boys (Series opens November 10, 2020)

The Secret of Cyprus Farms (coming February 2, 2021)

The Thing in the Cellar (coming June 8, 2021)

Sweeny's Return (coming October 12, 2021)

Stand Alone Novels:

Morgan's Run

Finding the Bassline

SLIPPAGE

Spore - (Coming Soon!)

Short Stories:

Fire (A Lars Hargrove Story)

Endorphins

SID

For Sarah
You can be anything you want to be,
but you're already amazing.

ONE

"WAKE UP," JAKE WHISPERED IN THE DARK. "WE GOTTA GO. Gotta go *now*."

Meg groaned and raised her head. She sprawled facedown in her bed, heavy, woozy, and still wearing yesterday's clothes. Her mouth tasted like rancid NyQuil, but she hadn't had a cold since winter before last, and her dreams had been weird, senseless things she barely remembered. "What?" she mumbled, squinting into the dark. "Jake? Why are you in my room?"

Jake stood at her dresser and stuffed clothes into her Hello Kitty backpack. "Where are your boots?"

"My what?" she asked, pushing herself up to her elbows and tottering there before managing to sit. *Boots? I never wear my boots.* She vaguely remembered kicking them under the bed when Mom had commanded she clean her room a couple of days ago, but the memory, like her fading and twirling dream, was wispy smoke at best. She held her head to capture its unbalanced spin before her thoughts twirled onto the floor. "Why do you need my boots? Why am I dizzy?"

"I'll tell you later." Jake left her dresser and knelt beside the foot of her bed, rummaging around until he pulled out the boots. While she tried to rub her face awake, he put them on her. "Your coat? Where's your coat?"

"Shi..." Meg blinked at him and managed to stop the word before it fell out of her mouth. Mom didn't let them cuss. "Um. The kitchen? I dunno. Why do I need my boots and coat? Where are we going?"

Jake stood and she noticed he was already wearing his coat. "Shit," he muttered, then whispered, "Stay here. Stay quiet," before slipping out her bedroom door and disappearing into silence down the hall.

Meg moistened her lips and struggled to stand. *Why is my mouth so dry and taste so nasty? Why was Jake in my room, in my dresser, in the middle of the night?* Curious, she tugged at the backpack he'd left by the bed and found it heavy, stuffed full. *How long was he in here before I woke up?* she thought as a loud popping bang filled the house, like a firecracker, only much, much louder. A heartbeat later, another loud bang, echoing, with a third right after.

Startled, she staggered away from the noise, her legs hitting the edge of her bed, and she fell onto it, sitting, her mouth open and her heart slamming. No one set off fireworks in December. *Is that a gunshot?* She managed to stand and took a hesitant step toward her door. *Mom? Matt? Jake? What's going on?*

A fourth bang filled the dark and she took a step backward again. Jake burst through her door and grabbed her hand a moment later. "Quiet," he whispered, his voice barely audible over the ringing in her ears. "For God's sake, stay quiet!" Then he grasped her pack and dragged her stumbling to the hall—*it stinks!* she thought, trying not to cough at a horrid stench like fireworks and blood—then they were out the back door and into a bitter dawn filled with swirling snow.

Fuck, fuck, son of a duck, Huey thought, slamming his thick palm on the steering wheel as the Channel 13 News van pulled up and parked beside his Navigator, completely boxing him in. Two more cop cars stopped behind the news van, dozens of neighbors gawked from porches and sidewalks, and a coroner van lumbered toward them over a hill two blocks ahead.

Dammit! Gonna have to wait this out, he thought, rolling down his tinted window to flag over a passing patrolman. "Yo!" he called, putting on his best I'm-late-for-work-scowl as the phone on his dash-jack chirped the opening for Such Great Heights. *Warren has the best timing.* Scowl deepening, Huey grumbled, "How long's this gonna take?"

Officer Joel Griffin, according to his golden nameplate, glanced over the clots of cruisers, paramedics, spectators, and filthy mounds of plowed snow, everything tinted lavender in the dawn. "A woman died, so it's gonna take a while, buddy," Griffin said. "Just sit tight. We'll get you out as soon as we can."

He moved on before Huey could comment, which was

probably a good thing since Warren hated waiting. But at least it wasn't the job chewing his ass. Yet. Huey let out a harsh sigh and picked up the phone while rolling up the window. *Fuck, it's cold out there.*

"Hey, Babe," he said as a pair of cops hauled Matt Adamson out of the house. The dipshit wore flannel PJ pants, sheepskin slippers, and nothing else. *Sucks to lose your sister, don't it Matty? If I'd been on time, you'd be dead too and I'd have the fucking kids.*

"Don't *hey Babe* me," Warren snapped. "My mother is bawling."

Fuck my life. Huey leaned his head back against the heated headrest and closed his eyes. "I told you not to call her until we'd figured it all out."

"She called me, like she does every morning. What was I supposed to say? Oh, yeah, we'll be there for sure tomorrow, when I know you'd already bought matinee tickets for The Nutcracker? Tickets I *told you* not to buy because my mother *always* does Christmas Eve?"

Huey heard a slurping sound, probably Warren sucking up the last of his morning kale-and-mango smoothie. "I thought it might be fun to—"

"Every year, Hugh. Every goddamn year you try to get out of Christmas at my folks' place and every goddamn year you make my mother cry. Then what happens?"

Sighing, Huey blandly watched the news folks haul equipment out into the snow, their plumed breath whisked away by the wind. "We end up going anyway."

"Exactly." Timberlake blared from the phone, signaling the start of Warren's cardio. "And what then?"

Huey banged his head against the headrest over and over again as he cursed this wretched frigid morning. "We spend the next three months making it all up to her."

"Exactly!" Warren snapped. "We're her eager fucking little slaves 'til Easter because you just can't go to fucking Christmas at my folks!"

A pair of plain-clothed cops entered the house, a young, bleary-eyed woman and scrawny middle-aged dude with a viciously receding hairline. *The detectives?* Huey took their picture with the phone. "Sorry."

"Sorry's not gonna cut it this time, buster. She's expecting a new back deck. A deck! You know how I feel about power tools!"

"You only want one thing vibrating in your hand, and it isn't a saw?"

"Exactly! So you'd better—"

The phone chirruped again, this time an excerpt of The Imperial March.

Aw, fuck. The job wondering where the hell I am.

Warren fell silent. "Tell me you picked them up and you're on your way in?"

"Can't do that, Babe," Huey said. "It all went to shit and they rabbited."

"Aw, Christ. Go. Deal with that. Be careful."

Always am, he thought, then clicked over to the other phone. "Yessir."

The nameless male voice from SynAg said, "Have you secured our property?"

Huey looked into the rearview mirror and the unopened duffel of prepped zip ties, blindfolds, and pressure injectors of Propofol on an otherwise empty backseat. "No sir," he admitted. "There was an accident on I-80, a total traffic stop. I arrived a few minutes late, but the package had already bolted and... um..." He looked out to the snarl of rescue personnel tromping through the snow, "the cavalry arrived."

"Fix this. Now."

"Yessir," he said, but the phone had already gone dead. He leaned back, took a deep breath, and tried to appear bored while watching the cops and wondering where the fuck the kids had fled to.

SILICONE EXAMINATION GLOVES on both hands, Detective Lester Fawkes stood in a clothes-strewn bedroom and tried not to fixate on the stink of brains splattered over the bed, walls, and bedside table while feeling a pang of thanks a cat wasn't licking up the mess this time. Three adopted cats were enough. As Fawkes turned his gaze away from the splatter, he reminded himself to pick up Fancy Feast on the way home before the horde decided to mutiny.

Jennifer Garrel, his partner back from extended maternity leave all of three days since her newborn son Noah had taken ill, stood at the foot of the bed with the camera. She covered a yawn with her fist then took another set of preliminary pics. Despite the lingering aroma of spit-up and wipes, Fawkes was happy to have her back. The kid knew tech.

The victim, Cheryl Adamson, laid on her right side, slightly curled, one hand beneath her head and her eyes closed. She'd look asleep if not for the bullet holes in her head and shoulder. Or the blood and brains soaking the bed and headboard. She wore flannel pajama pants and a faded Bart Simpson t-shirt. *Guess she wasn't sexing it up last night.* Matthew Adamson had said he woke hearing shots and found his sister dead. He was already being taken to the station for questioning. "How long 'til techs get here?" Fawkes asked as he took in the mess of blood, clothes, and bedding surrounding the corpse. Something seemed off.

Garrel checked her phone. "En route. Should be any minute."

"Take extra pictures of the brain spatter," Fawkes said, glancing past Garrel as a uniformed policewoman tapped a gloved hand on the doorframe. "Every angle."

"Detective? Looks like there were two kids living here. No sign of either of them. A little girl and..." she said, her voice dropping off.

"And?" Fawkes asked, picking his way over dirty laundry.

"It's, um, shiny." She pointed toward the living room.

Les followed her across the house to a hallway leading to the converted garage. He eased the door open to see a pair of officers searching a dresser and closet. Every wall, the ceiling, and floor was coated in dull, silvered foil. Duct-taped foil over the window crackled in the leaking breeze. One lone CFL bulb hung loosely from the ceiling as the only illumination, with wads of foil encircling the dangling wire. More foil arched over the bed, shaped over a half-pod hobbled from parts of clothes baskets someone had taped and twist-tied together.

The room was tidy otherwise, just a worn desk with a desktop PC monitor beside a purple model-robot-in-progress, a couple of GhoulBane comics, a wooden chair, bookshelves, and an old braided rug on the foiled floor. No posters, no art, nothing personal except the robot and the comics.

Just foil.

Footsteps sounded in the short hall and Les stepped out to wave the pair of forensic techs toward him. He knew one well, but the other was apparently a new hire. The new hire blustered on past Fawkes and into the foil room

"Who's the new guy?" he asked black, petite Becca Hodginson who stood beside him, shaking her head.

"Tim something," she sighed. "He just started Monday and isn't supposed to be in the field yet. The boss stuck me with him since we're so short-staffed."

"It looks like kids are missing. I need you to treat both of their rooms like crime scenes, along with the victim's."

Becca pulled on fresh gloves. "I'll treat the whole house as a crime scene."

"Just do the best you can, the quickest you can." She nodded and Fawkes glanced toward the girl's room. The chances of this being a typical homicide were minuscule at best.

He'd taken just two steps toward the hallway's archway to the kitchen when Becca called out, "Detective!"

"Find something already, Hodginson?" Fawkes asked as he turned around.

She stood just outside the foil room's doorway "Officer Lawson found a gun in the closet of the foil room, beneath some dirty laundry. Thought you might want to take a look. I've already told Tim to bag and tag everything near the gun's location."

"Thanks. Good job." Fawkes knelt in the closet and, after Becca took photographs, lifted the gun and checked the clip.

Four 9mm bullets were missing, and it reeked of recently-shot rounds. Becca held out an evidence bag and Fawkes slid the gun in and sealed it. "Put this and other initial samples in my car," he said, writing on the bag with a Sharpie. "Want to get them to the lab right away. Unless something unexpected pops up, take whatever time you need."

"Yes, sir," she said.

His cellphone beeped and he flicked the screen to see a message from Garrel. Tax records indicated Cheryl Adamson had two children. Ten-year-old Meghan and fifteen-year-old Jacob.

"Hope they're off visiting relatives for Christmas," Fawkes muttered as he called in a potential kidnapping, and dodged the newbie tech. "'Cause they sure as hell aren't here."

MEG STUMBLED, tottering on her feet and struggling to maintain her balance in the snowy alley. She kept slipping, falling on her butt, but Jake helped her up and begged her to hurry while more police cars screamed down the road and alley toward their house. So far, none had stopped for questions, they merely drove by without slowing.

Jake pulled her upright for the third or fourth—sixth?—time and Meg wobbled, holding her head. It felt like her brain was made of rocks and mud. "I don't feel so good."

"I know." He guided her toward garbage cans behind the Gunderson's place, about half a block from their house. "It's the drug you took. Just do your best."

She managed three steps then tripped over a stupid Pepsi can, her legs buckling to send her sprawling.

Jake tossed the Pepsi can aside then offered her an encouraging smile as he held out his hand. "C'mon, Meg, we really have to get out of here and find a place to hide before he sees us."

She sat in the snow, looking up at her brother with vision that smudged and tilted. "What happened?" she asked, not hearing the weak slur of her voice over the wail of another police car. Or maybe it was an ambulance. She heard something with a siren anyway, and it seemed like the whole block was packed with flashing lights. "Why are we outside? Did you tell me?" She licked her lips and swallowed against the nasty taste in her mouth. "Why can't I think?"

"You were drugged. Take deep breaths. It'll help. I think. Surely it won't hurt." Jake looked toward their house even as he reached out to pull her upright again. "The Kirkland's have an old doghouse behind their garage. Maybe there's room to hide in there, at least until you can walk. Only a couple more houses down. Let's go."

She blinked up at him and refused to grasp his hand. "What happened? Why are we out in the *alley*? Why are there so many cops?"

He grasped her upper arm and forced her to her feet. "Because Mom was shot and there's a really, really bad man looking for us. If we're caught out here, we're dead. We have to *move*, Meg, and you have to help me."

"Mom?" she asked, her throat tightening. "Is she gonna be okay? Jake, tell me she's gonna—"

Jake stared toward their house again and shook his head, his mouth set tight and his eyes glistening. "She... She's not..." He wiped at his nose and lowered his gaze.

"Oh, God, no, not Mom!" Meg slumped to her knees,

weeping, her world tilting, but Jake gave her a mere moment of grief before gently pulling her up again.

"We can't sit here," he murmured, coaxing. "We've already been noticed twice that I'm sure of. We need to find —" His head snapped up and he took a sharp breath. "Shit! They're letting him go! Shitfuck! We gotta move. Gotta move now!" He yanked her forward, dragging her despite her stumbles. Then he jerked to a sudden, trembling halt.

Through her haze, she smelled her big brother's fear, her lifelong protector's quaking terror, and, for a moment, thought she might pee herself like a baby.

Jake? she thought, too scared to speak.

He stood still, head turning to follow a black SUV she barely glimpsed beyond winter-bare trees and bushes filling the gap between two houses. It passed out of her line of vision, but Jake still tracked it like a rabbit watching a fox slink past its nest.

He turned to face away from her, and he lurched backward, onto her foot, as a small noise escaped his throat. "Gotta hide, gotta hide, gotta *hide!*" he said, frantic. "He's coming this way!"

The Kirkland's old doghouse was at least fifty, maybe a hundred feet ahead. *Too far,* Meg thought as he grasped her arm and dragged her two steps forward. Jake then shifted course toward the snarl of old juniper along the bottom of the Gunderson's deck, just a few steps away. He ran, and she did the best she could while being half-dragged across the uneven mess of a yard full of snowmen, snow forts, snow angels, and wintry toys, abandoned when the Gundersons left for holidays in Colorado a couple of days before.

Meg heard the crunch of tires on icy gravel before they

reached the deck and she didn't resist when Jake stuffed her under, didn't voice a single complaint about ripping the right knee of her jeans on a busted branch or getting a mouthful of winter-dry dirt as she sprawled, face first, beneath the deck.

Jake followed, scrambling through the juniper, his breath coming shallow and fast. She crawled beside him and grasped his hand as the SUV backed into the Gunderson's driveway and turned off.

Both sucked in a breath when a man eased out.

Tallish in height, his build was hidden beneath a police coat, but his black hair had been bleached at the tips in triangular flashes like teeth and he wore sunglasses that seemed to wrap clear around his head.

A cop? Meg thought through her stumbling mind. *We're screwed.*

She saw no expression as he stood, sniffing, head turning about and the blue gemstone in his earlobe sparkling like a beacon in the morning light. He removed the sunglasses. His dark gaze passed over the Gunderson's house and their deck then moved on. Meg held her breath until he prowled down the alley and out of sight.

GROWING INCREASINGLY aggravated and deciding the kids could have fled in any direction, Huey eased away from the scene as soon as a path had cleared and even managed a disgruntled wave to the assisting officer. Instead of leaving the area, he drove a couple of blocks down and doubled back, into the alley running behind the Adamson's house. He pulled a fake police photo ID from the glove compartment and ran a comb through his hair to loosen and smooth the gel he'd so carefully spiked that morning. He climbed out of the SUV and walked to the back, opened the hatch, and peeled up the carpet to reveal three rubber tubs: one blue, one white, and one red. Huey popped open the blue tub then took off his wool coat and replaced it with a generic police-navy windbreaker. Not quite weather appropriate, but it would have to do.

Notebook, a pocketful of evidence bags, pen—properly clipped into his jacket pocket—walkie-talkie, silicone gloves, and a flashlight gathered, he slammed the hatch closed and climbed into the driver's seat again.

He coasted down the alley and backed into a driveway a few doors down from the crime scene. He reached for his Sig Sauer, wanting nothing more than to shoot a slug right between fucknut Jake Adamson's eyes and put an end to it. He grumbled as he pulled the pistol from between the Navigator's heated leather seats and checked the ammunition. A contract was a contract and just one botched job, accidental or not, could ruin his reputation and Warren would ride his ass like a bitch. Huey pushed the Sig Sauer into his underarm holster and exited the vehicle, taking a moment to make sure no local police were watching. He let out a hissing breath to calm himself after the morning's fuckaroo. *Blend in, get what I need, then get the hell out so I can find those fucking kids.*

He walked slowly down the alley toward the Adamson's house, his head lowered as if searching the alley for evidence. A young black woman in a similar uniform took photographs of footprints in the backyard snow then walked inside the house.

Huey thought, *Shit. Shoulda grabbed the Nikon.* He put a slightly smashed Pepsi can into one of the bags, along with a crusty shotgun shell casing he found lying beside a dilapidated garage, and a hefty sample of dog shit. Approaching the back door, he took care to shuffle his feet and wreck his footprints. He saw no sign of camera girl, but one tech worked in the bedroom closest to the back door, taking foil samples from what Huey suspected was Jake Adamson's painfully tidy room.

"Thank God they sent somebody to help," the tech muttered, barely glancing at Huey with exhausted eyes. "You from state DCI?"

"Yeah," Huey said, putting a working-class lilt into his voice. "Hired me right after Thanksgiving. Feels like I'm the only sap without vacation time this week."

"You and me too, brother," the tech muttered. He turned toward Huey and offered his hand. "Tim."

Huey used his standard bullshit everyman name, "John."

They shook and Tim said, "The gal's Becca. She's primary, but she's okay."

"Damn right I'm okay," she chirruped from across the house. "You boys wanna quit yanking yer dinkies and get back to work? I'd like to get at least *some* evidence to the lab yet this hour."

"Go ahead and keep on trace," Tim said, winking, "but leave the main scene to Becca. There's blood in the hall, living room, and under this bed, but I got this one covered already. Get all the fibers you can, and whatever else you find."

"Sure thing." Huey turned toward the short hall. *Kitchen, computers, get the fuck out.*

"Hey, John?"

He paused to glance back at Tim. "Yeah?"

"Just thanks, man, for helping out. We're slammed and it's fucking Christmas."

TWO

FAWKES LEANED BACK IN HIS CHAIR AND MUNCHED ON A breakfast burrito, trying not to listen to Garrel's conversation with her husband who'd taken their newborn to the hospital that morning for more tests. Whatever it was, it sounded bad. The victim's brother slouched sullenly in an interview room. Fawkes itched to question him, but Matthew Adamson could wait. Jenn and Dan's son could not.

Garrel sighed as she clicked off the call.

"You all right?" Fawkes asked. "Need more time off?"

"I'm fine," she said, turning to face him. "I'm good."

"You sure? The baby..."

"Yeah. Doctors have decided he's got a chromosome issue. Something about calcium tracks or something. Dan's got it under control. We're fine."

She sighed again and flicked on her tablet. "It's better I work. Keep up the insurance and all. So," she said, swiping her screen and ending that avenue of conversation, "The crime scene techs are still on-site and we're waiting on preliminary labs for the few samples that have arrived." She skimmed the notes on her tablet. "But it *is* barely 8 AM Monday."

"And right before Christmas," Fawkes mumbled around his mouthful of food. "Half the lab's on vacation."

"Yeah. The techs found blood on the bed in the foil room. They're sending it for ID, to see if it matches any of the blood in the victim's bedroom, but don't expect lab results on anything until tomorrow. If we're lucky. After New Years if we're not." She flipped the screen. "So far, we've found only four identifiable sets of prints in the entire house, and one set matches the suspect. Looks like the Adamsons didn't get many visitors. Doesn't rule out the killer wearing gloves, though, and tech is collecting roughly a million bits of trace. They still might turn up something." She tapped the screen with one finger. "This is interesting. The foil room had seven flaps cut into the foil, small ones, about the size of a fingernail, but only on an interior wall. Looks like they lifted up to reveal the wall beneath."

"Sort of like miniature tent flaps?"

"Yep. Nothing beneath them, though, at least not that the techs identified on-site. Just blue paint. The lab's supposed to run UV and blacklight scans on them once they come in."

"Anything on the gun?"

Garrel swiped her tablet screen. "Positive for gunshot residue, but we already suspected that. It's registered to the vic. They're still running ballistics, prints, and a second round of trace."

Trace? Fawkes raised an eyebrow. "They found something on the gun?"

"Blood. No notation yet of where it splattered or whose it is, but it tested positive, and no word from the coroner about what gun or caliber killed the vic. We might have the murder weapon, we might not."

"What have we got on the victim?"

"Cheryl Suzanne Adamson, thirty-two. Parents both deceased, and she lived with her only sibling." Garrel ran her finger down the report. "Was a B student, but apparently got pregnant her senior year in high school, dropped out, got her GED, and never went back to school. Been working a cash register at gas stations and convenience stores ever since. No credit listing, not on any utilities, but she did collect WIC when the kids were little. She and the kids were off and on Medicaid and food stamps as her jobs changed. Currently on Medicaid but not food stamps. Never had housing assistance and she's lived with her brother since their dad died, heart attack, back in 2013. She got a speeding ticket in 2009, for doing forty-two in a thirty, and was listed as the mother on two birth certificates. She's a registered Democrat and votes state and federal elections. Subscribes to a couple of housewifey magazines and a home educator website. Otherwise nothing on record."

Fawkes finished off the burrito as he thought of the four shots to Cheryl's head and chest. "There's something. Somewhere. Even poor, working-class mommies get murdered for a reason." He crumpled the wrapper and tossed it in the wastebasket. "Any background on the kids?"

"Not much. They're homeschooled, so dead-end for anything but academics there. Other than the uncle, there's no other obvious family in the state besides Meg's father, who rarely pays child support and is not involved in her life. Jake's father is deceased, killed in Afghanistan, and his folks died in a collision last year. There are some distant relatives out in Ohio, none of whom have heard from the Des Moines Adamsons for a decade or more. Said Matthew told them to all fuck off back in '05 and apparently meant it. There's nothing notable in their mail or address book, no incoming calls other than charities, bill collectors, and salespeople. Outgoing's all pizza places, Medicaid, auto parts stores, and Walgreens pharmacy. Still waiting on the subpoena for their prescriptions because the medicine cabinet was ransacked. I've sent Gretchen to comb records to see if there are more grandparents or long lost aunts or something, somewhere, but it's not looking good. These are the best pics of the kids we found so far, but I think they're a couple of years old."

She handed Fawkes copies of two photographs. One of a cherubic little girl around seven years old making a peanut butter sandwich while grinning with both front teeth missing, and the other a retro-dork boy of maybe thirteen, slouching on the couch in flannel PJs with a fleece-lined leather bomber hat tied beneath his chin. Regular looking kids. Missing. One with a possible murder weapon in his room.

God, I hate missing kid cases. Fawkes sighed. "Uncle say anything?"

"Nope. Just asking who killed his sister. Before you ask, the lab says he tested negative for gunshot residue."

Fuckadoodle great. "Kids have any friends?"

"Doesn't seem like it. Neighbors all saw the little girl once in a while, no mention of the boy. Except..." Garrel swiped forward a couple of screens. "Kid across the alley said she's talked to Jake a few times. No one else seemed to know he existed."

"Ask her folks to bring her in for a statement," Fawkes

said, returning the photos to Garrel. "Find out why Matthew Adamson discarded his relatives, if Cheryl kept any contact, and get copies of these pics out to the news. If Gretchen doesn't turn up an estranged Ohio relative they're visiting, we're probably looking at a kidnapping."

"Yeah," Garrel sighed as she clicked her tablet screen off. "I just hope Jake Adamson didn't kidnap his own sister."

THE WITNESS AND POSSIBLE SUSPECT, Matthew Adamson, sat slumped over the interrogation room table, hair bedraggled and eyes red and downcast, as Garrel read him his rights. Since his clothes had been collected for evidence, he wore clean cotton scrubs and elastic booties, but blood still smeared his hands and cheap digital watch.

Before Garrel could confirm Adamson wanted to talk to them, Fawkes took a breath and said, "Here's what we know. You and your sister lived in a filthy dump with two—"

Adamson raised his gaze. "I don't give a shit what you *think* you know. Someone broke into my house and shot *my sister*, then you brought *me* here in fucking hand-cuffs? Jesus H. Christ, I called you guys! Why the fucking hell are you questioning me instead of catching the shit?"

Fawkes had heard it all before, the anger and bravado, from both the innocent and the guilty. He merely said, "We will figure out who did this, Mr. Adamson, but to do so we need to ask you some questions."

Adamson flung himself to sit upright and flicked his hand toward the ceiling. "Fine. Ask me anything you want. Whatever I need to do to catch the shit who killed my sister."

Fawkes saw Garrel click to a note-taking screen. "Let's start with what happened. When did you and your sister go to bed?"

Adamson slouched again and let out an exhausted sigh as his gaze wandered. He wiped at his nose. "She works 'til eleven, so she got home ten, quarter after or so. Least she usually does. I was already asleep. Didn't even hear her come home." He shook his head and said, "I was supposed to be at work by eight this morning. Guess that ain't gonna happen."

"And the kids?"

"Every night, it's nine o'clock bedtime. At least that's when I tell them lights out. Then I go on to bed myself."

"Any problems with Jake and Meg last night?"

"No," Adamson said, sniffling as he looked at his hands and tried to rub blood off his thumbnail. "Got 'em to bed about nine. It was a typical boring evening."

Fawkes glanced over to see his partner type that the kids were home. "Lock the doors? Check the windows?"

"We don't..." Adamson sighed. "No, I don't think so. We don't ever do that. There's never been a problem and we don't think about crap like that."

"What then? After everyone went to bed?"

"Nothing," Adamson said, shrugging, "until there was a loud bang. It woke me up. I was all what the hell?!, you know? Then there were more. Three, four, I dunno. I was frozen. All I could think was gunshots? In my house?" He let out a harsh breath, then another, his head shaking, as Garrel slid a box of tissues toward their only witness. "I... I got out of bed, made it to the hall, and her door was standing wide open. It's never open, you know, because she's such a slob

and I don't want to see the mess. Goddammit, I never want
—" He snatched up a tissue and blew his nose. "I never want
to see my sister's mess. Fuck."

"It's all right, Mr. Adamson. Go on."

"So I go in and she's there," he says, his voice coming in
frantic gasps. "In bed. Asleep. But she's not, she's not asleep.
And I try to wake her, but she's covered in blood. I keep
trying, but she's dead. My baby sister's dead. I don't know
how long I stood there, trying to wake her, but I finally
thought I ought to call you guys. Everything else is just a
blur. A big, terrifying, fucking blur."

"Did you see anyone? Hear anything else?"

"No, not even footsteps," Adamson said, meeting Fawkes'
gaze for a moment before dropping it again to weep. "By the
time I got the guts to check my sister, they had gone."

Garrel tapped away on her tablet while Fawkes watched
Adamson's grief. Some parts seemed genuine; the grief, the
horror at all the blood. But for other answers, especially
about the kids, Fawkes wasn't as certain. Adamson's hesitations weren't quite right, the looks aside, the way he cleaned
his thumbnail when asked about the kids.

"Tell us about your sister," he said.

"Not much to tell," Adamson replied, shrugging as he
looked aside. "Working mom. Slob. Occasionally bitchy. You
know. Boring, normal shit."

"She have friends? Enemies?"

Adamson blew his nose and shrugged again. "There are
a couple of gals from work she'd hang out with sometimes,
but no, no one who hated her, at least no one I knew about."
He gave the names of Cheryl's three friends without
hesitation.

"Boyfriends?" Fawkes asked.

Adamson shrugged again. "Sometimes. But not often. Not serious enough to count, anyway."

"Then how'd she get the two kids?"

Adamson chuckled and shook his head. "High school sweetheart and an ass she was serious about but dumped her when she got knocked up."

"You got names?" Garrel asked.

"Yeah," Adamson said. "Jake Davis, he died in Afghanistan before my nephew was born, and Chad Lyton. Scumbag sends child support when he feels like it, which is almost never."

No lies there, Where'd you get the welt on your cheek?

"Oh, this?" Adamson said, rubbing it with his knuckle. He sighed then said, "My nephew decked me, night before last. Got mad when I told him to clean his room. We both yelled, then we, um, fought."

"He hit you often?" Fawkes asked, mentally noting the hesitations in Adamson's statement, as well as the oozing freshness of the welt, while Garrel typed away. "Do you ever hit him?"

"Paddled the boy's ass a few times when he tried to run into traffic or touch the stove, back when he was maybe four. Otherwise, no, I've never hit him."

"Do you drink, Mr. Adamson?" Garrel asked.

Adamson turned to blink at Garrel. "Yeah, I have a beer or two once in a while if I'm watching a baseball game on TV. I party hearty with bratwurst, beer, a can of Pringles, and my ass in the recliner. But only for big games."

Fawkes asked, "Were you drunk last night? Or the night before?"

"Nope," Adamson said, turning his head to face Fawkes. "Last time I had a beer was game six of the series. Months ago."

"So, why did Jake punch you the other night?" Garrel asked.

Adamson leaned back and rolled his eyes. "He didn't want to clean his room, like I told you. What does this have to do with what happened to my sister?"

"That's what we're trying to figure out," Fawkes asked.

"Look," Adamson said, leaning forward, "the boy's an awkward, homeschooled, socially-isolated teenager with no friends. All that testosterone builds up and he gets pissy once in a while. Anybody would."

"Has he hit you before, Mr. Adamson? Hit anyone else in your home?"

Adamson merely blinked.

Fawkes and Garrel waited, letting the silence stretch until Adamson filled it.

"He loved his mom, adored his sister, and put up with me. He wanted to assert some dominance, maybe be the man of the house, I dunno, and didn't like me making him do shit he didn't want to do. That's all it was. A one-time thing. Just punching the head bear. Bastard even missed. He was aiming for my nose."

"What did you do after Jake struck you?" Fawkes asked.

"Sent him to his room then put ice on it." Adamson shrugged. "The kid's a lightweight. Barely left a mark."

Fawkes nodded. "What did Cheryl think of your fistfight?"

"I dunno. I didn't see her to tell her. She worked late. Like I told you."

"Jake ever shoot your sister's gun?"

Adamson shrugged and dropped his gaze to the corner of the table. "Not that I know of, but plenty of kids shoot cans and stuff. I sure did when I was a kid. He ain't supposed to touch it, but, hey, he's a boy. Right? I don't think he'd shot it but he might have held it a time or two."

"Did he pull that gun on you, Mr. Adamson?" Fawkes asked.

Adamson looked up and met Fawkes' gaze. "Of course not."

Fawkes heard the swipe-click of Garrel noting the inconsistencies of Adamson's timeline. He changed the interview's direction. "Where are Jake and Meg?"

Adamson blinked then sucked in a breath and scrambled to his feet. "What the fuck do you mean *where are they*?" he asked. "Don't you have them?"

"They weren't at the house when we arrived."

Adamson paced, his hands clenching and unclenching. "Then whoever killed my sister musta took the kids!"

"Why would someone want Jake and Meg?" Fawkes asked.

Adamson shook his head and continued to pace. "They wouldn't. They're just..." He paused to let out a shuddering breath. "They can't be gone," he said at last. "They're special."

"Special?" Fawkes asked.

"Oh, God," Adamson shook his head and paced. "They... They have a brain abnormality. It happens in our family sometimes. Genetic shit, ya know, controlled with medication, but they're good kids. And now you're telling me they're *gone*?"

His breath shuddered and he reached for his chair, leaning onto it, his head hanging. "Jesus. Everybody's gone. What the hell am I gonna do?"

Then he wept.

Fawkes and Garrel stood, gathering their belongings. "We're gonna take a little break to notify the media about the kidnapping. Can we get you anything? A cup of coffee? Something to eat?" Fawkes asked as Garrel left the room to call the Chief.

"No," Adamson said, sitting again, his gaze near the base of the exit door. "I'm... I'm okay. Just... reeling."

Fawkes patted him on the shoulder. "Hang tight a little longer. We'll be back in a few minutes."

Adamson laid his head on his arms and sighed, "All right."

Out in the hall and the door locked behind him, Fawkes raised an eyebrow at Garrel.

"Told the chief the uncle says the kids were taken," the younger cop said, "but I have to admit, I dunno if I trust this guy."

Me either. They walked down the hall. "He never used their names. Never Cheryl, always my sister, same with the kids."

"Yeah. I noted it, along with claiming last night's punch was the night before last," Garrel said, flicking through a couple of screens as they walked. "We can review all of the audio. Some of his pauses seemed overly long."

Yeah. Maybe he got tired of babysitting kids with mental problems, got pissed and offed the kids, then his sister. "He's all we've got, though, until labs come in. At least he hasn't asked for a lawyer."

Garrel nodded as she checked her text messages and sighed before replying.

"News about baby Noah?" Fawkes asked on the way to their shared cubicle.

"Yeah," Garrel said, fingertips flying over her phone screen. "Dan says this specialist wants to run more tests insurance won't cover. What are you gonna do, right?"

"Hey, it's just me and the cats. I have a pretty hefty 401k. Be happy to help—"

"We've got it," she assured him, then finished her text and clicked off her phone screen.

———

THE CONDO'S garage door automatically opened as Huey pulled into the drive, and he eased the Navigator into its space between the kayaks and Warren's Jeep. Muttering to himself, he popped the cargo gate as lean, redheaded Warren came through the kitchen door in jeans, a flannel shirt, and delightfully-freckled bare feet.

Toes curling against the chill, Warren stepped down into the garage with a steaming mug in his hand. "Hey Babe," he said when Huey exited the Nav. "Sorry it went to shit this morning. Any luck?"

"Not really." Huey headed for the cargo. "The target rabbited and I was blocked in long enough to lose 'em. Could be halfway to Morocco by now."

"I doubt they're in Morocco." Warren's baby blues winked as Huey glared at him. "Seriously, Babe, be reasonable. They're still in town. Somewhere."

Huey hefted the duffel out of the back. "Yeah. Somewhere. At least the newbie tech crew didn't give me any trouble. I walked out with half their case. Hopefully, it'll help me find the targets." He faced Warren and sighed, wishing to hell he had a different job. He never kidnapped children, never shot middle-aged men, made young women disappear, or torched businesses, he always acquired targets or eliminated competitors or simply *did the job*. Six years as an acquisition and elimination specialist. Six years of narcotics, suppressors, ropes, explosives, and body bags always handy in the back seat, just because the pay was good. And this time the target was two kids who'd never harmed a soul. Two fucking orphan kids. He had no idea why anyone wanted these poor-ass kids, but the client did, wanted them bad enough to put a three-million acquisition order on them.

That's a lot of fucking money, and, hell, he and Warren both liked the lifestyle.

Huey took a deep breath and thought, *fuck my job, fuck my life, fuck the big-screen 3D plasma TV and our upcoming trip to Malta. Fuck the newest gadgets and Egyptian cotton sheets and our marble bathroom. Fuck it all. We could live in a tent in the woods—hell knows I survived worse in the sandbox—but my baby loves his bling.*

He sighed again, wanting a hot shower and a blowjob to calm his nerves, but had no time for either. Gesturing to the mug he asked, "Mocha?"

"Vanilla caramel, double espresso." Warren held out the mug and his empty hand. "Trade ya."

"Thanks, Babe." Huey traded the duffel for the steaming mug and a kiss.

"How many hard drives?" Warren asked as he trotted toward the kitchen.

Huey followed, sipping and watching Warren's ass and the sweet, slender line of his back. "Two. Both PCs, both older than shit. Probably nothing worthwhile on either of them." He paused then added, "The client's called me three times already. They're starting to panic." They reached the kitchen and Huey smelled bacon frittata and baking cinnamon. He took another sip of espresso and vanilla caramel so good he almost smiled.

Warren plunked the duffel on the kitchen table and unzipped it. "So it's a rush. How long can you give me?"

"Fifteen," Huey said as he pulled a camera and a trunked radio from the duffel. "Maybe. I have a couple of threads I can yank before I get desperate."

Two hard drives in hand, Warren glanced at the kitchen clock. "How about eight? That's when the pecan rolls will be done," he said. "I'll send everything I find to your phone and be back out here well before the oven goes ding."

Huey thought eight minutes sounded just fine.

MEG LICKED her dry lips and blinked awake, her breath pluming and everything smelling like dirt. She lay outside, in the dim dark behind scraggly bushes, and, when she tried to sit, she banged her head. "Ow!"

"Hey," Jake said from beyond her feet. "You all right?"

She rubbed the sore spot on her head and shifted to look at her brother. "I think so. Where are we?"

He curled against a cinderblock wall, his knees drawn up and his arms clenched around them. His teeth chattered as he said, "Under the Gunderson's deck. Don't you remember?"

"Kinda," Meg admitted. The only clear points within the fading fog of her mind were gunshots and her mother. Her heart clenched and, for a moment, her vision wavered. *"Mom?"*

"Yeah." Jake straightened one leg, then the other, shivering. "Do you think you can walk?"

Oh god, oh god, oh god, was she shot?! "What happened to Mom?" Meg asked, struggling not to blubber.

"What do you think?" Jake muttered. He winced as he crawled past her toward the bushes. "That guy left more than an hour ago, but there are still cops at the house so we have to be careful. And quiet. We need to find a place to hole up for a while. Somewhere *warm*. So we can figure out what we need to do. He paused beside the bushes and stretched his hands, slowly opening and clenching them. They moved as if he was eighty instead of fifteen.

"Shouldn't we tell the cops?" Meg asked. "If they're at our house, shouldn't we—"

"No. Not yet," he said, still stretching his fingers. "I don't know if we can trust them." She gaped and he said, "I just don't know, okay? I've kinda had my hands full this morning, saving you. Dammit, Meg, you were drugged and the best I could do was get you down the alley and under a deck before that guy found us. Cut me a little slack here. At least we're both still alive."

That guy. A fuzzy memory of a dangerous looking cop in a big, black SUV flickered in her mind. *No wonder Jake hid us.* Meg's lower lip quivered. "Okay, okay. I'm sorry."

"No need to be sorry, just... be able to walk. Maybe help me a little. Can you do that?"

"Yeah," she said, nodding. "I think so."

"Okay," he said, pushing aside part of the bushes before crawling through. "Stay close and stay quiet."

She followed, crawling, her hands melting the snow beneath them to slush. She stood easily and helped Jake stand fully upright as she looked toward their home. She nearly sobbed, but clenched it back. *Oh, Mom!* She glanced at Jake and asked, "Where's Uncle Matt? Was he shot—"

"It's just us now," Jake muttered. He paused, lowering his head for a moment before meeting her gaze. "I did the best I could, Meggy. I didn't have much time, and I did the best I could."

He took a deep breath, dragged off his aviator hat, and slowly turned around in the Gunderson's back yard. He made it about halfway before he sucked in a pained breath and paused to wipe clear fluid from beneath his nose.

At least there isn't any blood. Meg reached out and grasped his arm. *Oh, Jake, be careful. Don't hurt yourself!*

He panted, nodding once, then finished his turn. He yanked his hat back on and tied it beneath his chin. "I think we're okay," he said, his voice tight and raspy, "but we need to get somewhere safe, somewhere warm. Where there might be news."

"McDonald's has TVs in the booths," she said, grabbing her big brother's hand. "The bus stop's this way.

THREE

THE MISSING CHILD ALERT FOR MEG WITH HER BROTHER AS A person of interest officially went out at 8:23 am, more than an hour and a half after Matt Adamson called to report the murder. *Too slow. Always too slow,* Fawkes thought as he paced in the break room with his coffee. No vehicle and no description of the suspect meant no AMBER alert, the kids' pics were roughly two years out of date, they'd been gone for God knew how long, and the boy might have kidnapped his sister. *And* Adamson hadn't given them any good leads. Yet.

Garrel walked in, her tablet in hand.

"Tell me you have something," Fawkes said as he dumped the last of his coffee in the sink.

"Neighbor kid and her parents are here," she said. "They're waiting in the interview room. The lab says we might get ID of the blood in the foil room by the twenty-sixth, if not sometime next week, which *sucks,* but they did say it's not aluminum foil on the walls. It's a heavier metal. Lead, nickel, zinc? They're still testing and waiting for the rest of the crime scene collections to arrive. There's some hold-up on scene, apparently."

"Great," Fawkes muttered as he walked toward the open door. "Anything else?"

"T.O.D. is about 6:40 AM. Prelim says any of the shots could have killed her, but we'll know more after a full autopsy and drug screen. Maybe later today, but probably not until the day after Christmas, like everything else. That's it so far there. Five lab rats have called in sick, so the lab's fucked. We're competing with three drug busts, two gas station holdups, and Saturday night's stabbing of a stripper behind Big Earl's, so we're fucked, too."

"Homicide and kidnapping trump—"

"Not when the primary suspect in the stabbing is a state senator's nephew," Garrel interrupted. "But you didn't hear that from me. We're lucky to get anything until that mess's been processed."

So maybe more than two hours gone and we're not primary in the lab. Christ. Fawkes muttered an expletive and took a quieting breath before knocking on the interview room door.

Terrified Trinity Jackson and her ticked-off mother sat at the interview table with a straight-backed young woman, her braided hair piled high and wrapped in brightly-dyed cloth.

Fawkes maintained his hopeful smile. *The kid lawyered up. Lovely.* "Good morning, Monique."

"Detective," the lawyer said, nodding hello as she opened a leather-bound legal notebook. "You've brought in a fourteen-year-old black honor student to question about a murder simply because she lives across the alley from the victim? That's unethical, even for you."

"It's ridiculous, that's what it is," Mrs. Jackson said, her voice tight but furious. "Trinity was at home, *in the shower*, when we heard the shots. I got her up at 6:30 and she was in the bathroom, *showering*, when it happened. And if you think for one moment—"

"She's not a suspect," Fawkes said as he and Garrel sat. "She's the only person we've found who's ever talked to Jake Adamson."

"Jake?" Trinity asked, blinking and jerking back. "What'd—"

"Don't say a word," Monique said, leaning forward.

Mrs. Jackson, however, turned to her daughter and snapped, "You spoke to that weird kid? When? Did he hurt you?"

Trinity shook her head and scowled at her mother. "What? No! Was just out in the alley. He's nice, not weird. I'm allowed to talk to Elijah, why not Jake?"

"Because Elijah's isn't from a family of crazies! God only knows what they're doing over there!"

Monique continued to insist they stop talking, while mom and daughter argued unabated.

"Stop!" Fawkes said, in his *'I'm a fucking cop and you will fucking stop'* voice.

Three pairs of eyes turned to stare at him and he clasped his hands and smiled his practiced smile. "Mrs. Jackson, we would love to hear all about the Adamson family. In fact, we're ready and able to take your statement at your earliest convenience, but I want to insist, to all of you, that Trinity is *merely a witness*. We have a murdered mom and two missing kids. We'd like to know why, and where the kids are. Since the Adamsons have no close friends we've been able to locate, and little extended family, we have to rely on acquaintances, such as Trinity, to help us find these kids before they're seriously hurt."

Monique conferred quietly with Mrs. Jackson for a few moments then nodded. "All right. Go ahead."

"She was crazy," Mrs. Jackson muttered, glaring at Fawkes. "Let that little girl play outside in all kinds of weather. No shoes, no coat. It's a wonder she didn't catch pneumonia. And that boy..." She pursed her lips and shook her head.

"What about the boy?" Fawkes asked, noting Garrel typed in "neglect?" with a reminder to question social services.

Mrs. Jackson rolled her eyes. "He'd lay outside on the picnic table. *At night.* His head was always wrapped in tinfoil. Was nuts."

"He'd only come out on moonless nights, Mom," Trinity sighed. "And it wasn't *always* in foil."

"He wrapped his head in foil?" Fawkes repeated as Garrel typed away.

Trinity sighed as if talking to idiots. "He got really bad headaches," she said. "*Really* bad. But they weren't as bad if the moon wasn't out. He said it reflected. No moon, no reflecting."

"Told you he was crazy," Mrs. Jackson muttered. "Crazy damn white kid. Any black boy saying shit like that would've been hauled off a long time ago. Only time he ever left the house was late at night. The whole damn family's crazy."

"How'd you meet him?" Fawkes asked Trinity.

She shrugged. "Couldn't sleep one night. I was so hot. Sticky. It was breezy outside, and he was out in the alley, just sitting, enjoying the relief. I startled him. He said he couldn't hear me," she murmured, her eyes distant, remembering, then she shrugged again. "He found it funny, not hearing me. So we laughed, then we talked."

Before Mrs. Jackson could interrupt, Fawkes asked, "When was this? July? August?"

"I dunno. Summer when I was seven or eight. I think." She lowered her head for a moment then raised it again, as Monique put a quieting hand on Mrs. Jackson's arm. "We had like a standing date. Kind of. Meet under the new moon, in the alley, and talk. Didn't matter what the weather was. Rain, snow... We'd done it ever since."

Fawkes nodded for her to continue.

"I... I was the only friend he had," she said, her voice cracking. "His family... There was a medical thing. He never really said what it was. I think it embarrassed him." She glanced at her mother. "His sister, she has this thing where she gets too hot sometimes. That's why she'd be outside barefoot or without a coat. To cool her down."

"Did he get along with his uncle?"

Trinity shrugged. "I guess so. Jake didn't mention him much. Said he mostly sat around watching TV and barking orders. Not great, but not bad or anything. Just *there*, ya know? The token grownup while Jake's mom was at work."

Garrel asked, "Was he active on social media? Facebook? Instagram? Snapchat? Reddit?"

"Jake? Nah. He said he heard too much crap already. Didn't need to read it, too. Besides, he doesn't have a cell phone."

Garrel noted the info. "So what did he do online?"

"Nothing," Trinity said, shrugging. "Classwork. That's

about it, as far as I know. He never gave me his phone number or an email."

"Did Jake Adamson have a medical thing?" Fawkes asked, thinking of the foil and Adamson's mention of a brain problem.

"Yeah, everyone except his mom. For Jake, everyone was too loud, he said, except me He always said it's so nice to *hear* you." She smiled, her cheeks darkening to mahogany. "That's why he used the foil. Except when he was talking to me."

"When did you last talk to him?"

"Night before last. New moon. We sat at the picnic table in the Morris's back yard. Over by their snowman."

Mrs. Jackson blinked and scowled, but said nothing.

"What did you talk about?"

"Nothing, really. School, siblings, TV. Regular stuff." She paused, moistening her lips and collecting herself before returning her dark gaze to Fawkes.

Fawkes had seen many deflective statements before and saw no reason to tolerate one now. "Did you have a romantic relationship with Jake Adamson?"

Disgust snarled Trinity's face. "Not like you think. We'd hold hands sometimes and talk. Just talk. Other than a goodnight kiss sometimes before I had to go home. That's it. So put your filthy thoughts back in your head."

"Did he say anything unusual the last time you talked?"

"Not, really. We just talked about whatever." She took a shaky breath and composed herself. "But he sighed once and mumbled, *I keep telling her but she won't listen. She won't listen.* When I asked him about it, he just shrugged and asked about my music class."

Garrel showed Fawkes her tablet with one sentence typed on the screen, *Did Jake get pissed and kill his mother?* then pulled it away again.

"Who's 'she'?" Fawkes asked.

"I don't know. He never said, even when I asked. He didn't talk much, really. He mostly wanted to listen to me."

"You're thinking that weird boy shot his mother, aren't you?" Mrs. Jacobsen asked, standing despite Monique's hand on her arm. "The same weird boy who kissed my baby girl. Is he gonna show up at her school and start shooting there, too?"

"He didn't shoot his mom or anybody!" Trinity threw back. "Wouldn't! He's a nice guy and he loved his mom. Needed her."

"Why do you say he wouldn't?" Fawkes asked.

"Because she's his mom and he loved her," she replied, staring the detective in the eye. "And because he couldn't hear her, either. He *really* liked that. *No way* he'd kill his mom. He said she was the only silence in the house."

SHARING the same bench seat at the back of the bus, Meg leaned away from Jake and stared at her hands while he pressed himself into the corner and took heavy, shaky breaths. The few other passengers—folks on their way to work, Meg guessed—didn't seem to notice two nervous kids in the back.

A young guy stood waiting at a bus stop far ahead and Meg watched him with growing hope. *Maybe I can—*

"Don't," Jake said, eyes still closed, the bus not yet slowing. "It's not safe."

I'm not sure if you're safe, she thought, dragging her gaze from the bus stop coming ever closer.

"I'm your brother," he said, his voice soft and assuring despite the tinge of pain within it. "It's my job to protect you."

"What about Mom and Matt?" she whispered, her throat trembling. "Are they—" The bus eased to a stop and she choked back the heavy thickness in her chest. *Are they both dead?*

The bus door opened. "Don't think about that," Jake said, a low moan escaping his throat. His hand clenched, gripping his thigh, squeezing, when the young guy climbed in and showed his bus pass. "We can't fix it, can't stop it, all we can do..."

He let his breath out as the door closed again, and a trickle of clear fluid flecked with blood leaked from his right nostril. "All we can do is run. At least until we figure out what's going on and find a safe place to hide."

Crap. Jake, she thought as she opened her backpack and pulled out a pair of socks. She daubed one at the base of his nose. "Why aren't you wearing your hat?" she whispered.

He nodded toward the front of the bus. She saw the bus driver's face in the mirror, safety rules, ride rates, and a camera.

"Oh," she said as she tucked the sock into her coat pocket. She thought, *No one's paying any attention to us yet, so I'm pretty sure you can put it on.*

"I can't take the chance. Not yet. Not 'til you're safe," he whispered.

But how can I know you didn't shoot—

"Because I'm telling you I didn't," he sighed.

Then who did? I didn't see—

"It doesn't matter now." He reached up to pull the call cord for the stop near McDonald's and she saw a smear of blood between his glove and the cuff of his coat sleeve. "Let's get something to eat and figure out a plan."

She felt the bus brake and he stood, tucking his glove further down his wrist before wiping at his nose. She followed, trying not to let her thoughts churn too much.

FAWKES and Garrel left Trinity's interview to find a uniformed cop hurrying toward them. "There's been a hit on the mom's debit card. QuikTrip then McDonald's, both at 6th and University. Black and white on the way."

"How long ago?" Fawkes asked, following the cop to the radio room.

"Three, four minutes."

Garrel muttered, "Hopefully the perp decided to stay and eat breakfast."

They entered the radio room. One of the dispatchers met Fawkes' gaze and shook her head. "You wanna repeat that, Seventeen?"

"Blond teenage male bought a couple of breakfast combos. No sign of him in the restaurant, so we're conducting a drive-by search."

Fawkes leaned close to dispatch and said, "Have him get whatever film McD's has. Least we can see who we're looking for."

The cop confirmed the instructions and promised to run it right in.

Garrel's phone rang. She promptly muttered, "Fuck." She listened a few moments more then barked, "I don't care what happened, *find* it."

"What now?" Fawkes asked as they stepped to the hall.

"Tech lost the crime scene camera and at least one case of evidence bags. All the positioning pics, the victim before she was taken by the coroner, evidence pics before collection... *All* of the original pics and other evidence. Gone. The scene's been potentially compromised."

Can this investigation get any squirrelier? Fawkes blinked twice as he struggled to find his voice. "What the hell? How?"

"Apparently someone from State DCI showed up to help process the scene, then he, the camera, and God knows what else disappeared."

Fawkes clenched his teeth. *Murdered woman with two missing kids and this shit happens because almost every tech with fucking sense is on vacation.* "Christ. What a goddamn mess. Get ahold of DCI and get our stuff back. They'd better have not fucked up our evidence chain."

"Will do," Garrel said and clicked on her phone.

Fawkes paced. *Dead woman, smoking gun, missing kids, unreliable witness, and now lost evidence. Jesus.*

"Hey," he said to Garrel. "Once we finish with Adamson, send over the photos you took. At least they're something. And get a copy to me. Don't want to lose them, too."

"You like the uncle for it?"

"Not sure. Depends on what he's hiding."

"He's definitely hiding something," Garrel muttered.

"But a gun was in the boy's room," Fawkes said. "Maybe he murdered his mom, regardless of what his little girlfriend says. Think how much media attention a teenage holiday rampage murder and kidnapping will bring."

"Yeah. We gotta find him before he hurts his sister, too."

A familiar clerk from the front desk hurried toward them, "Les? Can I see you for a sec, hon?"

"Maybe we should've called in sick, too," Fawkes muttered. As Garrel sighed her agreement, Fawkes strode down the hall to the front desk clerk.

"Sorry to interrupt," the clerk said, "but there's a lawyer insisting to speak to your suspect immediately. Never seen him before, but his suit costs more than my car. Just thought it was kinda strange."

What? Adamson didn't request a lawyer and we didn't call the PD's office. "Did Adamson make his phone call?"

"Nope," the clerk said. "Been watching him on my monitor. He hasn't left his interview room."

Fawkes scowled at Matt Adamson sitting quiet and forlorn beside the plain, metal table. *He's so poor his family lived in a rattrap yet he can afford a swanky corporate lawyer? I don't fucking think so.*

"Send a uniform to fetch him," Fawkes said, "but leave the suit to me. I'll be right there."

How'd you cut your fingers? Meg thought as she munched a second Egg McMuffin. They ate breakfast behind a furniture store a block-and-a-half from McDonald's, hidden beneath an old mattress and a sprung couch that leaned against each other and the building wall like a soft, warm tent. A little sunshine leaked in from above her and fresh air trickled in where the mattress met the brick wall, but their triangular cave was cozy and quiet otherwise, except for the occasional chatter of two Latinos loading a truck at the store's dock around the corner from them.

She had removed her coat before leaning against the store wall, but Jake had only removed his gloves. He pressed against the couch and shivered, his bandaged fingers clenched around a steaming cup of coffee while he studied a bus route map on his lap. She stared at the red-and-blue Spiderman bandages covering his shredded fingertips and wondered again how he'd cut his fingers so badly.

He continued to sip coffee, so she frowned and said aloud, "Thought you wanted to get warm."

"An old woman recognized me from this morning's news." He shrugged. "At least she thought I looked like the kid the cops were looking for. She was calling her daughter to tell her when I was walking out the door. And, my fingers are none of your business."

Meg heard sirens again and she eased further from the gap at the edge of the stained and sagging mattress, but Jake didn't seem to notice or care. He didn't even seem to be mourning Mom.

Tears welled in her eyes. "Do you think we'll get rescued?" she asked. "Do you think the cops will catch who hurt... who killed Mom?"

"I don't know," he replied. "I'm too busy trying to figure out what to do and if we can trust—" His eyes grew distant and his mouth opened as his breath fell shallow, his face slack and dull, then he blinked and was Jake again, munching on his McMuffin. "They're all looking for me, not you, so that's something. And we've been kidnapped. Supposedly."

"We've *what*?" she asked before slurping her soda. "I thought we were on the run?"

"We are," he assured her. "Pretty sure 'kidnapped' is the default police setting when kids are missing. So let's just sit tight a little longer until I can hear enough to—"

He paused again, eyes narrowing this time, and he sucked in a sharp breath. "It's *him*," he said, gaze turning toward the furniture store, but as if looking to the busy street beyond. "He's listening to updates from McDonald's on the radio. He knows we were there because I used Mom's debit and they had surveillance. He's looking for us, too."

Him. The big guy with the black car and shark-teeth hair. There's no way he can see us under here. "Is he really a policeman?" Meg asked, afraid to know the answer.

"I don't know," Jake said, his hand shaking as he took a sip of coffee. "I just know he wants us because we're worth a lot of money and Warren wants to go to Malta."

He paused and let his breath out slowly. "Don't ever think I don't miss Mom, okay? I... I just can't dwell on it right now. My first priority, my *only* priority, is keeping you safe."

He took another sip of coffee and moved his map into the tiny shaft of sunlight. His hands shook, the coffee sloshing in the cup. "I promised her I always would. No matter what."

"AH, YOU MUST BE DETECTIVE FAWKES," the suit said, standing and offering his hand as he and Garrel entered the interview room.

"And you are?" Fawkes asked as he, then Garrel, accepted the handshake. The clerk had gauged the compact, middle-aged man correctly. His suit did appear to cost more than any vehicle cheaper than a Lexus, and his haircut likely cost as much as the rust protection on the car's undercarriage.

"Malcolm Grant, from Hunters, Grant, and Stanhope," he said as he withdrew his hand and sat. "I'm here to procure the release of my client as expediently as possible." He pulled a shimmering pair of reading glasses from a pocket inside of his jacket and opened his portfolio. "Has he been officially charged?"

Fawkes and Garrel sat and Garrel showed Fawkes her tablet screen. Hunters had retired two years previously, leaving Grant the sole remaining founder of an LLP focusing on legal representation for agricultural chemical giant Synthetic Agricultural Solutions, with offices located in Chicago, Los Angeles, Manhattan, and Washington. None in Iowa.

You're a long way from home to represent a warehouse worker who did not call you, Mr. Grant, Fawkes thought. "No, not yet," he said, patient smile securely placed. "We've just begun the investigation."

"Perhaps," Grant said, sliding a paper from his portfolio to Fawkes, "but we have an unlawful arrest hearing sched-uled for..." he consulted his watch, "nineteen minutes from now with Judge Henderson. Both you and my client need to appear."

Grant did not smile, did not blink, did not show one

glimmer of emotion at all. "Time's wasting, Mister Fawkes. I suggest you fetch Mister Adamson immediately before you find yourself in contempt."

"Detective Fawkes," he corrected, holding the lawyer's steely gaze while Garrel tapped away on her tablet. "Adamson is on his way, but may I ask you a question?"

Grant opened his mouth to speak but paused when a knock sounded from the door.

Garrel rose to open the door a crack, listened a moment, then said, "We'll be right there." She typed onto her tablet before showing it to Fawkes. The five words made him scramble to his feet.

Adamson escaped a locked bathroom.

FOUR

FAWKES LEFT GARREL WITH THE LAWYER AND HURRIED DOWN
the interrogation hall. Three officers stepped aside as he
approached the witness restroom, but a fourth stood steady
and held Fawkes' gaze. "I followed procedure to the letter,
Detective," he said. "But he's not in there."

"What happened?" Fawkes asked.

"I entered the interrogation room and informed the
witness his lawyer would meet with him in a larger room. He
said sure, and I directed him to the hall where he asked if he
could use the restroom first. We walked here together and I
opened the door for him. I did a quick look inside to ensure
the restroom was vacant and clean. It was, so I let him in and
told him to knock when he was finished. I closed and locked
the door with my key, as per procedure in a murder case."

Fawkes glanced at the closed restroom door. "Did you
leave your post?"

"No sir. After three minutes, I knocked and asked if he
was all right, but he did not answer, so I knocked again, then

a third time, with a warning that I would be coming in. Then I unlocked and opened the door."

The door remained closed and Fawkes scowled. "It's an interior room. No windows. Concrete all around."

"Yes, sir. You can check hallway footage if you doubt me, sir."

"Did you go in?"

"No. I locked it again and sent for someone to fetch you," the officer said, then he unlocked and opened the door.

The bathroom looked pristine and untouched except for an inexpensive man's watch sitting on a pair of disposable elastic booties, and what appeared to be a pair of bright-green men's polyester briefs partly embedded, at hip level, in the far wall. The air smelled of cleaner and hand soap. No more, no less.

How does this happen? Fawkes thought. *How is this even possible?*

"No one came out, sir. I never left, not even one step."

"I believe you. Did you *hear* anything? See, maybe *smell* anything?"

"No sir, I don't think so. Just..."

"Just what?"

"He'd only been in there a few moments, not even a minute, and I thought I heard a wet, squishy sound, kind of like stepping on a rotten piece of fruit." The officer shrugged. "I honestly thought he was taking a shit."

THE LITTLE SHITS have to be around here somewhere, Huey thought, driving up streets and down alleys for the second time. The confiscated hard drives had held nothing but homeschooling crap, educational programs, and a kid-appropriate YouTube account, but the police scanner paid great dividends. Warren had hacked stoplight cameras in the area and none had shown the kids crossing the big intersection after getting breakfast at McD's, nor the next intersection in any direction. Unless they crossed without a traffic light, they couldn't have gone far. Huey wanted to check neighborhood sheds, dumpsters, and truck beds, but cops were everywhere on foot, searching for the same quarry.

He'd noticed sprung, stained furniture piled in the alley behind a dumpy used-furniture store. A mishmash of crap, sure, but maybe a skinny teenager and his little sister could squeeze inside. Maybe. Surely they were cold. Surely they were tired. Surely a soft cave would call to them.

He turned the corner and parked in front of a tired ranch house then called Warren. "I've got a shitty furniture store mid-block just north of the McDonald's. Thought I saw a camera high up, in the back. Can you get it?"

"Hold on," Warren said and Huey leaned his head back and rubbed his eyes while Warren clicked his magic. "Oh, their network sucks, and their security system's worse. Sending the digital feed to your phone now."

Huey lowered his hand to watch two Latino men loading a truck at the right-side edge of the downward view. The dumpster and part of the furniture pile were just visible on the left side.

Looked exactly like it had when he'd driven by minutes before.

"Can you roll back, to about the time they bought breakfast, then roll forward?"

Two clicks later, the image remained almost the same, but the timestamp had changed. As had the angle of a shitty, stained mattress.

"Here we go," Huey mumbled, watching as a skinny teenage boy in an aviator hat and carrying a pair of McDrinks walked into view at the left side edge of the screen. The kid lifted the mattress, peered beneath, then waved for someone to crawl into the hole. A sullen, shell-shocked little girl in jeans and an unzipped coat crawled in, taking a McBag with her. Fuck-nut-Jake followed and the mattress shifted, falling to cover the hole. It shifted again then held still in the position he'd seen when driving by.

"Got you, you little fucker," Huey muttered. He thanked Warren then drove to the furniture store's loading area, off a driveway connecting the street to the alley.

The pair of Latinos loading the damn truck hadn't finished and three cops poked around yards and dumpsters well within hollering distance, one in a backyard kitty-corner from the furniture store. Far too many to just go in and take the kids. But maybe, *maybe,* if he parked to block the cop's view, and sedated the kids. But he'd have to get minimal approval from the Latinos to go through their discards. They barked worse than Dachshunds when something was amiss.

"Yo!" Huey called out to the truck loaders. "*Puedo ver tus muebles de basura?*"

The younger of the pair turned, scowling. "What the fuck, gringo?" he snarled, jumping down while his partner continued to strap an armoire to the truck's interior. "Here you   are   in   your   *lujoso*   car   and   your designer *maldito* sunglasses. No, you can't look in our *maldito* garbage. Fuck off."

Huey resisted the urge to glance down the alley at the furniture pile. He had no guarantee the kids remained under there, but the police were still searching and Warren had not spotted them on traffic cams. Most likely, completion of his contract hid, trapped, not twelve feet away.

"Look," Huey soothed, "my wife's into rehab projects and I just want to give her something fun and unexpected for Chris—"

"Hey *policía!*" the young Latino hollered. "You said to let you know if I see something and I'm *seeing something!* I'm seeing this entitled asshole asking stupid ass questions about our garbage!"

Huey glanced over to see the cop in the backyard turn to look at them and trot their way, while the other cops at the ends of the alley turned as well, but had not yet moved.

Fuck.

"Garbage? What's going on, Miguel?" the nearer cop asked, and Huey recognized him as the cop who'd told him to sit tight in his SUV at the Adamson house. The cop who'd later told him he was free to go. The cop he'd spoken two at least three times that very morning. A cop who'd recognize his face and the SUV and fuckinggoddamnhellonastick!

Huey grabbed his Sig Sauer and he almost put a round into the young Latino backpedaling away from him, but lifted his arm and put two bullets into the forehead of the sure-to-snitch cop instead.

Then he floored it, speeding down the alley to a side street and driving over *that* cop before squealing away into residential Des Moines.

"Just sit tight," Jake soothed as the black SUV eased down the alley behind the furniture store. "We're well hidden, and he's trying not to be noticed because there are cops nearby." He took a sip of coffee. "Shh. It'll be okay. I hope. He can't do anything right now."

"It'd be better if I could see," Meg whispered. She'd finished her breakfast and only ice from her pop remained. She chewed on a few half-melted cubes. "How long will we stay here?"

"Until the cops have moved on," he replied, shrugging. "There are still three out there. One's almost right across the alley and he'd notice for sure."

A man near the dock spoke quietly to the men loading the truck but Meg barely heard what they said, until one Latino called out, "Hey *policía!* You said to let you know if I see something and I'm *seeing something!* I'm seeing this entitled asshole asking stupid ass questions about our garbage!"

"Aw, shit," Jake muttered, flinging aside his coffee and reaching for Meg. "Shit! He's seen that cop at the house!"

He yanked her away from the wall and to him, rolling to press her upper body against the softness of the couch and covering her smaller body with his while one hand clamped hard on her mouth.

"Garbage? What's going on Miguel?" a different man said. Footsteps passed their hiding place then two shots rang out—bip, bip—both ricocheting off brick, and Meg felt the couch shudder as one bullet punctured through. The mattress slumped over them, cloying and heavy, collapsing their secure cave. She grabbed at Jake's coat then yanked her hands away to splay them, hard, against the icy concrete beneath her hips.

We've been shot!

"No, no. He's not shooting us," Jake hissed in her ear, one hand covering her mouth as she struggled to scream. "Hold still, hold still, please, Meg. Please. *No one* knows we're here!"

His spilled coffee soaked into the leg of her jeans, still warm as she panicked, then it sizzled ozone-stink and evaporated dry. The Latino men hollered, their voices barely heard over an electronic whine, and a car sped away, its tires squealing as it reached pavement at the end of the alley.

"Ow, fuck," Jake whispered, his breath harsh in her ear. "Jesus, stay calm. Meg, please! We're safe, we're safe! Calm down."

She wailed silently, sucking vicious breaths through her nose since her brother's hand remained clamped onto her mouth. The air stank like it had that morning, of gunpowder and blood.

And death. Just like her mom.

Her dead mom.

God.

Who died? She thought, still sucking in terrified breaths. *Are you shot?*

"The cop," Jake whispered. "You're hurting me, Meg. C'mon. Calm down. Please! We're okay, we're okay. And, no, I'm not shot."

Footsteps approached, running, and she heard radio chatter mixed with hollering Latinos and a policeman. Then other voices, neighbors, customers, other people, all over by the dock and the far end of the alley, none coming closer, none giving them any care at all.

Jake released her mouth and eased off of her, holding his right hand as if it had shattered. He leaned against the brick wall, a bright chip out of it near his left shoulder, right about where her head had been, and he panted, staring at the blistering skin of his palm.

"Oh, Jake," she whispered aloud, her heart slamming somewhere in her belly. "What'd I do?"

"Nothing you could help," he said. "You okay?"

"I'm fine." A thin line of stuffing hung out of the mattress and waved in the slight breeze. It was tinged with blood. Looking at it made her want to vomit, but she knew it'd make too much noise.

The chatter outside continued as Jake shouldered the mattress upward again, giving them more space. Meg held perfectly still as he dragged his backpack to him and opened the flap. He pulled out burn ointment and a roll of gauze with his unburned hand, not that either hand was all that great. Spiderman bandages on the fingertips and wrist of one hand, blistered palm and fingers of the other.

"You never told me how you cut yourself," she said, watching him wrap his palm.

"And I'm not going to, so you might as well stop asking."

She nodded, helping him with the bandage when he needed it.

"We're gonna have to time this right," he said, wincing as he pulled his wallet from his pocket with his Spiderman hand. "There are three busses coming by in the next few minutes, one right after the other, and we really ought to get out of here before too many more cops arrive."

He tossed her his wallet with Mom's debit card and the little bit of cash he'd withdrawn.

"I don't want anyone to notice my hands," he said. "It'd just be one more thing they can track us with. The kid with the bandaged hands."

Yeah.

"So you need to go on the bus first and pay our fare, okay? Pay for anything we need to buy. I'll keep my hands in my pockets."

I can do that. Sure.

"Good. Get your stuff. A bus will be driving by in less than two minutes. Get a transfer for each of us when we board, but we'll get right back off where this route crosses four others. It's just a couple of blocks. So, we're gonna push the couch away from the wall enough to squeeze through, then walk, calmly and silently, away from the shooting and around the building to the street. The bus stop's a block from there, to the right. Hopefully, we'll make it across University on time to catch Bus 3. If not, we'll take Bus 60. Just make sure you get a transfer for each of us, okay?"

She shoved his wallet in her jean's front pocket. *Two transfers. Got it.*

"You ready?"

She nodded and wrapped her hand around an arm-strap of her backpack. "Yeah. I'm sorry about your hand."

"Don't be," he said, sliding the couch aside and letting a blast of cold air in. "Just part of keeping you safe."

He crawled through the hole and Meg followed, then they stood and walked to the sidewalk in front of the store as if they belonged there, and down the block to the bus stop. They waited less than a minute before boarding.

WHEN THE CALL came in about a shooting within the McDonald's search area, Fawkes and Garrel rushed to the new crime scene. Fawkes popped the trunk and radioed his arrival before exiting his car. Garrel following, he walked the few steps down the alley to where Officer Joel Griffin had been shot twice in the middle of his forehead. Griffin had fallen on grimy tire-packed snow, face-up, eyes open, the back of his head a mess of bone and brains.

"My sister babysits his kids," Garrel said, then shook her head and jogged back to the car. She returned with the digital camera and began taking pics.

"What'd you see?" Fawkes asked officer Hardy, who had searched the southern end of this stretch of alley. Paramedics at the northern end tended Officer Branston, who the fleeing assailant had run over with his SUV. There'd been little word on Branston's condition beyond him being alive and conscious.

"Was looking for the kids," Hardy said, "then I heard someone yell about garbage. I turned and saw Joel approach a black SUV parked beside the furniture truck and the two boys loading it. Then the driver just shot Joel and sped off. He turned the corner before I got a bead on him."

"What kind of SUV?"

"Navigator. New. Black. All the options. The windows were tinted, but the driver's side front was down."

"See the plates? You get a good look at him?"

"Yeah. Mid-thirties, dark hair with bleached tips. Clean-shaven. He wore sunglasses, the kind that goes partway 'round your head, and a dark coat. A nice one. Plate was Juliet Alpha Kilo Niner Seven Four."

Fawkes handed his notes to Garrel who radioed in the info.

Fawkes heard a crunch well behind him, footsteps on crusty snow, and he turned, hand reaching for his gun. A pile of nasty furniture stood at the corner of the shop and he approached it, gun drawn. A stained, saggy mattress mid-pile had two tidy bullet holes in it, but he kept walking, circling the pile, past a broken, up-ended sofa near the corner of the furniture store with a sprawl of disturbed snow beneath. Two sets of boot prints in fresh snow departed from the sofa, one large, one small, both headed toward the street. More snow crunched ahead of him and he looked up to see five spectators all vying for good observational position and obliterating the last prints Jake and Meg had left before fleeing down the sidewalk.

"Fuck," Fawkes muttered then called Garrel over to take photos of the furniture and footprints in the snow while Fawkes followed the prints back to the furniture pile. He pulled on silicone gloves before lifting the mattress and peering beneath. He saw fast food mess, coffee spilled on streaked, crusted concrete, and, scattered near the brick wall, Spiderman bandage wrappers in the narrow space between the mattress and the busted sofa.

He grabbed his radio. "It's Detective Fawkes. I need a second forensic team out here for the Adamson case. No idiots this time. And have every single officer on search duty to report to me and explain why none of them bothered looking in this goddamn pile of furniture!"

Aw, crap, Kate McLean thought, rifling through her purse for her car keys. *It's freaking cold out here. At least I got a little overtime tonight.*

Her door lock fought her, as it always did when it was cold, but she got it open and tossed her purse onto the passenger seat before pumping the gas pedal twice. "C'mon and start, honey," she coaxed as she turned the key. Her dented Kia finally sputtered to life, the radio blasting *Jingle Bell Rock* but the heater blowing ice cold, unlike the Dodge Caravan she'd given to her mom a few weeks before. The minivan was warm and comfy, but simply burnt too much gas. On mornings like this, though...

Sighing, she rubbed her hands together and waited. There was no use trying to drive until the car warmed up a little. It'd just die the first time she had to turn a corner. Unlike her old van.

Dangit.

So she took off her nursing-home ID badge and tossed it in the car's ashtray alongside her frozen pack of spearmint-flavored gum and the parking lot key-card.

What a night, she thought, relaxing against the headrest while she shut her eyes for a few moments. One old man had died during her shift, three people had shit the bed, an old woman vomited up all her meds, and Frank, randy 'ol Frank, had tried to visit Mary for some midnight delight and give her the clap. Again.

Frank was a walking plague of horn-doggery, but some of the ladies didn't care.

"He does love to share," she muttered, smiling as she braved putting her car into gear. The Kia complained but backed out of her assigned spot and groaned as it turned toward the parking lot exit, then she was on the road and on the way home.

Her home.

Divorced for more than two years—most of it spent mooching off her mother—she'd only lived at her own place for three weeks. Sure, it was just a little low-rent one-bedroom apartment, but *still*. It was hers. Paid for. Full deposit and everything, all by herself.

It got a little lonely sometimes, but she was living all alone for the first time in her life. It wasn't so bad.

Heck, nobody hit her when she ate ice cream straight out of the tub or left a dirty dish in the sink overnight or watched sappy love stories on TV.

Smiling, she left downtown and headed south, past the fire station and toward the river, humming along with a perky song on the radio. She'd just pulled away from a stop sign when she glanced at her rear-view mirror, then stared, her mouth working to find her voice.

A man, brown-haired and probably decent-looking if he shaved, sat in her backseat, yawning and rubbing his face awake.

"Hey," he said, meeting her gaze in the mirror. "Sorry. I fell asleep back here."

Kate's vocal cords finally got with the program. She screamed and slammed on the brakes, nearly getting rear-ended by a minivan. Her purse flew forward and spilled everything onto the passenger seat floor and her heart slammed in time with the dippy pop tune on the radio.

"What... What the *hell* are you doing in my car?!" She panted, hands clenched on the steering wheel and her gaze still riveted on the mirror.

The minivan surged past her, its driver and passenger flipping her the bird.

"I just wanted to get out of the cold for a few minutes," the freaking stranger in her car said. "I saw the blanket back here and the door was unlocked. I was gonna warm up then go on my way, no harm, no foul, but," he rubbed his face again and gave her a sad smile. "I must've fallen asleep. Sorry about that."

"You're sorry about breaking into my car?!"

"I didn't break in. It was unlocked. Like I said, I saw your blanket and just wanted to get out of the cold—"

"I always lock my car!"

"Really? The back door was unlocked, otherwise I couldn't have got in. This is a very nice blanket by the way."

"It's a quilt," she snapped. "And I think you need to leave."

"Oh! A quilt?" He glanced down and said, "Did you make it? It's lovely."

"Please get out of my car. I don't let strangers in my car."

"Oh. Well, hi. I'm Matt, Matt Adamson," he said, extending his hand. "And you are?"

"Kate," she said, cussing at herself as she started to reach for his hand.

His brow furrowed. "Didn't you use to work for Manpower? Or maybe someplace that used day labor?"

"Yeah," she said, squinting at him. "A long time ago. I work full time now."

He snapped his fingers and grinned. "Thought I recognized you! Action Warehouse. You were one of the gals packing boxes—"

Ah! Now I remember. "And you pulled a pallet jack, right? Spiderman t-shirt?"

"Yeah! Nice to see you again, and congrats on the full-time work."

"Thanks," she said, accepting his handshake, then she clenched her fist and put her hand back on the steering wheel. "You still need to get out of my car."

"Okay," he sighed, looking around. She'd stopped on a snowy stretch of road with an empty little league park on one side and houses on the other. "Let me be honest with you for a moment."

Kate wanted to bang her head on the steering wheel. "Oh, gawd. I have a crazy man in my car."

"I'm not crazy. I don't see anywhere to go around here, and, well, it's really cold out there and I don't have shoes."

This time she turned her head to look at him. "It's late December! Almost Christmas! Why don't you have shoes?!"

"It's, well..." he sighed and rubbed his eyes. "It's been a really long morning but, basically, someone shot my sister and, since we share a house... *shared* a house... Shit." He rubbed his eyes again. "And, well, her kids are missing, and everything's all sideways, you know? I'm not thinking right, I guess. Anyway, I had to talk to the cops, right, and they took all of my clothes to rule me out as a suspect, even my shoes. But I left the police station before I remembered I needed my stuff back, it's been that kind of day and, well, I found your car and here we are."

She stared at him. *"What?"*

He frowned and tried again. "My sister's been murdered, my niece and nephew are missing, and the cops have my shoes."

"Are you the guy on TV?" she asked, finally recognizing him. "From that house? On the north side? The little one?"

The nursing home residents had been riveted watching news of the holiday murder/kidnapping on TV.

"Probably," he said, shrugging. "There were news crews there. Look, if you could please take me somewhere warm, I'll get out of your hair."

Yeah, it's him, she thought, her grip on the steering wheel relaxing. The guy whose sister was murdered by her son. "You were in your pajamas, right? You looked like you were in shock."

"I'm sure I did. I woke up, found my sister dead, and called the cops. I didn't find out my niece and nephew were missing until I was at the police station."

Sorrow ached in her chest and forehead. "Wow. That's *awful.*"

"That's an understatement," he sighed. "I really am sorry I fell asleep in your car and scared you, but can you give me a lift to somewhere warm?" He managed a sad smile. "Please?"

He looked pitiful. Like a lost puppy.

And I'm a sucker for puppies, she thought. "Aw, hell," Kate mumbled under her breath before turning back to her steering wheel. "I guess I can help you out."

"WHERE ARE THEY, WARREN?" Huey asked, slipping into traffic on the freeway.

"I don't know yet," Warren said from the phone clamped onto the dashboard. "So much was happening, I didn't see them come out from their hidey-hole. The pile of junk extends outside of my camera view."

"Yeah, it did," Huey sighed. "Gotta give me something, Babe."

"Do you know how much traffic goes past there? It's one of the busiest roads in town. Plus traffic light cams, business surveillance cameras... There's a hospital nearby, a post office... that's the Feds, Hugh. Fuck!"

Huey drove, listening to Warren cursing on his phone and police chatter on his truncated radio. The cop he'd shot was dead at the scene, but the one he'd driven over was on his way to the hospital in an ambulance. Then his SynAg phone rang.

Fuck.

He wanted to let it go to voicemail, but picked it up anyway.

"Where is our property?" the voice on the other end snapped.

"Still rabbited," Huey replied. "Found them, but the area's crawling with cops. One saw me and I had to leave in a hurry."

"You're two hours late."

Huey took the next exit. "Yes, sir. I know, sir. I'll get them."

"You'd better. We've invested a lot of time and money in you, Rawlins."

Then the call went dead.

Huey clicked off his phone. "Get all that?" he said to Warren, still on speaker.

"Yeah. I have several dozen feeds to go through, but as soon as I see them, I'll call. Until then, keep looking."

Not much else I can do.

Huey turned north and worked his way back toward the furniture store.

MEG STARED out the bus window as a nice neighborhood gave way to a rolling expanse of snow broken by a few grave monuments and an iced-over pond. It looked peaceful. Open. Lovely.

Will mom get buried? she thought, her heart clenching. *How will we plan a funeral? How will we manage without—*

"Meggy, shh," Jake said from beside her, his bandaged fingertips gliding over the back of her hand. "It'll be okay."

What happened? She thought, glancing at him before returning her gaze to the snowy hill now covered with tidy brick houses and plowed streets. *Who killed Mom? That man? That awful—*

"Doesn't matter right now," he said around a tired sigh. "We'll worry about all that stuff once we get to your dad's."

She turned her head to glare at him and said aloud, "I am not going to my dad's."

"What's your backup plan, if we can't go to your dad's?" he whispered after several minutes of silence. "We're kids with about ninety dollars, no place to live, and no adults watching out for us. Mom's dead, Matt's who-knows-where, and there's a killer after us."

Meg wiped at her stinging eyes. *Jake, don't.*

"It's reality. I have to keep you safe. *Have to.* What'll happen if we're picked up by social services and put in foster

care? We're both freaks and Jacqui can only help so much."
He sighed and shook his head. "What else can we do?"

"We can find Uncle Matt! He knows how to take care
of us."

"Uncle Matt's gone. The cops took him away. And even if
they let him go or he got away, he's not... He's not a good
choice, Meg. You know that."

At least he loves us, Meg thought, scowling at her
knees. *My dad can't stand me.*

"Yeah, but he's still your dad, your next of kin. He'll come
around." Then Jake reached past her and pulled the cord.

Meg looked up to see fast-food joints and a WalMart
outside the windows. "Where are we going?"

Jake stood as the bus slowed. "Shopping."

FIVE

"HOW MUCH SECURITY FOOTAGE HAVE WE COLLECTED?" Fawkes asked as he sat beside Garrel and Carrie, a digital tech in the video lab. Officer Griffin had been dead for two hours, and there had been no reports of the kids or disappearing Matt Adamson.

"Almost every bus in town, the furniture store, McDonald's, QuikTrip, several traffic lights... The early parts were easy," Carrie said. "They caught a bus three blocks from their home at nine-eighteen, and rode it to—"

"Nine-eighteen?" Fawkes asked, wondering where they were for almost three hours after their mother's murder. "You're sure?"

"Yeah," Carrie said, pointing at footage of a bus interior about half-full of passengers. A pair of shocked, poverty-stricken kids sat in the back—a blond teenage boy in a black coat and a pre-teen girl with light brown hair and a pink coat. The girl rarely spoke and the boy often winced as if he was in great pain. No one on the bus seemed to notice them.

"Roll back to when they got on."

The film reversed then moved forward again as Fawkes watched snow-speckled Jake Adamson pay their bus fare with loose change while his sister sagged, sobbing, beside him. Jake wore gloves, Meg did not, and neither looked directly at the camera. Their fare paid, Jake took maps from the holders and followed his sister to the back of the bus. Fawkes watched the boy skim the maps while he spoke to his sister and, once, he looked directly at the camera for a few seconds, his blinking erratic as if he was crying, but no tears flowed down his cheeks and his face wasn't weepy-red.

"Pause and go back. Can you get a clean shot of his face?"

Carrie found and printed a decent image. "I can crop it out, if you want."

Fawkes sipped his coffee. "Yeah. And get it to local TV."

"What's wrong with his hand?" Garrel asked and the tech scanned back then forward again. "Something's up with his fingers and left palm."

"Blood, maybe?" Fawkes asked, squinting at the screen. "It smeared his map."

Garrel nodded while Carrie scanned through the footage. "Can't find a good image of the girl. The rare times she looks up, someone's head's in the way."

"How about when they got off?"

"Nine-twenty-eight, a block south of Sixth and University." Carrie showed Jake pull the cord then both kids stood, Meg in front, as they exited the bus from the rear-side door. Meg gazed downward the entire time.

"I have them at QuikTrip at nine-thirty-one," Carrie said, switching to convenience store footage. Jake entered first, pulling off his aviator hat as he walked through the doorway. Meg followed, her eyes downcast. She visited the restroom while he used the ATM, and she returned to him without looking toward the store's back door.

Fawkes leaned back. "He's not forcing her to stay with him. She's reluctant, maybe scared, but her mom just died. She's grieving, and he's all she's got."

"He's not grieving, though," Garrel said. "Is he trying to be strong for her, or..."

"Or what?" Fawkes asked as Carrie booted up the ATM's footage.

"Or he's left her no other option. Maybe he's using 'mom's dead and it's just us now' as leverage against her."

Jake, again, stared right at the camera, erratically blinking while his transaction failed to process.

"He got an even hundred," Carrie said, printing the pic of Jake at the ATM. "He tried two hundred first, then worked his way down, twenty bucks at a time. Only a hundred eighteen in the account."

"Yeah, I have the report," Fawkes said. He leaned forward, watching Jake wince then wipe a thin line of blood and mucus from beneath his nose before trying the card again. His fingertips were mangled with narrow cuts, leaving them bloody and scabby. For a moment, sorrow washed across his face, then was gone.

"What sliced up his fingers?" Garrel asked.

"Don't know yet. Can you print that one?"

"Yep!" Carrie said.

"Tell the lab to sample that ATM for blood residue and prints," Fawkes said to his partner. "No telling how many other people have used it, but we might get something."

Garrel tapped away on her tablet. "Done."

Carrie put the ATM and store footage on a split-screen.

Meg left the bathroom and returned to Jake while he got his hundred bucks from the ATM. They watched the kids pay cash for a small box of cheap Spiderman bandages then leave the convenience store.

"Got 'em crossing the street at nine-thirty-four," Carrie said, showing the kids walk into then out of view of the west-bound traffic cam. "He goes into McDonald's alone at nine-thirty-five. He finished off most of the debit card balance for breakfast, then he's out the door and off-camera until nine forty."

She typed and the screen changed to the back of the furniture store. Jake wore his aviator hat and examined the pile of discarded furniture then motioned his sister to come in from off-camera before opening a gap for her. He followed her beneath the stained and sagging mattress.

Carried leaned back. "That's it. That's all I have, so far. I've been searching bus cams, but I don't know when they left their hiding spot. I don't know what direction they went, or if they even left the area. If they walked off-site and stuck to residential streets and alleys, there's nothing for me to track."

"Do you think that's what they did?" Garrel asked.

"I dunno," Carrie admitted. "They took a bus to one of the busiest intersections in town, got some cash, a hot breakfast, then evaporated. Hell, maybe they walked a couple of blocks into a residential area and called an Uber."

"They could have flagged a cab," Garrel said, rubbing her eyes. "Hitchhiked..."

"He's watching out for his sister. It's too dangerous to hitchhike," Fawkes said. "Show us Griffin's murder."

Carrie ran the footage and paused, capturing the killer's

face in near-profile. "He fired his first shot twenty-three minutes and forty-two seconds after the kids went under that mattress. They might not even have been there."

"I hope they weren't," Fawkes sighed. "And this might have nothing to do with them."

"I've been through the footage four times, back and forth, frame by frame. That's the best frame of the fucker I have," she said, printing it. "The plates were random bullshit. Not even in the system."

"Get us a digital, too. Face and plates." Fawkes stood and stared at the dark-haired man, his face half-obscured by sunglasses. "And send it to the feds, every frame he's on-screen. Maybe they'll have an idea of who he might be."

"Looks like he uses a Sig Sauer," Garrel said, squinting at the screen. "Hard to tell for sure."

Carrie nodded. "We're pretty sure it is. Shape matches a 229. Hell, half the force carries one."

"Think he's a cop?" Fawkes asked.

"Maybe a freelancing out-of-towner? I dunno," Carrie said around a sigh as she handed Fawkes his prints. "Hope not. We've had too much bad press lately. But this asshole needs to be strung up by his nuts."

"All right, so what've we got?" Fawkes said as they left the digital lab and headed toward the break room. "Two bodies, two missing kids—"

"Might be two separate murders," Garrel reminded him, checking her messages on her phone.

Fawkes saw only her husband's photo and a short block of too-small-to-read text. "Yeah, I know. The furniture loaders said the guy with the Sig Sauer wanted to search through the pile of furniture the kids hid under."

"Yeah." Garrel texted a response and put her phone away. "Some craft project for his wife."

"And it was an efficient kill, unlike Cheryl Adamson. We get anything back from ballistics for either murder yet?"

Garrel checked her tablet. "Just caliber. Ms. Adamson was killed by a 9mm which might be her own, Griffin a .40. Probably nothing else for a couple of days at the earliest. Everyone's—"

"Gone for the holiday, yeah," Fawkes muttered. "So we're probably looking at two unrelated shootings. How about Matt Adamson?"

"He evaporated," Garrel said.

"And left his briefs behind." Fawkes poured a fresh cup of coffee then stepped aside so Garrel could grab one too. "So, besides him somehow freeballin' out of here, what do we have on him, Jenn?"

"Not a lot. No priors, no traffic tickets, no nothing. Worked for Manpower, warehouse picking or inventory, mostly, some forklift driving. Showed up regularly. Didn't fuck off, didn't bust his ass, didn't have any desire for full time work, didn't cause trouble." Garrel sighed. "Just a nobody who's barely scraping by."

Hip leaning against the break-room counter, Fawkes sipped his coffee. "A nobody who apparently walked through a second-floor concrete wall."

Garrel watched her coffee pour. "C'mon, you know that's not possible."

"Yeah. But we've got nothing else." Fawkes sighed. "What if he did it?"

"Killed his sister?" Garrel said as she stirred sugar into her coffee. "I dunno, I'm leaning toward the kid."

"Me too, but I like to leave options open so we don't miss anything. Why would Jake kill his mother, hide the gun in his room, *then* leave? Why not dump it in a snowdrift where no one will find it until March?"

"Because he's a kid and real life isn't a video game. He killed his mom, panicked, then bolted, taking a hostage. It happens."

Fawkes sighed and sipped his coffee. "What if Matt Adamson actually walked through that wall?"

Garrel turned, cup in hand, and her brow furrowed. "You can't be serious."

"He escaped a locked room, under video surveillance, while guarded by a good cop who never left the door."

"Les, come on."

Fawkes snagged a cookie off a Christmas snack tray. "Like Sherlock Holmes said, once you eliminate the impossible, whatever remains, no matter how improbable, must be the truth."

"Walking through walls is impossible."

"How else do you explain it? Rationally? We have a locked door, video, and a guard, all of which prove he *did not* leave through the door. Yet he's gone without his booties or his watch, and his underwear is *still* embedded in that wall. Something happened in there, Jenn. Something pulled Matthew Adamson through that wall. Somehow."

"Les..."

"Okay, then. Forget the underwear. We left Adamson sitting in interrogation. He never asked for a lawyer, never even made a phone call. Yet a spendy Ag-corp stiff shows up asking for Adamson by name? How? Why? Then —*after* Adamson's told he has a lawyer—he asks to use the john and disappears from a locked, guarded, videotaped room."

"That was weird," Garrel agreed. "Running makes him look guilty, with or without the surprise lawyer."

"But does it make him a murderer?"

"Maybe. But the gun was in Jake's room, with blood on it, and we saw blood on his fingers on the bus surveillance video. We've *gotta* look at Jake. You know as well as I do that a lot of fifteen-year-old boys are pissed-off, testosterone-fueled assholes wanting to gorge on pizza, shoot up their school, and get a wet dick. I'd call the vic's son more likely than her brother. Cheryl had a steady job, steady income, a checking account... Why would a slacker bump off his meal-ticket sister?"

Why would a boy kill his mom? Fawkes thought, then other cases, some big some small, flashed through his mind and he sighed.

Garrel said, "Where'd he take his sister for three hours before getting on that bus and what'd he do to her? She was awful subdued on every frame of video."

Yeah. "And where's he taking her now?"

"Don't know," Garrel said, finishing her coffee. "I just hope we don't find her raped and dead in a snowdrift."

———

HUDDLED against wind diluting *Frosty the Snowman* playing somewhere, Kate crossed Walmart's parking lot with a pair of cheap sneakers, socks, a pullover hoodie, and a bargain-basement bottle of Merlot in her sack. Part of her expected backseat-crashing Matthew to have traded-up to someone else's nicer-yet-unlocked vehicle, but he sat there, plain as day, dozing in her front passenger seat.

She'd left him in the back.

The doors were locked when she reached the car and she wondered if he'd climbed over like a little kid.

"Hey," he said, opening one eye and smiling at her as she slid into the driver's seat. "Thanks again for doing this."

"No problem." She pulled the wine bottle from the sack and tucked it beneath her seat before handing him the rest.

"These are great!" he said, pulling on a pair of socks. "How much do I owe you?"

She started the car. "About thirty bucks, but don't worry about it. Sorry I couldn't afford a real coat."

"God, don't be. Hoodie's fine." He checked the label before putting it on. "All cotton. Thanks."

"You said cotton," she said, backing out of her spot. "So. Where can I drop you off at?"

He tugged on the hoodie then returned to putting on socks. "How about my house? It's over by Park Fair Mall. Got money there. I can pay you back."

She paused, waiting for another car to back out. Heavy snow or not, the holiday shoppers were out in force. "I... I thought you said it was a crime scene."

"Yeah," he sighed. "But I have nowhere else to go. No money. The cops even have my wallet and ID and everything."

Shit.

Kate yawned and drove toward the end of her aisle. "Look, I feel for you, I do, but I've been up all night working and I can't just drive around. I gotta get some sleep." *With some help from Merle Merlot,* she thought, turning toward the parking lot exit. *Couple of glasses and I'll sleep like a baby.*

Matt pulled on his second shoe. "Okay. But I can't pay you back without money, and my money's all at the house."

"Then don't worry about it. Just keep the stuff. Pay it forward someday and help somebody out."

"Okay," he said, as she turned onto the street. "Hey, Kate? You've been really great."

"Thanks. So. Where can I take you?"

He sighed and pointed at the streetlight ahead. "Just right there's fine. Maybe I can catch a ride home."

"What? I can't leave you on the street! Don't you have friends, or family or—"

He wiped at the corner of his eye. "Just my sister and her kids. Everyone else is out of state and, frankly, they're no help. I'll manage to get my stuff and find the kids. Thanks, Kate. Promise I'll pay you back."

"C'mon, Matt. There has to be someone, somewhere..." She stopped, just one more car in the line waiting for the light to change, but he opened the door and stepped out then started walking opposite the direction she was heading.

"Shit," she muttered, watching him in her rearview mirror, then the light changed and traffic moved forward, so she did too. He was soon lost to distance, cars, and snow.

She drove, muttering and cussing herself for being a hard-assed bitch. Yeah, she'd never met him before that morning, and he did take an uninvited nap in her car, but he hadn't said one threatening or sexual word toward her. He'd been nothing but nice and apologetic for costing her time and money and gas, and had said only kind, concerned things about his lost family.

He's a decent guy, who's sister just got murdered, his niece and nephew are missing, he doesn't currently have a home, and I have to boot him out of the car on Southeast 14th, in a blizzard, just a couple of days before Christmas?

She reached another stoplight and sat there, hands clenched at the wheel while the radio played *I'll be Home for Christmas. And he's in ten-dollar tennies and a thin hoodie because I couldn't be bothered to buy him something warm.*

Gawd, I'm a bitch.

She yelled, "Arrgh! You have got to be insane!" at her windshield before taking the next turn and doubling back toward Walmart.

When she drove past on the opposite side of the road, Matt had walked a little less than a block breaking through fresh snow, and he huddled over, arms wrapped around himself, his breath blowing out in plumes of white before being whooshed away by the wind. She had to drive two more blocks before she managed to turn around and drive back toward him.

Slowing, she rolled down her passenger side window and pulled alongside him. "Hey," she said. "I'm sorry. Get in. We'll figure it out."

"Nah, you're right," he said. "I'm not your problem and it's not your fault things went to hell this morning. I'll be all right."

The SUV driver behind them honked, then cut off another driver and sped around, hollering, 'It's fucking Christmas, Bitch!' through his open window on his way past.

Matt glanced at the speeding SUV and frowned at it before looking back at Kate. "Go on home," he said as another ticked-off driver sped around her. "I'll get you the—"

"Just get in the damn car!"

His eyes widened and he opened the door and hopped in.

They drove in awkward silence pasted over by holiday music. "Where are we going?" he asked after a mile or so.

"I don't know where else to take you besides my apartment," she muttered, white-knuckling the drive on holiday-crowded, snow-slick streets. "You can sleep on the couch until you get your house back."

HUEY HAD hot-wired a silver Taurus and sipped a cup of coffee in a parking lot off Carpenter while wondering where in the hell the kids had gone. He'd driven down every side street, every alley near the furniture store, dodging cops and working his way outward, block by block, circling their initial hiding spot. He'd found no sign, no trace, no anything, for a mile out.

They'd apparently evaporated.

Police chatter after the shooting had been frantic but had finally slowed. The clients called every half hour and Huey muttered a curse when his phone rang again, but it was Warren, thank God. "Hey babe," he said, picking up. "What've you got for me?"

"You and Jake Adamson on breaking news alerts, every local channel. They're showing you shooting the cop."

"Sunnuva bitch," Huey muttered, pulling out of the lot

and heading toward where he'd hid the Nav. "What about Jake?"

"Wanted for questioning in his mother's murder."

"At least that's something in our favor." *Not much, though,* Huey thought. "I'm heading home. Can you pick up the Escalade and tell Rico we need another rush paint job?"

"I'm on my way and will call him as soon as I'm done with you."

"Thanks."

"It's what I'm here for," Warren said. "Be careful. See you at home. I'll have hot food waiting."

TRYING NOT to think about underwear in a wall, Fawkes sat at his desk and ran through the list of Polk County residents who owned black Navigators. His desk phone rang. "Fawkes," he said, picking it up.

"Detective Fawkes? This is Lieutenant Hicks, DCI. We understand—"

"I have two murders here and you don't understand shit." Fawkes leaned back in his chair and rubbed his eyes while, across the desks, Garrel set aside her tablet. It was two-seventeen and Cheryl Adamson had been dead almost eight hours, Griffin more than four. "Where's our evidence?"

"We don't have it."

You have got to be kidding me, Fawkes thought. He leaned forward, elbows on the table. "What do you mean, you don't have it. You sent one of your techs—"

"No, we didn't," Hicks said. "We're short-staffed, just like you. We didn't have anybody to send."

"Then who the hell was at our crime scene?"

"Don't know, but he wasn't one of ours. Nobody requested us. The Adamson case didn't even show up on our call sheet. Hell, nothing from you guys showed up today until your patrolman got killed. Did you try County? Hell, did your guys *call* County for Adamson and think it was us?"

"I'll have to check," Fawkes said, rubbing his eyes. "Any progress on Griffin?"

"The Nav had Michelin tires with little wear, and we're still running the casings and slugs. Lots of people there, lots of footprints, lots of trace, all in the snow. Don't hold your breath."

"You got *anything* useful?" Fawkes asked.

"Ammunition was wiped clean. No fingerprints, no hairs, no other trace. We're still running impressions on the casings, but the slugs have almost no rifling. They're damn near pristine. We're guessing a new gun or at least a new high-end barrel, but there are three good firing marks on the casings. Hopefully, they'll turn up something."

"What about the kids' hidey-hole?"

"There's a lot there, got fingerprints on the food and bandage wrappers, plenty of hairs and other trace. The weird thing, though, is the concrete. We actually dug a chunk of it up and dragged it in here."

Fawkes flipped open his notebook. "What about the concrete? Blood splatter? Semen?"

Hicks chuckled. "Nothing so boring. Nah, this concrete was melted, bubbled up with a scorched handprint and squiggly lines pressed right into it. It'd look like a lightning strike if it wasn't for the handprint."

Fawkes scowled. *More unexplainable evidence, not unlike*

underwear embedded in a wall. "Send us the pictures," he said and exited the call. He then called County, who also had no record of their people sent to the Adamson murder site.

"So who the hell was it?" Garrel asked.

"I dunno. But they fucked us good." Fawkes dialed their lab.

"Fake DCI?" Garrel asked. "Maybe they're our shooter."

"Yeah, or maybe it's a nosy neighbor who's watched too many CSI reruns and wanted in on the fun."

"Hey, Carla?" Fawkes said when the lab picked up. "Can you send the Adamson techs over to me ASAP, please?"

"Both of them? Right now?" Carla asked. "We're drowning down here."

"Yeah. *Both.* Don't forget, I've got a dead cop, a dead mommy, and two missing kids up here."

Then he slammed down the phone.

SIX

A SILVER ESCALADE SAT RUNNING IN THE OPEN GARAGE BESIDE Warren's Jeep, so Huey backed in, easing the Navigator behind the Escalade. He left the Nav running while moving his three bins to the Caddy.

"It's full of gas and I put on new plates," Warren said, wearing shoes this time as he walked down the couple of steps to the garage. "Rico says, with the holidays and all, he can get the Nav back to us by New Year's at the earliest. I told him Rhapsody Blue this time."

"Sounds fine." Huey settled the third bin into its slot and covered it with the back carpet. "Find the kids yet?"

"Yeah, sort of." Warren bent into the Nav to fetch Huey's pistol. "They took the westbound University bus and got off at 68th."

"Why the hell'd they go all the way out there?" Huey asked on his way to get the duffel from the back seat.

"I have no idea," Warren said. "Family? Friends? Another heavy-traffic area?"

"Christmas shopping?" Huey sighed. "Need to do some of that, too, so I'll head out that way."

"One more thing," Warren said. "Figure out if we're seeing the Nutcracker or visiting Mom tomorrow."

Huey tossed the duffel into the Escalade and slammed the door. "That all depends on if we can get these two kids to the client before I'm arrested for killing a cop."

"Hey," Warren said, grabbing Huey's elbow as he turned away. "It'll be okay."

Huey turned back and accepted an encouraging kiss as Warren settled into his embrace. "I hate kid cases."

"I know, babe, but these two..."

Huey sighed, "Are worth a fuck-ton of money, I know. But they're still kids."

"You've got to look at it as just a job. Hell, if the heat's too much after this is all over, we could change our names and buy a house in Malta," Warren teased as he took off Huey's sunglasses and dropped them on the concrete at their feet.

Huey grinned. "Could we do it before tomorrow so we don't have to go to your mother's for Christmas?"

"Ha ha, fat chance of that," Warren said. He pulled out of Huey's embrace and crushed the sunglasses beneath his shoes before returning for one more kiss. "Got you a ball cap, different shades, and a fresh gun in the car, along with hot soup in a thermos, two hot-ham-and-cheese sandwiches wrapped and waiting in the mini crockpot, and a couple of cold Cokes. Call me if you need anything. I deliver." He winked. "*Anything.*"

"I know," Huey chuckled. He grabbed a little ass and one more kiss before opening the Escalade's door.

Warren hurried to the Navigator and looked back with a

smile. "It'll be fine, you'll see. We'll get 'em, get paid, and move on to the next job."

"Yeah, I know," Huey said over the open door. "Just maybe look for a place in Cape Verde instead of Malta. They don't extradite."

The Escalade started with a purr. As soon as Warren drove off in the Nav, Huey backed out and closed the garage. Cap and new sun-specs on, Huey munched a hot sandwich and listened to his trunked radio on the way to Jake and Meg's last known location.

FAWKES LED the pair of crime scene techs to a meeting room and made them sit down while Garrel pulled up her few crime scene pics on her tablet.

Fawkes locked the door and sat across from the techs. "Most of our evidence is missing, so you're gonna walk us through everything, one room, one step at a time from the moment you arrived on scene, all right?"

The newbie twenty-something-year-old tech named Tim Vert grumbled, "We don't have time to do all that, Detective. It could take—"

"I do not give one flying fuck how long it takes," Fawkes snarled. "I have two murders—one a cop—and two missing kids. You two shitbags lost the Adamson evidence and you're gonna help us figure out what we don't know."

"We didn't lose it," Becca Hodginson sighed. "But we didn't do our due diligence and it got stolen. What can we do? Specifically?"

"Becca, we can't—"

"Shut up," she snapped. "You told me he was DCI. *You* did. *You* let him in the house. *You* assigned him duties. I barely saw him, but I was lead so it's *my* ass facing termination, not yours. Did you examine his ID? Did you ask him any questions at all?"

"You two arguing isn't gonna help." Fawkes kept his attention on Becca while Tim stewed, his arms crossed over his chest. "Talk me through the scene."

Becca pulled a notebook from her back pocket and opened it. "We arrived at 7:12 AM to a complete traffic jam and finally accessed the house at 7:26. The coroner was still there, as were the two of you. I told Tim to take initial assessment pics of every room, every closet—especially the boy's room—and the basement, from all reasonable angles. He finished the rough assessment pics at 7:38. Meanwhile, I focused on the victim and her room, at first, complete with measurements and flags, until the corner removed her at 8:18 am, then I moved outside to check for footprints and trace to flag before everything got trampled. I took numerous pictures there, circling the house twice."

"Did you find anything?"

"Lots of footprints, a man, woman, and two teenagery-kids here and there throughout the yard. But freshest were two sets, both leaving the house, both in boots. They looked like the boy and the girl's prints to me, and I took at least a dozen photos, plus close-ups of the clearest ones." She paused and looked up from her notes. "He was dragging her."

Fawkes and Garrel shared a look. "Are you sure?" Fawkes asked.

"Yeah. His prints were mostly clean, hers... they were

channels cut in the snow, mostly, or weird divots as if her ankles had given and she'd rolled her feet."

"Go on," Fawkes said.

"They went to the alley and got lost in tire tracks and slush. I think they headed north, but I wouldn't swear on it under oath." She paused and held Fawkes' gaze. "I got one partial boot print, hers, beside the northern next-door neighbor's garbage can. The alley was just slush and I didn't want to waste time wandering around instead of gathering evidence. I took more pics of the fleeing footprints on my way back in."

Fawkes made a note to search yards north of the Adamson house.

"What were you doing during all this?" Fawkes asked Tim.

"Trace," he said. "About a million fucking hairs. I don't think they ever vacuumed."

Becca rolled her eyes but said nothing.

"What else was in the closet? Did you find anything unusual in his room beside the gun?"

"Just dirty laundry in the foil room closet. Tshirts, underwear, socks, jeans. All cheap shit. I'd bagged it like Becca'd said. Found blood drops on the bed along with some rope fragments. Just strands."

Garrel brought images of Jake's bedroom to her tablet screen.

"Rope fragments?" Garrel asked. "Why weren't we told this?"

"Hey, I took pics of them and bagged them, it's not my..." Tim's voice faded and he stared at the table in front of him.

"We managed to keep two blood samples from the foil

room," Becca said. "I sent them out with the coroner and tested them myself once I got to the lab. The quickie microchip test said it's likely Cheryl Adamson's male child or close male relative. We'll get the full FISH back tomorrow, maybe the day after. I put an urgent tag on it."

"You're sure the sample wasn't from the girl?" Fawkes asked.

"Not in the foil room. The blood sample's definitely male with the same screwy Chromosome 19 as the victim, so they're obviously related. Besides, we didn't find any fresh blood in the girl's room. Possible smear of dried blood on her dresser and half-dried saliva on her pillow." She glanced at Tim as Garrel shakily swiped from Jake's room to Meg's and zoomed in on the pillow, but no saliva spot was visible. "I did her room after I finished Cheryl's. She was Cheryl's female relative, but the chip test of her saliva used up the whole sample."

"Did you want to test for something else?" Garrel asked.

"I dunno," Becca said. "Maybe. I have a kid, ya know? She's two, and I've seen plenty of sleeping-kid drool, but this... it smelled off." She paused and her hands clasped together as Tim turned his head to blink at her. "I asked my supervisor whether to run the DNA or a drug screen, and we agreed proving who the kid was, or was not, was the better use of the sample. It's good to know who missing kids are, ya know?"

"Do you think Meg Adamson may have been drugged?"

"Maybe. I really don't know. Maybe it was just cold medicine or residue from supper or a weird toothpaste or, well, anything."

"Well, that all kind of makes sense, right?" Tim said.

"The boy drugs his sister to keep her quiet, kills mom, then drags sister away? Right?"

"Yeah, maybe," Becca said, shrugging. "Anyway, I did all of the bedrooms except the foil one, plus the bathroom. Tim had the foil room, living room, kitchen, and basement."

"Just junk in the basement. All cobwebby and dirty," Tim said. "I took a few pics, but other than some footprints in the dust coming from by the furnace and water heater, I don't think anyone ever went down there."

"Was there anything interesting in Matthew Adamson's room?" Fawkes asked.

"Um, he likes girl on girl porn?" Becca said, shrugging as she examined the three photos Garrel had taken. "Not much else noteworthy. Just clothes and man-crap." She pointed at one image. "There were a couple of dried-up joints in the back of his nightstand drawer. I noted them in my log and bagged them. But they disappeared with the rest of the evidence."

"How about the girl's room?"

"Her dresser had been rifled through and I found what looked like a dried blood smear on a left-side dresser handle. I bagged the handle but it's gone. Bed looked slept in, but fine otherwise. The toys were messy. Looked like a typical kid's room."

Fawkes examined Garrel's pics and had to agree.

Becca had found nothing noteworthy in the bathroom other than an open medicine cabinet and an empty bottle of Excedrin in the sink, so Fawkes asked Tim, "All right, what about the kitchen and living room?"

The tech looked away and gnawed on his lip. "John did them. I mostly took foil samples."

"Jesus Christ," Becca muttered. "And I bet you fiddled with the kid's anime stuff too, didn't you? Even after I told you to quit playing with the damned robot."

"He was building an Eva Unit 01. I always wanted one of those."

"You can play with one at the unemployment office," Garrel muttered under her breath.

"So neither of you processed the living room or kitchen?" Fawkes asked.

Tim looked down but Becca grimaced, disgusted. "No. He delegated them to the guy. And the computers." She glared at Tim. "Both hard drives are gone. *Both* of them."

Tim continued to stare at the table. "I thought he was state DCI. He said stuff was piling up and was gonna take some to the truck. He promised to bring us back more trace bags before he walked out the back door."

Garrel slowly flicked through the pics for those rooms. "You have no idea what trace evidence might have been taken, or what might still be there?"

Both techs shook their heads, but Becca slid her notebook across the table to Fawkes. "Here's my notes, all of them. I found part of a box of 9mm shells in Cheryl's closet, top shelf, along with an empty shoebox that smelled like gun oil. It's listed in there, along with a list of the DVDs she kept under her bed—mostly Jennifer Aniston comedies— the forty-seven bucks in small bills tucked in the back of her underwear drawer, and the folded combat shirt she kept under her pillow. I bagged it, and it's gone now. Whoever her corporal Davis was, she loved him. She had check stubs and empty Diet Dr. Pepper cans and a few crumpled Fareway potato chip bags. I didn't find one single thing wrong in her room except for exhausted-single-mom life-mess and her dead body, nothing at all to show why anyone would want to kill her. Hell, as far as I could tell, she didn't even drink.

"All that's in my notes. I cataloged everything except her clothing and all of it was work uniforms, jeans, t-shirts, and sweats. She didn't even have a decent dress."

Becca stood, her eyes shimmering. "I did my job, and I was in Cheryl's room the whole ten minutes that thieving shit was in the house. So, sir, if you don't mind, I'd like to get back to work trying to catch whoever shot her and Joel while you and Tim discuss the lying shit who stole my evidence."

Fawkes nodded. "Understood. You're dismissed, Officer Hodginson. Thank you for your report."

Becca turned to go.

"At least we know who shot Joel," Garrel said, her voice soft. "Even if we don't have a name yet."

"You got a picture of him?" Becca asked, turning back. "So I can punch his face in if I ever meet him?"

Garrel flicked through her photos then slid her tablet to Becca.

"Looks like an asshole. I'll keep my eyes open." She nodded to Fawkes, then Garrel. "Sirs."

Garrel drew the tablet back to her and Becca had almost reached the door when Tim raised his head to glance at Garrel's tablet.

"Fuck me," Tim said. "That's him!"

Fawkes continued to skim Becca's precise notes. "We know. We have video of him shooting Officer Griff—"

Tim stood and pointed at the screen. "No! That's John! The guy who said he was DCI!"

Becca turned back, gaping. "No. It can't be."

"It's him!" Tim said. "He came in the back door, said he was there to help."

He sat again and met Fawkes' gaze. "Look, I know I fucked up. But I'll tell you everything I saw, everything he said. But that's him. Same hair, same sunglasses, same guy. I swear."

Fawkes set aside Becca's notebook and clasped his hands together as Garrel opened her note-taking app.

KATE TRUDGED up worn stairs to her apartment, Matt following, and she wondered what she was thinking, inviting a man she barely knew into her home.

"This is a nice building," he said.

"Thanks. It's okay, I guess. Was the cheapest place I could find. Took me a while to get used to airplanes flying overhead, but I'm not sure I'll ever get used to the neighbors."

"Fight a lot?" Matt asked.

Kate reached the second floor and turned right while the floors rumbled from the noise of an airplane descending over her building. "Yeah, fighting, screaming kids, loud music, an occasional drug bust, the usual."

They walked down the hall, Kate clenching her keys in her sweaty fist like a weapon and berating herself for being so damned stupid, so stupid she'd surely be raped, murdered, or both in ten minutes.

"My house was pretty quiet, I guess," Matt said. "My niece and nephew fought sometimes, but mostly it was just stupid kid stuff, like who got to use the Netflix account." He paused and she resisted the urge to look back. "Hope they're all right."

"I'm sure the police will find them," she said, then took a breath before inserting her key into the door lock.

Once they went in, she'd be trapped.

But he's been fine, she assured herself. *I'm just being silly.*

He's not gonna rape and murder me, is he?

God, I'm such an idiot!

She pushed the door open.

Lights on her teeny, twenty-dollar Christmas tree blinked in the corner, just like she'd left it, and the air still smelled like the cinnamon-cookie candle she'd burned before going to work the night before.

Her apartment was tidy—not that she had much stuff to make a mess with—and her furniture battered, but at least she had a place to sit, a place to eat, and a place to sleep.

What more did a girl need?

"Well, this is it." She almost tossed her keys on the kitchen counter, but caught herself and stuffed them in her pocket instead, just in case she needed to jab him with them. "It's not much, but..."

"It's great," he said, walking past her. "Kinda festive." He paused to look around the living room. "How many bedrooms?"

Oh shit, she thought, squeezing the keys in her pocket and taking a step back, one step farther away from him. "Just one."

"Oh," he said around a sigh and he turned to face her. "Is it okay if I sleep on the couch? Maybe just... Just for tonight? Or at least for a nap. It's been a really awful, exhausting day."

"Okay," she said, swallowing her fear. "I'll... I'll get you a blanket."

She kept an afghan her grandmother had made in the bedroom closet, and quickly returned to find him sitting on the couch hunched over, crying, his face in his hands, and his new shoes and socks set aside.

She watched him for a moment, silent, as the neighbor's kid started screaming about needing a Lunchable. Matt lifted his head and took a shaky breath before wiping at his eyes. He turned, shifting on the couch to look toward her room as if waiting for her, then saw her standing there. He looked away and wiped at his eyes again.

"Sorry about that," he said, still not looking at her. "My sister, the kids..."

"It's okay." Kate gently laid the afghan beside him and backed away. "I work the overnight shift and, um, I really need to get some sleep."

He drew the afghan onto his lap. "I understand. It's okay," he said, then took a ragged breath and turned his head to look at her. "Thank you for being so nice, the nicest person I've met in a long, long time. I don't know where I'd be if you hadn't helped me."

Then he nodded and stared at the floor again, his shoulders sagging.

For a moment, she wanted to sit down and comfort him, but she felt thankful when the moment passed. "Well, have a good nap," she said, backing away. "If... if you get hungry, there's some leftovers and apples in the fridge."

Then she retreated to her room and locked the door behind her.

With her senses on alert, sleep took a while to find her,

even after half of the bottle of Merlot. She woke several times for a moment or two to listen for any alarming sound or movement, but the only disturbance she had was to open her sleepy eyes and dream of his face like a picture in the middle of the wall, watching her. Just his face, no frame, no stand, just his face watching her sleep. She gasped a breath and, heart slamming, woke enough to sit up in bed, but she stared at the boring blank wall with only a crooked crack in the paint to mar its off-white blandness.

"I'm losing my mind," she muttered then curled around her pillow again, reaching desperately for sleep.

SEVEN

MEG SAT ON A BIKE TRAIL BENEATH A BRIDGE WITH HER COAT open and her battered notebook spread across her lap. Vehicles leaving Walmart's parking lot drove overhead, but she wrote and cried and doodled stories of her mom, wanting to keep them, remember them, while she still could. What soap her mom liked, how she laughed, how they splurged on Starbucks at Target, and how Mom'd dance to her MP3player while washing dishes and slide across the kitchen in her sock feet.

Meg lost track of time, of everything but the scritch of mechanical pencil on paper and the tear-soaked clump of sock clutched in her hand because her dippy brother hadn't thought to bring tissues or even toilet paper.

"I had like thirty-eight seconds to pack," Jake said from beside her.

We were in Walmart, she thought, but he merely sighed in response.

After a while, she sighed, "So what do we do?"

"Stick together. Be ready to run if we need to, or..."

Her heart thudded as his voice faded away. She closed her notebook and turned to her brother. "You mean hurt that... that monster who's looking for us."

"His name's Hugh." Jake sighed and looked away. "If we have to. Maybe."

You mean me, Meg thought, her hands shaking. *But I can't. Mom said—*

"Mom's dead. She was murdered, Meg. Killed in her own bed." Jake fished a blue M&M out of the bag they'd bought. "She'd want us to survive. I'll do it if you can't."

Meg rolled her eyes. "What are you gonna do? Tell him you know all his secrets so he'll run away screaming? That's pretty badass."

"Hey, he hasn't found us and we're still okay."

Meg reached over to grab the bag of M&Ms and glared at him while thinking, *We're hiding under a bridge two days before Christmas.*

"Come on. I know this sucks, but—"

She popped an M&M in her mouth and purposely thought about watching Scooby-Doo DVDs with Mom. Of helping Mom make grilled cheese sandwiches while dancing around the kitchen to Katy Perry on the radio, of cuddling in bed with Mom to read the *Little House* books and *Harry Potter's* first three novels, and the pack of 'perfect for teens!' pads Mom had stuffed into the back of her closet in preparation for her first period. How she and Mom had talked about boys and makeup and their special day of going to Target to pick out training bras then having frappes in Starbucks, just us girls.

"Don't do this," Jake sighed, wiping at his eyes. "I can't bring her back. I can't—"

"You can tell me who drugged me," she said, returning the pack of candy.

He shook his head. "I can't. I..." He plucked one candy from the bag and slid it into his mouth.

"You knew I was drugged," she said. "You said so when you woke me up, this morning, and again when I woke under the Gunderson's deck. Who drugged me? Who *thought* about drugging me so you'd know I was—"

"Who poured your apple juice at supper last night?" he asked, dropping his gaze. "I told you not to drink it. I tried—"

"Mom said it was fine," she snapped, then sucked in a startled breath. "*Mom* drugged me?"

He slowly chewed a second M&M. "I *told* Mom it had been drugged. I *told* Mom someone was going to try to kill her. I *told* her we—the three of us—needed to stay somewhere else last night, I *told* her—"

"Is that what you were fighting about yesterday? Why she left for work pissed off?"

"I told her what was going to happen," he said, standing. "And she didn't believe me. She thought I was just mixed up with everyone screaming in my head the past few days because we were out of my pills and I wasn't thinking right. She *died* because she couldn't get my pills until after Christmas and was certain I was just hearing too many crazy things. She told me she was sorry, Meg, but I'd just have to hold on, just a few days, and everything would be okay. To stay in my room where it was quieter and, even though I told her not to, *begged* her not to, she poured you drugged juice and you drank it even though I tried to warn you, too."

"So, there. *Mom* drugged you. Happy you know now?"

Meg wiped her sleeve beneath her nose. "Why do you have to be so mean?"

"Because I'm trying to save your life," he snapped. "I can't *make* you listen, I can't *make* you believe me, but if that guy finds us, if he catches us, he'll *sell* us, Meg, sell us to the same people who made us this way. He's pretty sure they'll do experiments on us, probably dissect us, and you know what? He doesn't care because he'll be taking a vacation on an island with some guy named Warren."

"No. Jake, he can't—"

"He *can* and he *will*. He killed that cop, remember? Do you really think he gives a single thought to two orphan kids? You need to listen to me. I've kept us safe so far, and I'll get you to your dad's. But you have to *listen*, and you have to do what I tell you to do."

She stared up at her brother. "So what do we do?" she asked.

"We catch another pair of busses," he said, sitting again. He stared at the far side of the bridge. "But not until dark."

Meg returned to writing and remembering and crying until she realized she *really* had to pee.

"Need to pee again," she muttered while stuffing her notebook into her backpack. She looked up and noticed the day had moved past afternoon and was sliding toward evening.

"Me too," Jake sighed, "But we need to stay put for at least another hour."

"I'm not gonna be able to wait another hour," she said without looking at him. "Mom wouldn't make me wait another hour. *And* I'm hungry."

"Have another snack out of the Walmart sack. I'm

keeping track of the busses overhead and I can't screw up my count. We need to wait until a couple of minutes after six to cat—"

"I *need* to *pee*." She turned her head to glare at her brother who shivered a few feet away, knees up and arms squeezed around him.

"Can't you just pee down there by the cree—"

"Where someone on the bridge might see?? Eeew. No!" She stood and pulled her backpack over her shoulder. "There's a Burger King *right over there*," she said, pointing. "Like a hundred feet up the hill. I'll run over there, pee, maybe grab us some burgers, and be right back."

"You *can't*," he said. "It's still light out and *he's* across the parking lot, by B-Bops, watching for us. *Looking* for us."

Meg turned back from staring out into the snow. "We rode the bus across town! How'd he find us clear out here?"

Jake snuggled deeper into his coat. "It doesn't matter."

"Yes it does, if we're trapped under a bridge by a freaking bike trail! Mom would never let us freeze under a bridge!"

"Well Mom wouldn't listen," he snapped. "So here we are. And we have to stay here until dark, at least, so he won't see—"

"I don't want to pee my pants like a baby!" she snapped back, then ventured out to the dimming day.

Snow swirled around her, soft and lovely, while, up the embankment to her right, cars pulled out of Burger King's drive-thru close enough to throw a snowball at. She turned toward the dim opening beneath the bridge. "Give me some money, I'll bring back—" Then she squealed as he yanked her back to the shadows and held her still, his grip tight against the skin of her wrist.

"He's on the move," Jake hissed in her ear. "He drives by every few minutes, and he's coming this way, again, like he has seventeen times already, looking for us. Maybe, *maybe*, when he heads back to the north end of the parking lot to wait a while before driving around again, *maybe* you'll have time to pee. Until then, we *have to wait!*"

She yanked her arm free. "I gotta pee so bad it hurts! I gotta go *now!*" She ran into the evening and up the embankment while her brother struggled to follow.

"He's coming. Please, Meg!" he called after her, but she continued up the embankment to the edge of the parking lot.

How can anyone see anything with all these cars in the way, she thought, pausing to gaze over the hundreds, maybe thousands of cars of holiday shoppers in front of Walmart. She waited for a minivan full of kids and a bearded guy she assumed was their dad to drive past her, then she walked into Burger King's parking lot and between parked cars. The crisp air smelled of snow and French fries as she weaved her way through the cars toward BK's entrance.

"He's in a silver SUV now," Jake hissed from close behind her. "Get down! Get down!"

She gave him an angry glare from over her shoulder, but he grabbed that shoulder and dragged her down between a rusted pickup and a Prius.

"Look," Jake whispered in her ear, pointing through the Prius's window, past the corner of Burger King, toward Sam's Club. "Right there!" he said. A lone man in a massive, silver SUV crept along behind a hatchback full of college kids. "That's him. He knows we have to be here. Somewhere."

The line of cars stopped, waiting at the stop sign for

others to enter or leave the parking lot, and the man driving the SUV turned his head as if searching down every row of cars. He wore a baseball cap, but seeing the rest of his face made her bowels clench. The same guy in the police coat at the Gunderson's house, the same guy who shot that other cop.

"Pee here," Jake said, letting her go. "We have a minute or two before he turns the corner and we have to move again. Just stay low. I'll look away. I promise. I'll be watching him instead. Just pee. I'll keep you safe."

Meg gazed toward the bright warmth of Burger King and the promise of a clean toilet and hot food, then she glanced again at the man in the silver SUV methodically looking across the parking lot rows. She pulled her pants down and squatted, being careful not to piss on her pants or boots.

Her bladder thanked her, but embarrassment and vulnerability fell like an icy weight, not only from exposing herself in a snowy public parking lot, but like a rabbit frozen and afraid to move while a hawk prowled overhead.

The pee wouldn't come.

"Hurry, hurry," Jake whispered and she closed her eyes and made herself relax enough to let go. The hot flood stank in the chilly air and flowed around her boots, staining the snow. She lowered her head. The Prius's driver would know, would see, would smell what she had done. After she pulled up her jeans but before she buttoned or zipped them, Jake grabbed her hand and half-dragged her in front of the Prius to crouch between it and the front end of a Chevy sedan. Her brother hovered close like a shield, but she peeked over the Sedan's hood and saw a glimpse of the SUV slowly creeping down the parking lot's entrance road, directly over their hiding spot while still behind the carload of college-aged kids. He looked between the Prius and pickup, where she'd peed, then he moved on.

How many times did that man drive right over us? Meg thought, her mouth going dry. *How many times was he that close to us and Jake didn't say a word?*

Jake slipped around her and took her hand again, staying low while leading her toward Walmart between pairs of cars, toward the bus-stop bench where they'd exited their previous bus. Just visible past Burger King, well to her left, she saw a bus in line with the rest of the vehicles trying to leave the parking lot.

"Take off your coat and turn it inside out," Jake said, peeling his jacket off. "So we'll look different."

Meg did as she was told, but said, "I don't think he can see us now. We're too far behind him."

Jake pulled his sleeves through. "He's not who I'm worried about. His husband's watching all the surveillance cameras. If Warren realizes we're on that bus, we're screwed."

"What about those cops?" Meg said, pointing to a Windsor Heights police cruiser parked in front of Walmart before she fastened her jeans. "Can't they help us?"

"I still don't know if he's one of them or not, but he *is* monitoring the police radio," Jake said as he pulled on his coat and reached for his backpack. "*He'll* know, and he'll kill them, just like he killed that cop this morning."

Meg's hands shook as she turned her coat inside-out and pulled it back on. Jake was standing by the time she finished.

"He's heading to PetCo so we're clear for now. You ready?"

Meg nodded. "Yeah."

He stepped out from between the cars and toward the bus stop. The bus was only three vehicles away and creeping closer. "Okay," Jake said, motioning for her to walk ahead of him to the bus bench. "Here's hoping this works. And remember, buy us both another transfer and don't look at the camera."

"WHERE THE HELL ARE THEY?" Huey asked. He sat in a parking lot beside B-Bops Burgers and watched the sun sink lower in the sky while wind blew snow-flurries around him. It'd be dark soon, within an hour or so, and he counted the third patrol car passing by—two on 73rd, one behind him across the massive parking lot connecting Sam's Club to Walmart, fast food joints, and a strip mall—in the last two minutes.

"I've got nothing," Warren said. "They walked out of Walmart and evaporated."

"That was six hours ago," Huey said, watching every pair of people he saw as they rushed, huddled, to their cars. "Two kids, no money... And this place is crawling with cops since DMPD saw them on the same bus footage you found. They've gotta be somewhere."

"I can't find any relatives, friends, or even acquaintances for anyone in the family in that neighborhood. They didn't cross Seventy-Third or University at any lights, and they didn't go into any of the other businesses in the lot. So they either managed to dodge holiday traffic to cross one of the busiest streets in town or..."

Or they holed up in one of the nearby residential neighbor-hoods, Huey thought, flicking on MapQuest for surely the umpteenth time. "Have you checked the cameras on Hickman? On 63rd?"

"Yeah. I've never stopped," Warren said over keyboard-clacking in the background. "I'm still monitoring all traffic and entrance cameras at every retail outlet, gas station, and restaurant between 8th and 63rd, and Hickman and the Freeway. Dozens of feeds. There are so many it's possible I missed something, but I've seen no sign of them."

"They could be hiding in someone's garage," Huey muttered. "There are hundreds of houses East and North of Walmart. Maybe thousands. 'Least the cops are still looking here too. They have no leads either."

"I'll keep watching."

"Me, too," Huey sighed. He put the Escalade in Drive and cruised over by Burger King, past the bus stop, then crossed 73rd to PetCo because, hell, maybe two kids decided to look at puppies.

AFTER STOPPING by his house to feed the cats, Fawkes sat off-the-clock in an unmarked car in the Sam's Club parking lot, drinking gas station coffee while listening to radio chatter about the search for his missing kids. Garrel sipped cocoa and swiped through security feeds on her tablet beside him. Walmart had volunteered their store entrance footage, but nothing more, HyVee volunteered it all, as did the gas stations, but none of the restaurants or chain stores could grant access, not without approval from their franchise owners who all seemed to be off for the holidays. PetCo's assistant manager had told them, "Not without a warrant," then hung up the phone.

But they had all of the bus cams, some of the cab cams, and most of the working street cams. With all of the snow and sleet, the traffic cam closest to HyVee had covered with ice.

Footage showed the kids had stepped off the bus in front of Walmart. Had walked into Walmart, then walked out eighteen minutes later with a bag of who-knew-what, then apparently evaporated. None of the traffic cams had shown the kids crossing a major road.

"They've got to be in the lot somewhere," Fawkes muttered for surely the hundredth time.

Garrel muttered her usual response. "What if they called somebody? A friend? An Uber? Hid in the back of someone's minivan? What if they left hours ago?"

"What if they walk right through walls like their uncle? They could be in that empty auto repair building, safe and sound, and no one would know."

She gave him a you-have-got-to-be-shitting-me sideways glance then resumed checking security feeds.

Fawkes sighed as his phone rang. The timestamp said 4:28 pm and the kids had been off-grid for about six hours.

Maybe Joel's killer nabbed them. Maybe we're just watching a dead trail.

His phone said the call was from the office. He accepted it.

"Hey, Les," Krista from the 911 call center said when he picked up, "I have a lady on the line who's positive she's looking at your kids *right now*. Thought I ought to keep it off the radio, seeing as how we have a cop-killer looking for them, too."

Holy crap!

Garrel glanced over when Fawkes almost dropped the phone.

"Can you patch her through?"

"Yep."

He heard a click, then open air with a slight engine-rumble. He put it on speaker.

"This is Detective Fawkes," he said. "How can I help you?"

"I'm on the Number Six bus, just crossing 22nd Street, heading West," a woman said, her voice soft. "I swear, those two kids from the TV news got on in front of Walmart and sat a couple rows back. They're quiet and they looked pretty scared when they walked by. I noticed the tags on their inside-out coats sticking out, and it got me wondering. Didn't want to spook them, but thought I ought to call."

Garrel brought up the bus footage and, sure enough, two kids, a boy and a smaller girl, sat together in the third row from the back. The girl's coat looked pristine white instead of grubby pink, and the boy's baby blue instead of gray. Jake Adamson crossed his arms over his chest and scowled at a middle-aged black woman on a phone, then he stared at the camera and blinked his odd staccato blinks before returning his stony, barely-blinking glare to the informant.

Jesus, Fawkes thought as he turned on his dash lights and drove toward the parking lot exit. *Are we really this stupid and missed something as simple as a turned-out coat?*

"Don't look back at them," Fawkes told his new informant. "Just pretend they're not there. We're on our way."

"Yessir," the woman said. "We're almost to 28th now. About to turn."

Garrel clicked away on her tablet while "I'm sending a text to the DART controller asking her to talk privately with the driver and to not let the kids off the bus."

The dash lights helped clear a path out of the parking lot and Fawkes kept them flashing, siren off, as he sped up Buffalo Road.

EIGHT

"We've got to get off this bus," Jake said as the bus eased to a stop and let a man off. "The cops know about us now."

He started to stand, but Meg put her hand on his arm. "Did you look out the windows? There's nothing out there but a couple of office buildings with mostly-empty parking lots. No place to hide!"

He leaned close. "If *they* know, *he* knows."

"You kids getting off?" the bus driver said.

"Just a second," Meg replied. She whispered to her brother. "We're almost to the mall, right? It's a couple of days before Christmas. Can't we can hide *in the crowd*?"

"I'm already running late, kiddo," the driver said, closing the bus doors. "Sorry."

Jake *fwumped* beside her and glowered ahead as the bus turned a corner. He quietly grumbled into her ear, "We've been found out. I *told you* we needed to stay there until dark."

She whispered back, "I didn't want to pee my pants."

"And I don't want to get a nosebleed from being closely surrounded by a couple-thousand stressed-out people in a damn mall!"

"Maybe... Maybe we can be quick. Get disguises. Maybe we can be gone before he finds us."

The bus paused beside more nearly-empty parking lots then turned another corner.

"Last time I heard him, he was still at PetCo," Jake sighed. "We went too far away, so the connection's gone. I can't pick his thoughts out of a crowd, not if I don't know where he is. If he sees us before we see him..."

"He won't," Meg said. "There's no way he can find us with all the people, all the stores."

"I hope you're right," Jake said as the bus turned again and drove on the road alongside Valley West Mall. He pulled the disembark cord and stood. "If you're not, we're done. All because you had to freaking *pee*."

———

DASH LIGHTS OR NOT, Fawkes didn't reach the bus before it left the mall. He saw the kids disembark on Garrel's tablet screen, saw Jake Adamson flip the informant and the security camera the bird, then they were gone, off-camera once again.

"Get every ounce of footage in and around that mall you can," he said to Garrel while barreling across 22nd St. and up Westown Parkway. He sighed as he passed the bus heading back toward downtown. *So close, so damned close!*

"I'll track the busses through there too," she said, tapping. "Shit. Multiple lines cross there. Four, five lines."

"Get mall security then DART on the phone. We need to find those kids before that murdering shit does."

HUEY DROVE from the back of PetCo toward the parking lot and saw a sedan speed by with dashboard lights flashing. "Hey, babe?" he said, tapping his fingertips on the steering wheel as a fat, middle-aged woman carrying a fluffy, mashed-faced mutt picked her way across the snow. "Just saw an unmarked cop car go West on Buffalo Road."

"That's a bus route," Warren said, clicking. "Bus six... Bus siiii... Fuck, it's them. They're... They're turning on 28th."

"Sunnuva bitch!" Huey snapped, then honked his horn. *Two miles, in this insane traffic? And the cops'll get there first? Shit!* He rolled down his window. "Get the fuck out of the way, bitch!"

The woman scowled but did not speed up, even when Huey leaned on his horn.

"I've got a stupid bitch with an ugly mutt blocking my way," Huey growled, wrenching the Expedition onto the sidewalk in front of the store while shoppers leaped aside. "I don't give a shit where Jake goes or what he does. Break into Google's satellites if you have to, but keep an eye on that fucker!"

The old bat finally moved enough for him to squeeze past, and he barreled out of the parking lot and onto the road into heavy traffic, well after the cop had disappeared around the curve.

"Where are they, Jenn?" Fawkes asked, skidding through slush into the parking lot beside the bus stop.

"They entered the mall through Penneys, over there," she said, pointing. "The door closest to the bus stop. We're minutes behind them."

Cars dodged out of his way as he sped toward JCPenneys. Leaving the lights flashing, they hurried out of the car and into the store. He looked right, Jenn left, and he saw no sign of two kids in the sparsely-populated store, just middle-aged people and a pregnant woman with a toddler shopping along to muzak *Here Comes Santa Claus*.

As they circled their way toward the store's mall entrance, Garrel muttered into her phone, "Do I sound like I give a shit? We need all security personnel to search for two missing juveniles..."

They separated to quickly search left and right of Penney's main aisle and he lost track of Jenn's voice as she moved out of range. She talked with DART when they converged near the mall entrance and stepped into the chaotic sea of shoppers.

Warren's voice said from the phone on the passenger seat, "I've got cops entering the mall from Penneys, but haven't seen the kids yet. They might have gotten ahead of me."

Heavy traffic held Huey's progress to a crawl as he crossed 22nd behind a rusted-out Ford with Sac County plates. "Keep looking. They're in there, somewhere, probably hiding in the crowd."

"A lot of people there, Hugh."

Lots of cars here too, he thought, slamming on his brakes to avoid a rear-end collision with the Ford. Its driver apparently decided stopping mid-block in front of a snowed-in dentist's office in bumper-to-bumper traffic was the smart thing to do.

The woman driver of the minivan behind him honked and Huey flipped her the bird. "I'm stuck behind this idiot too, bitch," he muttered. The old out-of-town car backfired then lurched forward again. Then stopped again. This time the taillights flickered and Huey resisted the urge to bang his head on the headrest. "Don't let 'er break down," he muttered. "Getting around you'll be impossible in this traffic. Only a couple of blocks to go. Come on! You can do it. Start that bitch and let's go!"

The Buick lurched forward about thirty feet then stopped again. Huey sighed at the ever-lengthening empty road in front of the goddamn-piece-of-shit relic.

"Come on!" he yelled at the windshield, but the old Buick didn't move.

"Goddammit." He flipped into 4x4 and cranked the Escalade wheel hard to the right. Crunching through plowed snow on the curb and sidewalk, he skirted around the Ford and into a motel parking lot packed full of cars. A couple of turns later, he crossed 28th and sped through another parking lot, then another, through plowed snow and over the curb onto 31st.

"Where are they, Babe?" he asked, pulling into Valley West's parking lot.

"Still looking," Warren said. "The cops are, too. I see them, no problem. They're upper level, in front of Bath and Body Works."

"I'm parking lower level, then. Between VonMaur and Penneys."

"Gotcha. You just pulled into range of the lot security camera. I'll blur you out of security footage and keep looking for the kids inside."

MEG PEEKED out of her dressing room and thought, *Are we clear?*

"Yeah," Jake said from outside the Ladies' Dressing Room archway. "I've got an idea."

"What?" Meg dodged a pregnant woman with a toddler who shopped near the dressing room entrance.

"There's a bunch of clearance stuff. Merry Christmas," he said, handing her a lightweight blue coat and a gift-set of snowflake encrusted earmuffs, snowflake scarf, and fluffy blue gloves. Jake held a flimsy duffle bag, a young man's parka, a plaid scarf, and a knit ski cap that'd partly cover his face. He gave her a worried smile and she saw his right nostril rimmed with fresh blood.

She tried to smile. The wool coat had a bad seam near the wrist but was still prettier than any coat she'd ever worn, the muffs and scarf were cute, and it was Christmas. But without her mother... cute didn't help much. "Can we afford this?" she asked, accepting the coat and accessories.

"Barely. But let's use different cashiers and everything so we can confuse our video trail as much as possible. It'll be dark soon. Maybe we can get out of here before anyone else notices."

She nodded and looked around, wondering if the awful man with the shark-teeth hair was nearby.

"Don't worry. I've checked every person in this store, and he's not here. The cops have moved into the mall to look for us." Jake handed her a fistful of cash. "Once you've bought your stuff, go out to the main area of the mall and turn left. Stay close to a family to blend in, if you can. There's a bathroom on the left side somewhere close. I just know it's ahead and left. Go in and change. I'll meet you there. Be right behind you."

She nodded and he walked toward the cash registers closest to the door they'd entered in. Meg took a breath and carried her new stuff to the registers near the mall entrance.

GARREL LEANED over the railing and looked down upon the center court. "We're never gonna find them in this chaos."

Fawkes finished showing two mall security personnel digital images of Meg and Jake on the bus. "They haven't tried to catch a bus yet, and they haven't left the mall. We're going to find them. West Des Moines cops are moving to cover every entrance and exit."

"Yeah, I heard." Garrel pushed off the railing and adjusted the radio plug in her ear. "Gawd, I hate Christmas crowds." She sighed and managed a tired smile. "Jake's running the show, right? Let's check out the game shop. He'd certainly fit in there."

"Sounds like a plan," Fawkes said. Garrel three steps ahead of him, they descended the escalator where a crowd of people watched someone in a Rudolph costume chase someone else in a Santa's Elf costume while a trio of Elves sang a kid-friendly song about hoarding candy canes and getting on Santa's naughty list. They turned toward the game store and Fawkes tapped Garrel on the shoulder to slow her.

He nodded his head forward. "Ahead. Well past the game shop. Looks like someone wants a pretzel."

MEG FOUND Jake lingering near the railing across from the restroom hallway, and he watched a silly show below with Christmas elves and some guy in a reindeer costume running around and singing. He still carried their Walmart sack, but he wasn't wearing his aviator hat. The tissue in his gloved hand was definitely bloody. He'd changed his hair, darkened it and slicked it to his head, and his new stocking cap had been stuffed into a coat pocket. It had no foil lining.

"It's just soap in my hair," he said without looking at her as she stood beside him. "It's a screaming storm of thoughts in here. Hurts. We should get moving soon." He touched the wad of toilet paper to his nose and drew back a thread of blood.

"Where's your aviator hat?"

"Bottom of the duffle. Everybody's seen it. I have to look different. Have to blend in." He pushed off from the railing and rubbed his temples as he walked toward Macy's at the nearer end of the mall. "There's a bus stop straight ahead, then through the store and out the lower-level doors to the left."

She wandered behind her brother, trying to look like they were strangers merely going the same direction. When he paused to pretend to tie his shoes, she walked around him and trailed close behind a man and woman about her mom's age down the stairs to the lower level. When he descended, she nodded up at him then looked away before anyone noticed.

"Want a pretzel?" he asked as he strode by.

The pretzel shop was ten, maybe twelve steps away. *Sure,* she thought, then sat on a bench near a grandma-aged woman with several shopping bags of toys.

She smiled at the grandma and told her she was waiting for her mom. Grandma seemed to buy it and Meg tried to relax.

Deep breath. We'll be out of here soon.

"WHERE ARE YOU?" Warren asked on Bluetooth.

"Approaching the Southwest entrance. Two cops are in the vestibule, just like the Southeast entrance. They're going to make extraction tricky. Why?"

"Because a cute little bird with a blue coat and snowflakes in her hair is perched on a bench at the bottom of the stairs behind you. Her shitty boots are a dead giveaway."

Huey turned and saw a young girl well ahead, sitting with her back to him beside a gray-haired woman. The girl wore a blue coat and big, sparkly snowflakes in her light brown hair. Hugh hurried, one hand palming an injector of Propofol from his pocket. He wondered if it could really be Meg Adamson and where her fuck-nut brother was hiding.

Then he released the security lock on his concealed Sig Sauer. Just in case the sedative didn't work on fuck-nuts. Knee-capping worked on everyone.

FAWKES WATCHED Jake Adamson blot his nose with a bloody tissue while standing in line for a pretzel, calm as could be, then spin on his heel and bolt toward the cluster of benches beneath the mall's southern staircase.

"Did he make us?" Garrel asked as they pressed forward through the crowd of shoppers. "Never saw him so much as glance this way."

"That's because he didn't," Fawkes said.

A large man wearing an expensive trench coat and a cheap ball cap strode around the corner past the pretzel shop, one hand in his pocket, the other within his coat, his gaze on Jake. Fawkes had studied that profile all day and he surged forward.

"Stop! Police!" he hollered, reaching for his service pistol. A sparkle-haired girl beside an older woman on a bench looked at Fawkes and gaped.

"Oh, shit, that's Meg," Garrel said, shoving through a clot in the crowd with her hand on her gun.

Jake, who did not glance at Fawkes or the cop killer, grabbed Meg's hand and dragged her off the bench, scattering the older woman's packages. Both stumbled, but Jake got his feet beneath him and tried to bolt for the exit, while Meg tripped and fell, sprawling belly-to-the-floor despite her brother dragging her.

The mall lights flickered.

Following the kids, the big man pulled a gun from beneath his coat and glanced over as he fired one shot, through the crowd, toward Fawkes. People screamed, panicking and running, obscuring the kids and the big man from view. Bright pain erupted on Fawkes' upper arm and a fleeing man directly ahead of him dropped like a bag of grain. Garrel tripped over the collapsed man and stumbled forward while drawing her gun. A high-pitched electronic whine filled the air and the mall's interior lights exploded, showering shoppers with sparks and crumbly shards of plastic and glass as they were plunged into darkness broken only by random flashes of store lighting.

Somewhere ahead, a girl's scream surged over the chaos.

Fawkes had time to think, *Oh shit, I'm shot,* then he flew backward with everyone else as a *whuuhhhBOOM!* filled the air.

NINE

"OH, GOD," HUEY GROANED, ROLLING TO HIS SIDE BEFORE struggling to his knees in a dust-filled haze that stunk of ozone while a high-pitched siren screamed in his ear. He'd landed with about fifteen other people in the back of a shoe repair store, all sprawled over each other, some bleeding, most not, while they and the shop's original contents tangled on crumbled concrete and tile. Only wires, cables, and dented rebar silhouetted against blue emergency lights remained from the store's front wall. The blast had obliterated most of the pretzel and ice-cream shops next door, leaving them utterly vacant of anything but spewing coolant and scattered pretzels, and, as the dust cleared enough to see through, folks in the destroyed stores across the walkway gaped at the chaos just as shell-shocked and lost as Huey's shoe-shop companions.

But moments had wasted and the quarry remained unsecured, so he struggled to his feet and staggered, coughing, into a dust-swirling atrium void of people, his boots crunching on shards of plastic, glass, and concrete.

He reached for his gun, but it and its holster were gone. Lost, evaporated, who the fuck knew, and, as he struggled to find his breath and balance, he noticed the right side of his coat and shirt had been shredded to tatters.

It took him a moment to realize he was apparently bleeding from every pore of his right arm, except where his watch had been. Gods knew where else. His skin felt like it had been lit afire.

He staggered forward, reeling on shifting rubble in the flickering blue haze.

The electric screech in his ear turned to a warbling, "Babe! Huey! *Babe!*"

I still have my Bluetooth? "I'm here. I'm alive," he choked out, wiping a smear of blood from his right eye.

"What the hell happened? The whole mall surveillance went dark. Police chatter is insane!"

Huey staggered forward, coughing through the dusty ozone stink, and nearly tripped over a twisted light fixture sprouting from a tangled wad of childrens' holiday pajamas. "She blew the place up."

MEG HALF-DRAGGED her brother among the tail-end of a mob of panicked shoppers fleeing the mall through Macy's while a pair of cops ran toward the terrified crowd, then past, then on to the destruction she'd left behind. Displays, merchandise, and mannequins littered the store's floor, slowing progress, but she dragged Jake forward anyway.

"He drugged me. Oh, hell, everything's wobbly. I don't feel so good," her brother said, stumbling. "Need to rest."

You need to stay awake. Hang on, she thought, skirting around a set of shelving. *I can see the exit. I'll get you through. Find us a place to hide. Somehow.*

He collapsed to his knees about fifteen feet from the exit, but she managed to get her shoulder under him and shove him upright again.

He was heavy, getting heavier, his knees weaker, but she pressed on.

The outer wall's glass had blown into the parking lot and shimmered in the snow alongside clothes, shoes, and housewares. Most everyone else ran straight through in a forward flood, but she paused to assess their options then dragged Jake to the left, toward a pair of semi-trailers stowed at the dock and a massive pile of snow beside a concrete divider wall.

"Officer down!" Garrel yelled from the dim and swirling, ozone-reeking din, then Fawkes felt her hands on him, searching for injuries. "Need a paramedic over here!"

He lay on his back over something jabby and something else that moved. He managed to choke out, "Shot. Left bicep," but his consciousness went sideways.

He blinked, and the air had cleared some. He sat, his back against a vertical support post that had curved like a barrel stave. Garrel crouched beside him, texting her husband. All around them, people were being carried away on stretchers or walking with assistance.

"What happened?" Fawkes asked, blinking when his vision tottered. Sharp pain throbbed in his left bicep.

"Same as I told you the last three times," Jenn said, giving him a tired smile. "Some sort of explosion."

He rubbed his aching arm and felt a good bandage. "Did you get the video?"

She laughed, and sat, facing him, on a hunk of concrete. "Not yet. We have to wait for someone to get the computers up again." She ran her hand over her head and dust poofed out of her hair. "Jesus, what a mess."

He took a breath and sat a little straighter before trying to pop the kink out of his neck. "I lost track of everything when he shot me. Did you see anything at all?"

"Yeah. He shot you then went for the kids. I saw him grab Jake's arm with both hands first, that's when the lights exploded. Then... Then he reached down for Meg..."

"And?"

"And I landed on a couch with four other people."

"So he set off a bomb?"

She stared past Fawkes for a long moment. "Maybe. I'm not sure what I saw. Dan's been texting from the parking lot. Noah's with him. If you're okay, I *really* need to go."

Fawkes grasped her wrist when she stood. "What do you *think* you saw?"

She took a deep breath, then another. "It's nuts."

As nuts as Matt Adamson leaving his underwear embedded in a wall? Unlikely. Fawkes coughed once then said, "Try me."

She sighed, shaking her head, and stared at the chaos for a long time. "I saw a ball of sizzling light come out of that little girl and it exploded on *him*." Garrel sighed again then met Fawkes' gaze. "Him, she wanted to *hurt*. We're just collateral damage." She swallowed and lowered her head. "Les... I..."

She let out a tired breath and stood, not looking at him. "You're supposed to see a doctor about your arm, so remember to do that. Get stitched up or antibiotics or something, I dunno."

He watched her stare off at something he couldn't see. "You okay, Jenn?"

"Yeah," she said, forcing a smile. "But I have to go. It's late. Dan's waiting for me and I'm going home now."

Then she put her phone to her ear and walked away.

TEN

MOSTLY ASLEEP, KATE SCRATCHED HER HEAD AND YAWNED ON her way to the bathroom, then stopped and sucked in a startled breath.

She smelled pork chops.

She didn't have pork chops. Not in her fridge, not in the freezer. No pork chops.

Scowling, she turned to see Matt in the kitchen, frying chops while a pan of water bubbled happily beside him and a pack of mint Oreos sat open on the table. "Oh, good, you're up," he said, glancing over his shoulder at her. While she stared, he dumped a box of macaroni and cheese into the water and gave it a stir. "Supper'll be ready in about ten minutes!"

"How did you get pork chops?"

"Bought them." He poked at the pan's contents with her spatula.

"Thought you didn't have any money."

"Oh! Yeah, well, I was sitting out on the stoop, and a buddy of mine walked by..."

In late December? she thought, watching him flip the chops.

"...He owed me twenty bucks and paid me. Merry Christmas and all that. So I thought I'd thank you by buying and cooking dinner." He flashed her a bright smile then resumed cooking.

She wasn't sure if she trusted him or his explanation, but the chops did smell good, so she continued to the bathroom to pee.

As she finished, she realized he'd *left* her apartment, but *came back*. Only one way he could've done that since her keys were locked in the bedroom with her.

"Hey?" she asked on her way to her bedroom, "how'd you get back in after you'd went outside?"

"Oh, I, uh..." He searched through her cupboards for her plates without looking at her. "I uh..."

She took a steadying breath and said, "There's some shady people in this building and that door stays *locked*. Please. I don't have much, and I don't want it stolen."

He lowered his head. "Sure. I'm sorry. I didn't know."

She closed her bedroom door behind her then flumped on her bed, glaring at the ceiling while breathing in the heady aroma of frying pork chops.

Way to go. He's cooking supper, so now I feel like a shit.

She reached for her bottle of Merlot and downed a gulp.

Forget supper, how am I gonna get rid of this guy?

———

ABOUT FORTY MINUTES after being shot and thrown backward more than fifty feet with minimal injuries, Fawkes lingered nearby while the West Des Moines detectives and crime techs from the city and county worked under battery-powered lights to survey the blast's epicenter. A blast that destroyed much of a major mall and gave innumerable bruises, contusions, and broken bones to mall patrons, but no known fatalities beyond the social studies teacher with four kids who'd died from the bullet intended for Fawkes.

The shift chief spoke to Fawkes directly. "You think this happened because of the two missing juveniles you'd reported?"

Fawkes nodded. "Due to their pursuit, yes."

"Were you aware they were carrying explosives?"

"No, sir, I don't think they were. But the man following them, the man we believe killed their mother and definitely killed our patrolman, may have when he attacked them." *Or, more likely, a ten-year-old girl blasted the murderous shit away from her and her brother, but if I mentioned THAT you'd escort me directly to a psych ward.*

A young uniformed cop approached. "Chief? We found a gun."

"Where?" the shift chief asked, following.

Fawkes remained in position but heard, "Embedded above the ceiling of the T-Mobile store," as the pair walked away.

Fawkes noted the site of Meg's explosion, then drew his gaze toward the blasted cell-phone store and saw how both locations intersected with the shooter's trajectory toward the kids to form a tidy triangle that pointed backward, away, and to the shooter's right. He nodded to himself. He'd bet good money they just found a Sig Sauer with firing marks matching the casing that killed Officer Griffin. Meg

Adamson had merely flung away the threats to her and her brother.

Random streaks of discoloration scrambled from her blast-center like roots or branches in all directions, growing ever narrower and more twisted as they cut into concrete and clouded store-front glass. Fawkes knelt to examine the tangle etched beneath his feet. Any mark wider than his index finger had cracked the cream-colored tile's surface, but all smaller rambles had merely stained their path red-brown with endless branches thinning to endless twigs thinning to endless hairs while leaving most of the tile's surface smooth.

He stood and looked outward, away from the epicenter. The mall's center court, where college kids in elf and reindeer costumes had recently danced and sang, had been shattered and dusted with broken lights and ceiling tiles. The destruction continued beyond, toward the Food Court and Von Maur, and disappeared into the flickering dark. Flashlights bobbed in the depths, surely officers and firemen searching for casualties and trapped victims.

"Detective Fawkes!" a county tech near the stairway called.

Fawkes trotted over. "What'd you find, Greg?"

"Walmart bag under the fallen ceiling. Dunno if it's yours, but you said you were looking for one."

Fawkes knelt and pulled on latex gloves before opening the crushed, torn sack.

It held part of a checkout-lane-sized bag of M&Ms, a box of store-brand granola bars, a pack of individually-wrapped cheese sticks, a pack of meat sticks, a tiny bottle of generic Excedrin, a box of cheese crackers, burn ointment, a receipt, half a bottle of water, and the crumpled packaging for whatever had already been eaten.

He examined the receipt. The kids had paid about twenty bucks in cash and had bought only snacks, ointment, and headache pills. It was time-stamped about a minute-and-a-half before video showed Jake and Meg leaving Walmart, and they'd carried their litter with them.

He sighed and stood. "Bag it all. Maybe it'll confirm their fingerprints, at least."

A ragged aviator hat lay not far away and Fawkes pulled an evidence sack from his pocket before lifting the hat from lighting shards, grit, and busted ceiling tiles.

The inside was lined with dark foil, just like Jake's room. Fawkes nodded to himself and stuffed it into the evidence sack.

HUEY DROVE with his right eye a blurry mess, and he mostly ignored the vicious stinging from his right side and face as he stewed over the fuckaroo at the mall.

Jake had known he was there and approaching. That in itself was not a surprise. He'd memorized Jake's file and the various tests of telepathic ability the boy'd shown while still a toddler, well before he and his mother fled to relative anonymity in Iowa. The girl, though... She obviously carried the family mutation, but, unlike her mother, her mutation was active, not suppressive, and there'd been *no file*.

He'd expected Meg to dim Jake's abilities as their mother had, not defend him. He assumed her to be a relatively-normal ten-year-old girl, not an explosive goddess.

He'd never make that mistake again, assuming he managed to survive the *again*.

Sighing, Huey pushed away the memory of terror in her eyes and called Warren. "Any video yet?"

"Nah, the power's still out. They're not on any busses, either. 'Least not yet."

"I'm on my way home. We need to figure out what to do about the girl."

Warren clacked on a keyboard in the background. "She's ten. Throw a My Little Pony at her and she'll be fine."

"Not this girl." Huey sighed and rubbed the blur of his right eye. "What if we weren't hired to bring in Jake Adamson?"

"What? Are you crazy? That explosion hurt you more than you'd thought? The kid's telepathic. Imagine the corporate espionage possibilit—"

"She blew up the mall, Warren. *She* did."

"It was terrorists. An atheist anti-consumerism group has already claimed credit. It's all over Reddit and 4Chan. Their statement is supposed to be on the news tonight."

Huey turned onto a narrow highway. "Nope. Happened right in front of me. Was a terrified ten-year-old girl."

"Hugh..."

"I need you to break into SynAg's system and find out what they have on Meg Adamson. *Everything*."

"She was only mentioned once in your file, and not even by name, only as 'the sister'. They probably don't want her at all beyond using her as a way to keep Jake calm."

"Find it anyway."

ELEVEN

"Hey." Matt cut up another bite of pork chop. "I'd like to ask you a favor."

Oh, gawd, here we go, Kate thought, keeping her attention on her plate. *These are decent chops, but they're not enough to buy me off. Not enough to let my guard down.*

"I want to go home," he said. "Get some clothes, then crash at my buddy's place. Can you drive me out there? I have money at the house. I can pay you for gas, and for..."

She looked up and said nothing while she chewed her macaroni.

"...for helping me? Putting up with me? You've been awesome, but I know this's been a pain in the ass. Just one last little errand, then I'm out of your hair."

She wanted to ask if he'd promise, if she'd have some guarantee this apparently-nice-but-odd man would actually go back to his own life and out of hers, but instead, she nodded and said, "Sure. We can leave after supper."

They finished eating without saying much. He volunteered to wash up the supper mess—even did a decent job of it—and he held the apartment door open for her when they left.

As she followed him down the stairs she thought it was *maybe* a little nice to have someone around instead of being lonely and all by herself. He seemed like a nice guy. Kind. Thoughtful. Sweet.

Then she shoved those thoughts away because they *all* seemed like nice guys until they weren't, no matter how hard she'd tried to make it work, no matter what she did to make them happy.

He hummed along with the radio on the drive north but didn't say much beyond directions and random comments about the snow. Despite herself, she found the cross-town drive almost pleasant, then she shoved that thought away too.

Better to be alone than with another abusive shit, she reminded herself and packed the rest away.

His house was small and shabby, even snow-covered at night. Yellow police tape across the front didn't help.

He had her drive up the alley in back. They stopped beside a neighbor's garage and he sat there a long time, staring at his house's back door.

"Can you..." he said, wiping the back of his hand across his eyes. "Can you come in with me? I... I don't want to go in there, and I definitely don't want to be in there alone."

"It's, it's a crime scene. I don't know if *either* of us should be in there."

"I... I can't survive without clothes. Without money. It'll just be a couple of minutes. Please. I'll get my stuff, then we'll go."

"I... I don't know."

He sighed, heavy and deep, then held her quaking gaze. "I lied, okay? A little. I know my sister was killed, I saw her, I tried to help her, but I have no idea what happened to my niece and nephew. The cops didn't know. The news just says they're missing. That's it. Yeah, I need money and clothes, but I *have to know* what happened to the kids. I don't think I can face whatever's in there alone. *Please.*"

Aw, crap. Kate took a shaky breath then pulled her keys from the ignition and stared out at swirling snow. *Maybe I misjudged him. Maybe he's playing me. Maybe I'm being an unreasonable ass. Crap!*

"Okay," she said at last. "Let's go."

FAWKES LEFT the mall a little after seven, his mind churning over the case on his way back to the office. He had a seasoned killer chasing the kids and he'd probably killed their mother, too. An uncle who apparently walks through walls. Two kids who remained unseen beneath a mattress despite police nearby, then hid for hours somewhere in a public parking lot under heavy surveillance. A teenage boy who knew, who *KNEW,* and reacted to that same killer walking toward his sister before he could've seen the guy, and then, a little girl who exploded *most of a mall* with a ball of light.

"I used to love the X-files," he mumbled. "Never thought I'd get one of their cases."

A bus drove toward him on its way to the station and he watched it pass.

"Aw, shit, where'd they go?" he muttered, then realized if

the kids had survived Meg's blast—which was likely, he reasoned, since there'd been no blood or tissue near the blast center—they could have picked up new coats in the mess, new boots, new anything, changed their look again, maybe ridden busses separately, and no one would've known. They could be anywhere in the Metro by now, anywhere in the entire county.

He reminded himself one or both of them knew how and where to *hide*, and how and when to *move*.

Jake Adamson had reacted to the killer walking toward him, even when the murderous fuck was hidden by a wall. Jake *knew*, and Jake *reacted* to save his sister.

Then his sister exploded a ball of light and they escaped. Again. Past police at every exit.

So, shit, maybe they walked through walls like their uncle, too.

MATT'S HOUSE smelled like death, the close and cloying metallic rot of blood and old meat. Kate resisted the urge to cover her mouth and nose with her hand. They'd entered from the back, climbing through an unlocked window into the kitchen by the table. The place was dark, stinky, and it felt like the walls were closing in. She spied a rumpled dishtowel on the counter and, hoping to remove her fingerprints, scrubbed it over the sill.

Matt coughed a little as he rooted in a kitchen drawer, finally producing a flashlight. "You can stay here if you want."

Kate gave the windowsill one last wipe and stuffed the dishtowel into her pocket. "I... I think I'd rather go with you."

"I think I'd rather not go at all," Matt said, taking a shaky breath. "But I need to get my stuff and figure out what happened to the kids."

"Let's get this done, then," Kate said, offering what she hoped was an encouraging smile. It felt more like a grimace.

Matt stood unmoving at the edge of the living room, and the tremble of his light cast careening shimmers across the walls like drunken ghosts on a sinking ship.

Before she got queasy and yarked up the pork chops, Kate reached out to still Matt's hand.

"Sorry," he said. "It's just... Did they have to make a mess?"

Drawers had been opened, cushions up-ended, DVDs and CDs strung about, the disks winking back from the floor. Black powder coated many surfaces, from doorknobs to the coffee table, with occasional paler rectangular patches.

Kate looked at her hands—clean—then Matt's. "You've smeared fingerprint powder. It's all over your hands."

"They've surely found my prints all over the house anyway," Matt said, walking toward the converted garage.

Yes, but now they'll know you were here after they'd left. Hands in pockets, Kate followed, her nose wrinkling at the stink.

The stench was worse in the cramped hallway, heavy and oppressive, the air thick with it. Matt hesitated, shuddering light reflecting back at them off of framed photographs on the walls, the images lost to glare. "I... I don't know if I can do this. What if it's not just my sister?"

"Do you want me to look?"

Matt shook his head and walked to the end of the short hall. "This is my niece's room," he said, the light on the door wavering. Powder coated the doorknob and frame, highlighting smudges and fingerprints. The door was unlatched, not quite closed, and Matt pushed it open with the flashlight.

The room looked like a cyclone had hit it, with black powder on every conceivable surface, dresser drawers hanging open, and toys strung about.

"Is it usually like this?"

"Not usually. She's generally tidy, other than her artsy crap, but she does have her moments." Matt took a step in and paused. "I don't see any blood, do you?"

"No." They stood quietly beside each other, their breathing harsh in the otherwise silent house. "Do you see anything missing?" Kate asked.

Matt licked his lips and seemed to steel himself. "There's such a mess," he said, stepping farther into the room. "Her fingernail polish's there, on the floor. Her favorite jeans..."

"What is it?"

"I don't see Blessy, a stuffed penguin she got for Easter when she was three. It's ratty and missing part of one foot but she loves the dang thing, uses it as a pillow."

Matt moved toward the bed and nudged some clothes aside with his foot. "Her shoes are supposed to be right here, next to her nightstand, so she won't lose them." He knelt and plucked a striped t-shirt from the floor and held it tightly in his fist.

"If her shoes and toy are gone, maybe she's okay. Maybe we can find her," Kate said.

"I hope so. Let's check on her brother," he said, then turned and walked across the hall.

Kate paused in the doorway to the other room and tried not to gape. Every constructed surface was covered with dark foil, leaving only a naked bulb and a pillow uncoated. A box-shaped structure about the size of a clothes basket lay on the bed and it, too, was encased in dull metal and dusted with black powder. Scuffed and torn foil on the floor was partially obscured by a ragged rug, and a purple robot lay on the computer desk. Otherwise, she saw only foil.

"Why is everything covered in foil?" Kate choked out, her throat clenching at the dead metallic scent.

"He says it makes things quieter," Matt said, rooting about in the closet before turning back to the room. "Three layers. Two of lead, one a nickel and tin alloy, at least on the walls." He pointed at the box on the bed. "He sleeps under that, otherwise... um, sounds keep him awake all night."

Weird. Kate nodded as if she understood. Even in shambles, the boy's room was tidier than the girl's but he also seemed to have fewer things to toss about. An old PC, a few books, pencils and paper... And all the foil.

Matt walked past Kate to the hall and sagged against the doorframe. "His shoes are gone, too. He always left them outside his door so he wouldn't tear the foil on the floor." He looked back at Kate and smiled. "My niece and nephew are alive."

TWELVE

AFTER VISITING THE EMERGENCY ROOM TO GET HIS STRAIGHT-through bullet wound checked and receiving too goddamn many infectious disease tests and preventative drugs, Fawkes grabbed a cup of coffee on the way to his desk and settled in with the Adamson File. He read his notes and cross-referenced them with Garrel's digital notepad on his desktop computer.

The gun from Jake's closet showed blood on the trigger and grip, which matched the wounds on Jake's hands, but did not explain them. The gun also had blood flecks on and near the muzzle. Fawkes noted on the sheet that gunshot residue on the gun indicated Jake's hand wounds preceded firing the weapon—*should the DNA confirm it was his blood,* he reminded himself—before moving on to the next report, and the next set of notes.

During Matt Adamson's questioning, Adamson had said the kids were special, with a genetic condition that ran in their family, a brain abnormality that was controlled by medication.

It was all right there in Garrel's impeccable notes.

So, Fawkes thought, *the crime scene techs had collected all of the family's medication as evidence, evidence the killer then stole. Did he steal them to block that path of inquiry? Do the meds have value on the street? With the holiday stalling the subpoena, is there another way to find what the kids were taking and why?*

He reviewed the notes again, looking for any mention of a pharmacy or physician or...

There we go. Walgreens pharmacy, and the kids are on Medicaid.

He flipped to a clean note page and called Social Services' late-night number. He explained who he was and waited for the on-call caseworker to confirm his identity, then asked her to look up who handled the Cheryl, Jake, and Meg Adamson cases.

He wrote down their caseworker's name, phone numbers, and email, then poured himself a fresh cup of coffee before calling Social Worker Jacqui Glees on her cell phone.

"Hello?" she yelled into the phone, her voice partly lost to loud music and shouting. "Who is this?"

"Detective Lester Fawkes with the Des Moines Police Department, Homicide Division. I have a few questions about one of your case files."

"*What?* Detective *who?*"

He repeated the info as the noise faded to a more manageable level.

"I'm in Boston, Detective. My college roomie's about to get married, and I'm not going to be back until January. I can refer you to my sub—"

He cut her off. "Do you remember anything about Cheryl, Jake, or Meg Adamson?"

"What? Oh, God. What happened?" he heard a door close and the noise disappeared. "You said homicide, right? How? Why?"

"So you do remember them?"

"Yeah. They're kind of unforgettable. Cheryl's a great mom, and I've never worried about the kids being safe with her. I was their facilitator for homeschooling, I fought to get Jake's meds tweaked, I handled the home visits when neighbors complained, and Cheryl used me as a reference for her job. They're nice people. Different, but nice. Especially the kids. Who'd hurt *them*?"

"That's what I'm trying to figure out. It's my understanding that the children both have a medical condition."

Silence stretched.

"Ms. Glees?"

He heard only more silence and was about to repeat her name again when she said, "How do you know about that?"

"It's my job, ma'am. But I don't know what *kind* of medical condition or what medication they're on."

"I... I can't discuss that. Um... HIPAA and all."

"Ms. Glees, Cheryl Adamson is dead. Murdered. I need to know why and if there's anything unusual about the family I ought to know about, including whatever their medical condition is."

"Oh, God. *Cheryl?* Shit."

"Yes, well, about that—"

"Are the kids okay? Did you put them with a temporary family or—"

"They're missing, Ms. Glees."

"Aw, shit, no. Goddammit. No!"

"Yes. There've been some odd events, and I need any information you can provide so I can—"

"I... I can't. My hands are tied, Detective. I'm sorry. I can't discuss their case with anyone except Cheryl."

Then the call clicked off.

He sighed and hoped he could get a subpoena for the meds tomorrow, holiday or not.

———

HAVE I taken my hands out of my pockets? Kate thought, pacing as Matt banged around his bedroom, stuffing clothes and stuff from the floor into a grocery sack.

Once. Didn't I have them out once?

The dishrag she'd wiped over the windowsill fluttered beside her wrist, stuffed into her coat pocket. *Did I touch something? Oh, Christ, did I?*

Headlights flashed across the living room wall and Kate froze, a small squeak escaping her throat.

"What is it?" Matt turned, shoving underwear into the sack. He wore an old coat, a grubby flannel-with-wood-toggles thing that made him look like a drunken lumberjack.

Kate glanced toward the living room where the windows faced the driveway. "Someone's here."

"What?" Matt lunged to the hall, pushing past Kate to see, and he muttered a curse before returning. "Come with me!"

"What?!"

Matt pushed past her, back to his bedroom, grasping Kate's arm as he went. "Come with me."

Once they were inside, Matt fiddled with the door latch and closed the door. He hurried to the single narrow window and pushed it open. "Come on! Take off your coat."

She took a step backward. "What? Why?"

"Because I need you to take off your coat. Now." Matt ripped off his coat then paused and looked down at their feet. Jacket off, he knelt to untie his new shoes. "Shoes too."

"I... Wha?"

"Now, Kate." Matt shoved his bag of clothes through the open window, dropping it into the side yard. His coat and shoes followed.

A door banged open in the living room, and Kate nearly squealed. She frantically unzipped her parka.

Matt pulled Kate's coat from her and shoved it through the window. "Keys are in the pocket, right?"

Kate nodded dumbly, the thudding of her heart almost drowning out the sound of someone searching the house. She fumbled out of her boots and flinched as something heavy overturned in the boy's room. *The bed? His desk? Oh, God.*

"Give me your hand," Matt whispered.

The intruder returned to the hall, a man, muttering, and Kate stifled a scream as Matt's hand, his fingers hard and cold, encircled her forearm. He yanked her off her feet and Kate fell to the side. She stumbled, sure she was going to slam into the wall, but the world twisted and careened dark, filled with gritty itch and the taste of plaster. Paint. Old wood. Age. Cold, thin metal sliced through her shoulder, coppery and sharp, while threads of glass tickled her throat, her sinuses, her belly.

Kate fell to her knees on wet, lumpy snow, coughing up

flecks of insulation and masonite siding. Her suddenly-underwire-free bra slumped forward, loose and unfastened inside of her sweater, and her jeans had unzipped, the button coming undone.

Kate staggered to her feet, barely feeling the cold soaking her socks as she tried to right her clothes, but her jeans had no button and the zipper was gone, just gone.

"Here. We've got to go," Matt whispered, tossing Kate her parka and boots. "Sorry your feet got wet. Hurry up though. We can finish dressing in the car."

Kate nodded, not trusting her voice. She stepped into her boots and stumbled after Matt.

JAKE LEANED against the cement retaining wall in an igloo-like tunnel Meg had made in the mound of plowed snow. He shook his head and looked toward her, his face barely visible in light reflected off the dock door. Blood smeared his lips and chin like a carnivore after a kill. "How long was I out?"

"I don't know. A while?"

"Where are we? Where's our stuff?"

"Um, we're by a loading dock? Um. Near Macy's? I wanted to get to the bus stop, like you'd said, but you couldn't walk..." She sighed at her knees. "I don't know where any of our stuff is. I just wanted to get us out of there, as far away from him as possible. I'm sorry, Jake. I didn't know what else to do."

"You did fine. Last thing I remember, I was standing in line for a pretzel."

"That's when he came. When that other man yelled to

warn us," she said, her eyes tearing. "He shot the man who warned us. I saw it. There was blood. Then he grabbed you, gave you a shot... With a needle, ya know?"

Jake leaned forward, his eyes narrowing. "He *injected* me?" When she nodded, he asked, "With what?"

"I don't know," she admitted, drawing her knees to her chest. "But you stumbled, then he tried to grab me. Oh, Jake, I'm so sorry. So... so..." Her voice fell to a whisper as she said the worst word she knew, "So *fucking* sorry!"

"It's okay," he said, pulling her in for a hug. "We're all right. How'd you get away from him?"

"I think I killed him," she whimpered against his chest. "I was so scared, I just *pushed*. Hard."

Jake's voice wavered. "Like you did this morning when he shot that cop?"

"*Harder*. And I couldn't ground out. I didn't want to kill anyone else, but... I think I did, Jake," she wailed, clutching at him. "It was so big, I think I killed people. A *lot* of people. Then I dragged you out of there, even though you were barely awake. I didn't know what else to do. And now we're in a parking lot in a snowdrift and I'm sorry. I didn't want to hurt anybody! I just didn't know what else to do!"

"It's okay," he soothed, gently rocking her and stroking her hair. "Shh. It's okay. Shh."

"I want Mom!"

"I know. Me, too. But she'd want us to stay alive, stay free. You did that. She'd be proud Meg, not mad."

She sniffled and raised her head. "You sure?"

"Alive in a snowdrift or dead with Hugh? I'm *positive* mom would be *fine* with this."

"Even if other people died?"

"Even if."

She started crying again and he held her, rocking her, until her tears ran out.

He wiped tears from her face with his fingertips. "There's a bus coming and no one's paying any attention. I think we can make it. You wanna try?"

She nodded. "Yeah. I want to get as far away from here as I can."

———

WITH NO VIDEO surveillance to track the kids' flight from the mall—if they had even left, they certainly hadn't caught a bus the first hour afterward—Warren had signed off to focus on researching SynAg's top-secret info on Meg. Despite the clerk's alarm, Huey picked up some burn ointment at Walgreens then parked at the apartment complex across the street from the mall. He glowered and spread ointment on his oozing skin while listening to chaos on his police radio.

At least the fucking cops didn't know anything either.

Restless, and with Warren researching, he decided to do a little recon at the Adamson's house. He drove across town and paused on a quiet residential street to put on his police gear, then drove the final couple of blocks to the house. *The kids had headed west, but why? Did they have any actual destination in mind at all? Any plan?* Surely that info was in the house, a place he didn't notice when he stole crime scene evidence, a detail that wasn't on a hard drive or in a crime scene photo.

There had to be a way to complete the contract despite

the kids going completely off-grid. Had to be a way to find them.

After parking in the Adamson's driveway, he strode through the snow to the front door, tore off the police tape, and shouldered the door open.

The house reeked of death—which he expected—but he felt and heard a breeze coming from the kitchen.

A window was open beside the crappy dining table, flurries blowing in. He saw little more than wet specks on the kitchen floor, certainly not a puddle. It hadn't been open long.

He turned, hand reaching for a gun that was no longer there, and, for a moment, he felt unsure and exposed.

Police tape remained over the back door, and no recent footprints had marred the snow near the front, so perhaps the interloper had exited through the window? He leaned out and saw two sets of prints coming in, but none going out.

He closed and latched the window.

Huey strode through the kitchen and locked the basement door then turned to the hall that connected the remodeled garage to the rest of the house. Fucknut's chilly room remained foil-lined and depressingly Spartan. No one hid under the bed or in the closet. Blast-o-girl's dollar-store-decorated room seemed messier than he remembered when he had left that morning. Again, no one hid under the bed or in the closet, and, despite Meg's blast-damage still stinging his right arm and side, he sighed. Kids deserved better than poverty and a dead mom.

Scowling, he walked across the house. Cheryl's room had been sealed with untouched police tape, leaving only Slippery Matt Adamson's bedroom and the basement to search.

Huey walked to Matt's locked door, ready to grab or punch or break whoever hid within, and rammed his shoulder against it twice before it burst open. He found only the rifled-through remnants of a slacker's tiny bedroom, complete with an open crank-out window. A window no one larger than a pre-schooler could have squeezed through, a window he'd noted as closed when he'd pulled in the driveway.

A window with fleeing footprints beneath it nonetheless.

He stared at the hand-length gap between windowpane and wall, then cranked the window closed. He had taken two steps toward the closet when something crunched beneath his boot.

Two zippers, jeans buttons and brads, bra hooks, a pair of underwires, and an outdated smartphone lay at his feet.

He crouched to examine his finds. "Ah, Matty. You were just here with your little girlfriend, weren't you?"

He left the clothing detritus, but picked up the phone and clicked it on. Kate McLean had no security features installed so he checked out her Facebook, Instagram, and Snapchat on his way back to the Caddy. As he drove away, he wondered whether Matt or Kate would break first.

For the first time that day, he smiled.

THIRTEEN

KATE DROVE UP EUCLID, HER HEART RACING. SHE FELT ALIVE, electric. Excited. "That... That was impossible!" She glanced at Matt then back to the sloppy street.

"You would think so, but obviously no." Matt chuckled. "Been doing it my whole life."

She glanced at him again. "Wow, just... Wow! We went *through a wall!*"

"Yeah, we did." He reached through the front of her glove compartment to pull out a tire pressure gage, flip it through his fingers, then put it back. "See? It's really not a big deal."

"Oh, god, that is so cool! But of course, it's a big deal! No one can walk through walls! But we just walked *through a freaking wall!*"

"Everyone in my family does stuff like that."

Kate paused at the stoplight and, seeing plenty of space, turned south. "For real?"

"Yeah, for real. There are much more interesting... *talents* than mine."

She drove for a while, grinning. "Wow. I don't know how

that's possible, but wow. Are you guys like mutants or something? Like that movie? Are you superheroes?"

"Nah. It's a genetic condition. My grandpa worked for a chemical company when he was young, doing testing on animals, and I guess there was an accident involving some monkeys who ate genetically-enhanced grain. I guess they all freaked out and autopsies showed they had an altered brain structure, but the company kept making its chemical. Anyway, my granddad stayed on the project and he *changed*. He could make anything he held disappear. And later, after he got married and had some kids, the kids were..."

"Like you?"

"Yeah. All of us different, all of us talented in our own way."

"So your niece and nephew? They're different too?"

"Yeah. Well, it's mostly in boys, I guess. Girls don't usually have much."

"Sure," Kate said, rolling her eyes. "Screwed out of the cool stuff, just like everywhere else in this world."

Her face flushed hot. *I can't believe I just said that.*

"If anything, girls quieted other talents around them. That's what my sister did, and it helped keep Jake from going insane. Granddad said it was a sex-linked mutation. Boys displayed their talents, girls... They diminished and absorbed."

She glanced at him and his fingers flicking through the seat beside his thigh. He had good fingers. Strong fingers. Fingers slipping in then out again.

Oh, god. What would it feel like if... if... if he did that to me?

She took a breath and kept her eyes on the road. *What*

am I thinking? Yeah, fine, I haven't slept with a guy in months, but I just met him this morning!

Picked up guys in bars, though, she reminded herself. *At least I know he's nice, right?*

She drove a few blocks then glanced over to see him watching her with a slight grin.

"See something you like, Kate?"

She blushed and returned her eyes to the road. "Maybe."

They drove for a couple of blocks, then she took a calming breath and said, "So. What talent does your nephew have?"

"He knows what someone's gonna do before they do it. Only it's not just someone he's next to, it's everyone, for a quarter mile or so. It's why we lined his room with the foil, so he wouldn't be bombarded by everyone's upcoming actions in the neighborhood all the time."

"Cool, but weird."

"Yeah. We had some trouble with him last year, breaking into houses and stuff. Since he could tell where people were and what they were doing before they actually did it, he could steal shit. Sometimes he goes crazy and we worry he's dangerous. I hate to admit it, but he's just a bad boy."

"He's a bad, bad, boy," she sighed, feeling a throbbing low in her hips as she glanced at Matt. "Are you a bad boy?"

He leaned close, his hand on her thigh, through her jeans but on her skin. He whispered, "Maybe. Wanna find out?"

She giggled, "Maybe," at the delightful tingle when he passed a fingertip through the side of her thigh, then nearly drove over the curb when he did the same thing to her right breast.

MEG SAT mid-bus with her brother and hoped no one had seen the blood-smeared pack of Sesame Street training pants she'd tucked beneath her coat. The parking lot outside of Macy's—probably outside of the whole mall, she reminded herself—was strewn with clothes, display equipment, and Christmas decorations. Jake had ripped open the training pants and used a pair to wipe away the blood, then they'd washed his face with snow and he wiped it clean again with the back-side of the undies. They'd dropped that gore-stained mess behind a semi-trailer and left it behind when they'd scrambled over the retaining wall.

After the bus came, he sat beside her, eyes half-closed, a wadded pair of toddler-undies clenched in his fist and pressed tight beneath his nose. Every once in a while he'd moan in pain.

None of the six other people on the bus seemed to notice. Everyone looked exhausted—including the bus driver—and no one talked.

Meg stared out at festive western suburban neighborhoods as they drove down the freeway, then the bright and cheery Christmas decorations and lights of Jordan Creek Parkway. Everything looked so joyous and pretty, especially with the glitz reflected on fresh-falling snow, but she thought only of her lost mother, her hurting brother, and the awful man she'd surely killed even though she'd only wanted to shove him away.

Jake slumped beside her during their bus ride and, once, she thought she saw blood in his ear before he wiped it away.

I have to get him out of here, have to get him away from so many people, she thought.

He staggered off the bus when they reached the mall, and she stood beside him, worried, until the bus gathered new passengers and drove away.

"Where do we go?" she said aloud. "What do we do? Am I going to need to hurt—"

Jake held the training pants to his face and pointed across the parking lot.

Meg saw a stoplight and asked, "Cross at the light?"

He nodded and fell in beside her as she guided him across the parking lot. She had to help him remain standing before they reached the road.

———

"HEY, GUYS," Fawkes said as he unlocked the front door of a bungalow near the fairgrounds. "Sorry I'm so late."

Fitz, a half-grown-marmalade-kitten who'd been the only witness to a suicide when he was no bigger than a teacup, chirruped a greeting and bounded across the couch toward Fawkes like he always did, but Carrie and Lexington were nowhere to be seen.

Fawkes tucked his armload of files beneath his sling and scooped up the rowdy young cat with the other. "What'd you get into today, you ornery little shit?" he asked, tickling Fitz's cheek.

Fitz purred and climbed onto Fawkes' shoulder as they walked to the kitchen. Lexington mrowed from the bedroom, followed by a dull thump of him jumping to the floor.

Fawkes set his folders on the kitchen table, refilled the food and water dishes, and did a quick scoop out of the litter box before pulling a Heineken and 3-day-old pizza from the fridge. Fitz crunched a couple of bites then batted a jingly ball around the kitchen while an overweight old Siamese rubbed alongside Fawkes's legs on his way to the kibbles.

"Hey, Lex," Fawkes said, reaching down to pet the old fella on his way past. Lexington mrow-wow-rowed in reply then settled around the bowl to eat.

"Yeah, I know I'm late."

Lex gave him a sideways blink. "Mow, mrrrowh?"

"Dead mom, missing kids," Fawkes said, pulling a paper plate out of the package. "Crazy case, though."

"Rwow?"

"No, no meth heads. Not this time. A brother who walks through walls and a daughter who blasted half of a mall. The son... I'm still trying to figure him out."

Lex paused chewing to blink at Fawkes.

"Really. Half the mall. And I got shot."

The old cat huffed and resumed eating.

Fawkes took a pain pill and his antibiotics, then ate pizza and reviewed the files one-handed, re-reading every word of Matt Adamson's interview, the preliminary coroner's report, and what little material the lab had received and processed. He spread Garrel's crime scene pics across the table while Lexington ate and Fitz batted his jingly ball out to the living room.

Pizza gone and only a couple of swigs left in his Heine, Fawkes sighed when his cell rang. "Fawkes," he said, reaching for his pen, and noticed Carrie, a petite, black-and-white longhair, washing her face just inside the kitchen doorway while keeping one eye on Fitz.

She'd had her pretty little face inside her human's skull when he'd first seen her three years before. The drug dealer'd been dead two days before anyone bothered to call the cops and, well, a cat's gotta eat.

"Hey, Les," Claire's familiar voice said. "I see you're finally home. Interested in a little toast on a cold winter's night?"

He leaned back and smiled, stretching. "Maybe. But I'm injured and on a homicide. No telling when I might have to get back."

"Understood," she said. "I'll bring the butter."

Fawkes carried his files to the office and headed for the shower.

KATE HELD her jeans closed and mostly held her curiosity in check, but as she followed Matt up the stairs to her apartment, he glanced back at her and wiggled his fingers through the banister. She wondered how much it'd tingle if he did that in her.

"Still have that wine?" he said as they reached her floor.

"Most of it."

Then he grabbed her wrist and pulled her through the wall into her apartment.

He kissed her, his lips warm and firm but not tingly, his hands on her back gripping her, then slippery-tingle, then gripping again.

She shifted and her jeans slid from her hips, partly due

to gravity, partly because he helped, and she tugged his down, too.

He wore no underwear and his penis sprung right into her hand.

They stumbled toward her bedroom while he pulled her panties through her and tossed them aside, then tugged his shirt through his chest.

He backed her to the bed, one finger in her, tingling as he stroked through her clitoris and into her vagina then back again, in and out, in and out, electrifying every core of her being. She cried out against his mouth, coming, coming hard, even before he pressed her onto her bed and pulled her on top of him, over him, and into her. He tugged off her sweater as she fucked him, riding the hot, heavy tingle of his penis within her, his fingers on and within her breasts, unbearably stroking her buried pleasure-centers as she came again.

FOURTEEN

FAWKES FINISHED EJACULATING AND SUCKED IN BREATHS AS HE eased off Claire, taking care not to wrench his bad arm or kick Lex off of the bed. "We should do this more often."

She popped her back and rolled to face him. "Maybe you should work less. And maybe not get shot."

"But who'd catch the bad guys?"

Claire rested her hand on his belly. "Someone who doesn't make me toast."

He laughed and staggered out of bed, his toes curling on the cold floor.

His wife had divorced him for a richer guy with a safer job seventeen years ago, followed by Claire's husband's fatal heart attack four years later. Their just-across-the-street friends-with-benefits arrangement started six, maybe seven months after the funeral.

She'd called asking him to unclog her garbage disposal on a lazy Sunday morning. While he lay on her kitchen floor with his head and shoulders beneath her sink and his hands full of disposal, she'd asked him if he ever felt lonely. He'd admitted he did, sometimes. When he crawled out, he saw she'd untied her bathrobe. He'd watched her turn away and walk toward her bedroom, letting the robe fall behind her. He'd washed his hands and followed the delicate swish of her nightgown right into her bed.

After, she made him toast. Then she fucked him again.

For twelve years, neither dated anyone nor wanted to. Both liked their independence and privacy, but they also liked a good toss once in a while. Sometimes he'd walk over to her place, sometimes she'd walk over to his. He'd never kissed her, but, before returning home, they always shared toast.

The snowstorm blustered against his windows. "You heading right back or staying 'til morning?" he asked on the way to the john.

"Probably stay over," she sighed. "It's getting nasty out there. I can head back if you want me to, though."

One of the cats scratched at the door. Probably Carrie. He ignored her.

"Nah, stay as long as you need. I'll be up a while."

"Sounds fine," she said and burrowed into the warm bed.

He cleared his pipe, wrapped his bad arm in plastic, and showered again, returning to the bedroom to find Claire holding out his phone and Lexington snoozing on her belly. "Your partner called."

He accepted the phone. "There must be news. Thought she logged out for the night."

"Say no more," Claire assured him as she slipped out from beneath Lex. On the way to the bathroom, she said, "I'll make tonight's toast. You want anything else?"

In all the time they'd shared a bed and toast, they'd never

expanded the post-romantic-munchies paradigm. He managed to pull on flannel pants and a sweatshirt. "Um. Eggs?"

"You got it, Detective. Go bag your baddy."

He heard the bathroom door close and the shower turn on before he reached his office and the stack of files. He sat, opened to a fresh notebook page, and clicked to return Jenn's call.

Garrel picked up on the first ring. "What kept you?"

"Toast," Fawkes said. "How's Noah?"

She sighed. "About the same. Dan..." She sucked in a breath. "He found a new, um, specialist. We're seeing him tomorrow."

Wow, on Christmas Eve? Fawkes thought, but said, "Oh, good. Hope he can give you some answers."

Niceties out of the way, Garrel returned to her usual brusqueness, "The mall finally came back online and we have security footage of the explosion. I've emailed the three best viewpoints to you. We've got several good shots of the big asshole's face this time, and brass's sent him up the chain to the Fed's database. With luck, we'll get an ID on the fucker soon."

"Anything in from the lab?"

"No. But we received the official casualty report from local hospitals. The only fatality in that entire mess was the guy who took a bullet for you. Some concussions, abrasions galore, and a few broken bones. Oh, and six people's pacemakers went bonky then settled back down. That's it."

"How is that possible?"

"I don't know, but I wouldn't want to screw with that little girl. We're not releasing video to the press. People will freak out, so we're calling it a power surge brought on by the storm taking out a relay or some blah-blah bullshit. The asshole in the dark coat injected Jake with something and tried to inject Meg, and I've already requested the search and clean up crews keep an eye out for it, but don't hold your breath. They've likely been tossed. And, with that, I'm heading to bed."

"Thanks, Jenn. See you tomorrow."

"Yeah," she said, then clicked off.

Fawkes downloaded the videos and watched them twice from each of the three viewpoints Garrel had sent him. All three showed cautious but broken-looking kids trying to blend in until the big man in the black coat approached. Fawkes selected the video with the best view of Meg and set it to watch in slow-motion. He zoomed his screen in to focus, frame by frame, on Meg as she sat next to an aging woman. The kid looked exhausted and on the verge of weeping, but who could blame her? Her mother'd been murdered just that morning and they'd been on the run ever since. Meg sat, sad and apparently unaware of anything but passing shoppers, until her brother appeared on-screen, running and grasping her hand as he continued past the bench she sat upon.

Fawkes saw her startle, saw her struggle to stay upright and follow, saw the older woman's purchases scatter, saw Meg stumble and land face-first on the floor.

His own throat tightened as he watched Jake turn to face his attacker. Lights flickered. The teenager was terrified but defiant as the man in the black coat pulled the boy toward him and injected his throat with a pressure-injector before efficiently shoving the boy and injector aside in one fluid movement. A light above them burst, sparks and shards of plastic tumbling from above like jagged snowflakes. Black-coat thrust his left hand into his coat pocket and reached his right hand down for Meg who'd just managed to get to her knees. Black-coat grasped her arm and she screamed, the air around her rippling. He'd barely pulled a second injector out of his coat pocket when scrambling, sparking tendrils of green-white light streamed from Meg's chest, her eyes, and her forehead. Like branches, roots, or lines etched in a shattered mall floor, lightning surged toward the assassin, tangling together into a blinding, writhing mass before bursting apart.

The next frame, the final frame, went near-solid green-white.

Fawkes clicked backward two frames, to the brilliant, basketball-sized electrical mass gathering in front of Meg. He leaned back and sucked in a surprised breath.

She'd made ball lightning.

Jesus.

HUEY CALLED Warren on their secure line while driving to the stop sign nearest the Adamson's house.

Warren sounded exasperated. "Whatcha need, Babe?"

Things must not be going well. "Just an address for a cell number. Found one at the house."

He heard the familiar patter of Warren's bare feet on the tile in the hall. "You went back there?"

"Yeah. Needed to find *something*, and I found a phone. It

belongs to a Kate McLean. She apparently wears an under-wire bra and knows Matt Adamson."

"All right," Warren sighed as he settled in. "Gimme the number."

Huey recited it back and let the Caddy idle at the stop sign. No reason to turn until he knew where he was headed.

"Katie lives in a dump off Scott Street."

Huey wrote down the address then flicked his turning signal. "I'm heading south."

"And I'm still trying to figure out what SynAg's hiding. Call me when you're done with Kate. Maybe I'll have something by then."

FIFTEEN

MEG HELPED JAKE ACROSS THE HIGHWAY AND INTO A QUIET suburban neighborhood where the residents focused more on their busy holiday cheer than a shattered little girl and her stumbling, bleeding brother.

They stayed to the relative smoothness of the recently-plowed road, its snowy banks blinking in cheery reds, blues, and greens from nearby holiday lights and giant inflated snowmen.

I can ask someone to help us, she thought. *Surely with all of these people, someone can—*

"No," he said, his voice muffled behind the wad of underwear. "They'll call the cops. Keep going. South. Go south."

After a few blocks, suburbia ended and rural fields began. Meg hesitated at the end of civilization, but Jake pointed ahead to a snow-covered field. Not long after, when most of the cheery holiday lights had faded into the storm, they took one step too many and sunk thigh-deep into a ditch that looked no different than anything else. Meg floundered and remained upright, but Jake collapsed sideways.

"Jake!" she called out, scrambling to pull his head and shoulders from beneath the snow.

"So cold," he said, teeth chattering and his face smeared with snow and frozen blood. "And so many people. It's all chaos. Colors and lights and anger and being upset for not getting the right Barbie doll and worry if the in-laws will make more snide comments. I can't tell what's real and what they're thinking. I just want to get away from them, I just want it to stop."

She dug through the snow to search his coat pockets but found nothing. Desperate, she looked back the way they'd come, back where most of their footprints had already been erased by snow and wind. Where the voices in his head screamed from. "Where are your meds?"

"We ran out two days ago and Mom was supposed to pick up the refill tomorrow," he sighed. "Back when Hugh attacked us. Back when Grassley ran for Senate against Pinkie Pie. I want some, it looks *sooooo good*, but it's not on my diet."

Oh, crap, she thought, looking around her but seeing nothing but a few scraggly trees and snow.

Jake hadn't hallucinated since the summer she was seven, when Mom was between jobs and the Medicaid hadn't kicked in yet to help pay for his medicine that dulled strangers' thoughts in his head. Even in his foiled room with an iron pot on his head, he'd ranted and wailed for days, had hallucinated and talked nonsense and bled from his ears. At one point, he'd begged Mom to kill him.

Then Jacqui had come through, forced through approval for his prescription herself, and Meg got her brother back.

But Jacqui wasn't here, and Meg had no idea how to

reach her without the little card in her mom's purse, let alone having a phone to call her on. The nearest houses were far behind them, a few hundred yards away across a field and lost in the snowstorm. *Would anyone help us? Would taking him back there make it worse? What do I do?*

"You leave me here," Jake said, grabbing her coat with both hands as fresh blood leaked from his nose, "and head south, to Patterson, okay? It's on highway ninety-two. About twenty miles south." He sighed and leaned his head back into the snow. "South. Twenty miles. Keep the interstate to your left. Just don't tell Brenda I'm getting her a new car for Christmas this year. Don't want to ruin the surprise."

"You need to get up. We'll find shelter. I can get you warm."

"I don't want any more purple spiders!" he screamed at someone she couldn't see, then his eyes locked on hers. "Patterson. Repeat it back to me, Meg."

She tried to lift him but failed and, crying, pulled off her new coat. "Patterson. Twenty miles south."

"That's my good boy. Want some roast turkey?" he said, his head rolling back again, then he whined, "Dammit, Pico, why do you always have to get drunk at my Mom's? Frankie never got drunk. Stoned, sure, but never drunk."

She covered him with her coat and cried while he ranted the random nonsense of other people's thoughts tangled in his brain. She lay beside him for a long time, trying to increase and share her body heat, but his rants turned to murmurs to whispers to silence, no matter how warm she made him.

Oh, God, she thought, crying and staring up through the

falling snow while her brother lay unconscious beside her. *Please. Help us.*

But no miracle came.

She heated her hands and touched his face, wiped the worst of the blood away, then she stood again, hoping to see signs of someone's home nearby.

Nothing. Nothing but night and snow and, far to her left, the rumble of an engine.

She clambered forward, arms reeling to stay upright, through the ditch and up to a road drifted over with snow. A pair of round headlights crested a hill to the left, the light turning the blowing snow afire. Meg tottered into knee-deep snow on the road, waving for the driver to stop. A truck rattled toward her, plumes of snow arcing from its tires.

The engine sounds shifted lower, more rumbly, as the truck eased to a stop. From the vertical slashes in the grille to the pair of straight-as-sticks wipers on the split windshield, Meg had never seen such boxy, straight lines on a vehicle before.

The driver's side door creaked opened and someone hopped out. "Gracious, child!" a woman said as her thick shadow came around the door. "What the bloody hell are you doing all the way out here without a coat in a snowstorm?"

"My brother!" Meg said, pointing to where she'd left Jake in the ditch. "Please help me! He fell and won't wake up!"

"Aw, shit." The woman rounded the front of the truck and followed Meg. Tall, bulky, and middle-aged, she plowed down into the ditch as if crossing a field of grass instead of a sea of drifting snow. "How long's he been unconscious?"

Meg knelt beside him. "Just a few minutes."

The woman's hands moved swift and sure over Jake's face and throat. "Why're you kids out in this?"

Meg lowered her head and tried not to cry. "Is he still alive? I gave him my coat... I didn't know what else to do."

"Yeah, he's alive, but he's surely hypothermic." She looked over at Meg. "Too cold. And looks like he might have bashed his nose. C'mon. Help me get him to the truck. I have blankets and a good heater."

"Thank you, Ma'am. Thank you so much!" Meg said, reaching beneath Jake's shoulder to help lift him to a sitting position.

"Nobody calls me Ma'am except bill collectors," the woman said as she ducked under Jake's arm. "Just call me Ginnie."

"I'm Meg," she grunted as she stood under her brother's loose weight. "And this is my brother Jake."

They half-carried, half-dragged him to the truck and managed to stuff him into the cab.

"Go on around to the driver's side and climb on in," Ginnie said as a fresh blast of snow billowed around her. "Get yourself buckled in the middle, and I'll get him to lean on you, okay? Then we can shut this door and get some heat blowing on him."

Meg nodded and did as she was told, trying not to stare at the flat, vinyl seats or the thin, two-spoked steering wheel. The bright-blue metal dashboard had only small, round knobs, the radio played a song about life in a fast lane, a bar of some kind split the windshield into two halves, and a weird metal rod with a knob on top stuck out of the truck's floor.

It was a crazy looking truck, but the heater blew toasty warm air.

While Ginnie supported Jake, Meg buckled herself in. She pulled on Jake while Ginnie pushed until he was in the truck, if sort of crooked and leaning on Meg. They managed to buckle him in and get his legs mostly arranged in a sensible-looking way. Ginnie covered him in a grubby blanket she'd found behind their seat then slammed his door and rushed around to the driver's seat. A flick of one knob sent hot air blasting into the truck cab.

After buckling herself in, Ginnie reached for the knob on the long metal rod and pulled it toward her. "Alright," she said as the truck staggered forward again. "We can get turned around up here a ways, then I'll haul you kids right into town. I think that Methodist Hospital on 60th is open. I think."

Meg reached for Ginnie's arm. "No, no!" she said. "We can't go to a hospital!"

Ginnie glanced at her but moved the rod forward and kept driving into the blizzard. "Why the hell, er, heck not? They'll warm him up, give him electrolytes or something, call your Mom..."

"Our mom's dead," Meg said, her eyes stinging. "A really bad man killed her this morning, and he's been chasing us, trying to catch us. He's why we're out here, why we were stuck in the snow. We've been running from him all day."

Ginnie moved the floor-rod toward Meg as the radio shifted from music to a winter storm update.

"A bad man?"

"Yeah. His name's Hugh. He kills people. He drugged

Jake, and if we go to a hospital, he'll know. He'll find us. And he'll sell us. Please."

"Honey, I can't—" The washers whooshed while Ginnie looked straight ahead into a vortex of bright snow. "Did you say he's going to *sell you?* Into *what?* Human trafficking or some shit like that?"

"I... I don't know what that is," Meg admitted. "But if we go to a hospital, he'll know. If we tell the cops, he'll know. Please."

"Honey. If your brother got too cold, he might die without a doctor."

Meg's hands shook. *What can I do? How can I save us?* She sucked in a harsh breath and struggled not to cry. *Maybe someone at the hospital will listen. Maybe we'll get a good cop. Maybe.*

I can't let Jake die.

"Okay," she said at last, her voice small behind the endless whoosh of hot air.

The truck slowed while heading down a slight hill, and the man on the radio talked about road closures and Christmas Eve cancellations. Ginnie pushed forward on the floor-rod's handle and the truck eased to a stop while Meg looked out to the intersection, trees at all four quadrants, the roads lost beneath snow.

"Interstate's closed," Ginnie muttered, her head cocked toward a speaker. Meg watched her stare out to the storm. "Shit."

The radio guy kept talking, but it was hard to hear over the heater. Meg asked, "What's wrong?"

"Everything south of 44's shutting down. We're looking at almost three feet by morning, with more to come. Global warming my ass." Ginnie pushed the rod forward and the truck resumed its straight-ahead trek. "Driving through this crap, it'll take me a good hour to get you to the hospital. At least. And that's assuming the goddamn Sheriff will let me past roadblocks at all. We can get to the house in ten, fifteen minutes. I think."

Meg nodded, hopeful. House sounded a *lot* better than hospital.

"Hang on, Kiddo." Ginnie moved the floor-rod-thing again as the road curved and sloped downhill. "This might get kinda bumpy."

SIXTEEN

DESPITE THE WORSENING SNOWSTORM AND HIS STINGING SKIN, Huey reached the ratty little house and pulled in its un-shoveled driveway. The mailbox alongside the road said K. McLean, but the house was dark. No car stood in the driveway and no tire tracks or footprints marred the snow.

After he backed out of the drive and reached a plowed road, Huey called Warren's phone and left a message.

"Hey, Babe. No one's home and I'm too tired to stick around. See you in a bit."

He worked his way north through light traffic, the memory of Meg Adamson's bright terror fresh in his mind. Streetlights flickered on his windshield as he passed them and, sometimes, the image of Meg in his mind flickered to the face of a little boy in Somalia, or a girl in Syria. Brazil. South Africa. Columbia. Uganda. Baltimore. Kids whose parents deserved to die. Kids who were killed in an explosion he'd set. Kids who simply were in the wrong place at a time when distant men who lusted for power quarreled with weapons and armies for trinkets and wealth.

He felt the weight of every child he'd killed following him like a ghost. He could forget freedom fighters, rebels, insurgents, gunrunners, mercenaries, and thieves, even the teenage ones. They became a blur in the festering bowels of his mind.

But the kids?

The kids stared. Even from death, from maiming, from utter obliteration, they stared.

How many looked at me like Meg did before they died? he thought while waiting at a stoplight. *How many had the guts or the chance to stare at me when I removed their future? How many?*

How goddamn many?

He blinked away the sting in his eyes and drove forward again.

Most never saw me, but she did. And she knew what I was going to do to her, to her brother. Just like I've done for most of my life. Kill or acquire. Not necessarily in that order. Complete the contract, then move on to the next, and the next. But Meg looked at me with green-glowing eyes, then flung me away like I was nothing.

He drove home, forcing his mind to go blank until he parked the Caddy beside Warren's Jeep and walked inside.

Their spotless kitchen smelled of peppermint, pecans, and nutmeg. Like Christmas. Huey peeled off the tattered remnants of his coat and dropped his duffel bag on the kitchen counter. Sighing, he grabbed himself a bottle of caramel Frappuccino from beside a chocolate-and-nut dusted cake in the fridge—*aw, hell, it's Mocha pecan. Christmas or not, I swear he's trying to fatten me up*—before heading down the hall to Warren's dimly-lit office. Two of

Warren's three monitors were filled with surveillance footage, a dozen images per screen mostly showing live feeds of bus interiors and traffic cams. The third was split into a running stream of data on the left—despite almost seven years together, Hugh still couldn't make heads or tails of Warren's search and trace program—and the right half of the screen in unmoving code.

Warren frowned in the corner with a laptop. He'd curled into the loveseat with his grandma's quilt snuggled over him and a steaming mug of coffee close at hand.

Huey lifted Warren's bare feet and the end of the quilt then sat beneath both, drawing Warren's feet onto his lap to rub them. He tucked the bottle of frappe beside his hip and started the massage. "Did you find her?"

"I have, um..." Warren took a sip of coffee and sighed, stretching his chilly toes. "I've found a hundred-and-twenty-six archives so far."

"Wow. That's a lot of intel on one ki—"

"No, Babe," Warren said, glancing up from his laptop. "This whole fucking database is encrypted to hell and back and, so far, I've found archives on a hundred-and-twenty-six *people* who've been genetically compromised by SynAg."

He took another sip of coffee and sighed. "I don't even know if she's in this set. Or in any of the other seventeen sets I think contain human samplings. The first three sets I found were pigs and I didn't realize it for I dunno how long because, fuck, Hugh, how many pigs can float above the ground? How many?"

"None I've ever seen," Huey admitted.

Warren muttered *goddamn genetically altered grain,* then looked up from his screen. He slapped the laptop closed and leaned forward. "What the holy fuck happened to your face?!? Are you okay?"

"Yeah, I think so. She just—"

"The little girl did that?!?"

Hugh shrugged and focused on rubbing the arch of Warren's foot. "It's just a burn. Stings like a bitch, sure, but..."

Warren pulled his feet away and set aside the laptop. "That is not *just a burn!*" He burst to his feet. "We need to get you to the hospital."

Huey gave him a you-have-got-to-be-shitting-me glare. "I've been hurt worse. It's fine."

"Have you seen it?!" Warren asked.

"Just in the car mirr—"

Warren dragged Huey off the loveseat and out of his office, down the hall, and to the main-floor bathroom.

"Babe, come on!" Huey said during the trek. "I can't go to the hospital. The cops are looking for me and they'll—"

Warren flicked the on the bathroom light and turned Hugh toward the big mirror. He'd never considered himself a good-looking man—too bulky, too weathered, too battered by life and occupation—but he took a step back from his reflection. The right side of his face and neck were scribbled with erratic red lines like roots moving up from his collar to his scalp.

While Huey stood there, staring at himself, Warren gently tugged up his scorched shirt then let out a trembling sigh. "You're covered in electrical burns. Take everything off."

Shit.

Huey stripped, wincing from both the pain of dragging fabric over the burns and the worry of what doing so might show. He stood nude in front of Warren and a full-length mirror and could not look away. The force of the blast had hit him mid-torso on the front right, leaving that area a blistered and angry red. Paler lightning streaks and tendrils scrambled out from it, across his belly, hips, and genitals; up his chest and neck to the right side of his face, ear, and scalp; and around his thigh and down his right leg to mid-shin and calf. A separate set covered his right hand and scrambled up his arm up to just past his elbow.

Huey stared at the burns, the marks Meg had given him.

She could have killed me, killed everyone there. But she didn't. She flung me away, and marked me, BRANDED *me.*

Warren examined Huey's side, near the epicenter of the burns, right about where he wore his pistol holster. "That's surely second degree," Warren said, not-quite touching the blisters. "We need to get you to a doctor."

Huey met Warren's gaze in the mirror. "You want me to get arrested? You want to visit me in prison?"

"What? No. Of course not."

"Then I cannot go to the doctor."

Warren muttered, "Shit," then pulled his phone from his pocket. He typed a few taps then said, "Okay. I need you to go to bed and lie down, scorched side up, under the covers."

Huey winked. "Love ya, Babe, but now's not the time for—"

Warren shoved his phone and its WebMD article toward Huey's face. "We don't have aloe or bandages, so lie the fuck down, on your good side, under the goddamn duvet, preferably with your feet up, while I get the supplies."

"The roads are shit, and I'm fine."

Warren pointed toward the stairs. "Go, or I'm calling an ambulance!"

Huey went, shaking his head at Warren bundling up to drive through a blizzard for aloe and gauze.

MEG SAW little but the blizzard until the truck stopped beside a spindle-railed porch. She climbed out to help Ginnie carry Jake then paused, staring agape at an aged but elegant house that surely came from a fairytale. A dog barked somewhere inside.

"It's just an old farmhouse, honey," Ginnie said. "C'mon. Let's get him inside."

They managed to pull Jake from the truck without dropping him, and Meg struggled to keep her grip while remaining balanced on the snowy steps, but she let go when she slipped and fell on her butt near the front door.

"Go ahead and open the door. Hold it open for me," Ginnie said, huffing under Jake's limp weight.

Meg scrambled back to her feet. "Where are your keys?"

The barking dog sounded closer, louder.

"Don't need no keys. Go on. Open the door."

Meg stared at Ginnie, blinking at the impossibility of her statement. *All adults had house keys, right?*

"Girl, he's heavy! Just open the danged door!"

It sounded like the dog barked from right there, right behind the door, but Meg sucked in a breath and tried the embossed knob, which turned easily. The door creaked a warm welcome when she pushed inward.

Darkness beckoned from within and a slender, thigh-high brown dog rushed out and barked circles around Ginnie.

"Damn fool dog," she muttered as Meg hurried to help her with Jake. "Go on. Get back in the house!"

The dog wriggled, sniffing everyone, then bounded into the yard, each leap poofing up clouds of snow. They managed to get Jake about halfway through the door when the dog ran back in, knocking Meg's legs hard enough for her to stumble a step aside.

The dog disappeared into the dark, Meg heard its toenails on hard floor moving away, then approaching, then it whooshed past her, across the porch, and leaped into the snow again.

"Never you mind Lady. I've been gone most of the day and she's just excited I'm home, with company, no less. We don't get much company."

They got Jake completely in the house and Ginnie pointed to the right. "Light switch is right behind you."

Meg reached to the wall, tentatively feeling for a switch. She found three, and, holding her breath, pushed them all upward with her forearm.

She flinched at the sudden brightness of a porch light, the light above them in the entryway, and a living room light flicking on. The house was warm, cluttered, and cozy in a retro style, but the wood floors and moldings shone.

"Let's get him to the couch." Ginnie nodded toward the massive navy-and-burgundy striped sofa and recliner to their right.

"Have him sit," Ginnie said when they lowered Jake onto the cushions, "so we can get his coat off."

Ginnie held him while Meg pulled, and Jake felt sweaty, not cold.

"Shit, I dunno if he's hypothermic," Ginnie said. "Was he sick? Did he have a fever?"

"Not exactly." Meg lifted her brother's legs onto the couch and untied his boots.

The dog had come back in and her butt wiggled as she sniffed Jake then Meg then Jake again.

"Not exactly?" Ginnie sighed and pulled an afghan off the back of the couch. "What does that mean?"

Meg helped her cover Jake with the afghan and the dog leaped onto the couch to snuggle down beside him and lay her head on his hip while gazing adoringly at Meg and Ginnie.

"It means he hasn't had his medicine." The dog licked Meg's fingers and her eyes stung as she reached out to pat the dog's head.

"Well... Where's his medicine?" Ginnie asked on her way to the front door.

"We ran out. Two days ago. Mom was supposed to get..." She sucked in a harsh breath and sat beside Jake while the dog whined softly and nuzzled her arm.

Now she's dead. What are we gonna do without Mom? What am I gonna do if Jake doesn't wake up?

Meg looked around the room full of furniture out of an old TV show, at a dog she only met three minutes before, and a blocky, graying-haired woman, the stranger who'd rescued them from the snow. Her throat clenched.

My brother's unconscious, I don't know where I am, and I'll never see Mom again.

She was bawling by the time Ginnie shut out the storm.

"Here, honey," Ginnie soothed a few moments later. She pressed a tissue into Meg's shaking hands.

Meg nodded her thanks and blew her nose while the dog nuzzled under her elbow. "I'm sorry," she said, without looking up. "It's just been a really awful day."

"Is there someone I can call? Someone who needs to know you're all right?"

Meg shook her head. "Maybe my Uncle Matt, but I don't know where he is or how to reach him. Jake said the cops took him for questioning." She sucked in a sniffle and looked at Ginnie who'd crouched before her. "I don't know what to do."

"I don't know, either," Ginnie said. "This is outside of my tool kit." She sighed. "Have you eaten anything today?"

Meg shrugged. "Since this all happened? Breakfast from McDonald's. Then a cheese stick and a granola bar. Some M&M's. That was hours ago."

"Well, I haven't eaten since a donut after lunch. How about I make us some soup?"

Meg nodded and managed a smile. "Sure. Soup sounds good."

Ginnie took a couple of steps away then turned back. "You can help, if you want."

But what about Jake? Meg thought, frowning at him. *Can I leave him after all that's happened? Even to go to the next room?*

"Honey, he's gonna be whatever he's gonna be. Sitting and staring at him isn't gonna make him any better any faster, or worse any slower. There's not much more we can do for him until this storm's over except keep him warm."

"Actually, there is." Meg took a shuddering breath and stood. "Do you have any foil?"

F AWKES PICKED up his phone on the first ring and slid out of bed. Claire sighed and rolled onto her belly.

"Whatcha got?" Fawkes said as he hurried, nude, down the hall.

"Detective, it's Becca Hodginson. From the lab?"

"Hey, Becca." Fawkes flicked on his office light and sat at his desk. "What happened?"

"I freelance at night sometimes at a testing lab at ISU," Becca said, her voice lowering, "and I ran one of Cheryl Adamson's blood samples. A specific test, on Chromosome 19. The screwy one, remember?"

"You what?"

"I ran a special test and found something. Look, I know the evidence chain is technically busted, but I thought the test could tell us something quicker than the lab downtown would get to it, considering it's Christmas and all, and, well, there's plenty of her blood to sample, and you could always request the specific test to make it official, and—"

Fawkes leaned forward and grabbed a pen. "What'd you find?"

She took a breath. "The short arm is a lot shorter than it should be. *Crazy* short. I thought at first it was because gene 13, the calcium channel gene, is just..." She sighed. "Okay, it's *all there*, but it's configured weird. Stuff's switched around, and I'm *pretty sure* there's been a mutation, a chemical substitution somewhere in there, which is nuts all by itself. But that's not the *really* weird thing."

Fawkes' pen kept up with her. "What was the really weird thing?"

"The gene that's supposed to be two slots down is *gone*. That's why the gene's arm is so short. NOTCH3 is *gone*."

"What? How can a gene be gone?"

"I have no idea. Everything has that gene. Everything with a brain, anyway, since it mostly controls neural pathway development. But it's just *gone*. Calcium channel, the big one on the short arm, it's there but *weird*, the next gene looks *perfect*, but the third one, NOTCH3... *It's not there*. After that, everything else looks perfect. I called you because this makes no sense. How was she even alive? Both kids showed a weird Chromosome 19, so if they're missing NOTCH3 too, how can *they* be alive? How can any of this—"

"It's okay. Take a breath. I have a question. Hypothetical, but... Unofficial. Off the record. Confidential. Just one question."

"You want me to keep my mouth shut?"

"Yeah. For now, at least. Everything you found tonight, *and* the answer to what I want to ask you."

He heard a door close and the sound of running water.

"Yeah. Absolutely. What's the question?"

"Hypothetically, could someone with that genetic abnormality, have, um..." Fawkes rubbed his eyes and wondered if he'd hit his head harder than he thought during the explosion. "Could this genetic arrangement cause some sort of... superpower?"

"You mean like teleportation or shooting lasers or something? Like in comic books?"

"Not precisely, but yes."

"Wow, um..." The water sound faded and grew stronger then faded again as she talked. "Well, the calcium channels control electricity in the body, but they're weird in this blood sample, plus the missing gene controls neural pathway development, so I guess it's possible that some sort of electrical function or structures in the brain that NOTCH3 impacted is no longer getting impacted and whatever electrical impulses *are* there are probably totally different than normal, and, hell, I've been awake almost thirty hours so, sure, put those two together and I'll say anything's possible. Even eye lasers."

Or ball lightning or walking through a wall, Fawkes thought, staring at his notes. "So you'd suggest this is potentially an electrical issue?"

"In the brain, sure. That'd make sense. Theoretically, anyway, considering those two genes. Maybe the nerves running through the whole body, or even cellular function, depending on how the genes are expressed. Or not expressed. Not that any of this makes any sense."

"Thank you for your diligence and candor."

"You're welcome, Sir. Sorry to wake you."

"Never apologize for waking a detective on a murder case, especially one with missing children."

"Yes, Sir. Goodnight, Sir."

"Oh, Becca? Before you go..."

The water sound disappeared. "Yes, sir?"

"Your job's safe. Get some rest, and see me in the morning."

WORK WAS ONLY three miles away but Kate skipped down to her car an hour early because of the storm. She grinned as she excavated her car and scraped the windshield, waved hello to every white-knuckled driver who cut her off, and released a delighted sigh while clocking in at work.

Sex with Matt had been *amazing*.

"What's got you so chipper?" Juanita asked when Kate all but danced to the nurse's station.

"Nuthin'." Kate ran through the resident assignments and the long list of daily tasks left to do from the previous shift.

Juanita sipped her coffee. "We're gonna have a tough night. Most of the staff called in sick, and we've been short-handed since right after supper. I agreed to stay until 3 am, but I might end up staying longer if no one else comes in. I can definitely use the overtime."

"Yeah, me too," Kate said. "The roads were awful, but I can't pass up the money. Besides, it's officially a holiday in an hour."

Juanita laughed. "Time-and-a-half to wipe asses, baby!"

Kate looked up to see randy ol' Frank striding across the hall.

"Back to bed, Romeo!" she called out.

He grinned at her. "I'm lonely, Katie-bell, and I know Paula's still awake. I hear her watching that Jimmy Fallon kid!"

Kate gave him a patient smile and pointed back toward Frank's room. "Paula doesn't need the clap. Can't you at least wait until the doctor clears you so we don't have over half of the floor infected again?"

"But I'm *lonely!*"

"We're all lonely," Juanita muttered. "Go on back to bed, Frank. It's Christmas. Let 'er sleep."

Kate walked to the coffee pot and tried to hide her slight grin. *I'm not lonely. Not anymore. And he's even a nice guy. Gave me grocery money and everything!*

Ginnie heated a can of chicken noodle soup and buttered bread for grilled cheese, wondering all the while what Meg was going to do with the roll of heavy-duty aluminum foil.

She sighed and glanced over her shoulder toward the living room—not that it did much good with a wall in the way—and decided she was probably going to jail for kidnapping. Oh, she certainly didn't bring the kids home by force, nor was she forcing them to stay, but it'd be just her luck that dragging the boy out of the damn ditch would be cause enough to get her in trouble.

People sometimes got awful touchy about kids. Even when folks were trying to help.

She sighed and put the first slices of bread onto the griddle, deciding it didn't matter. She no more could've left them behind than cut off her own leg with a toothpick. If that made her a criminal, then so be it.

I've certainly got room for a couple of houseguests, she thought while layering cheese and more buttered bread. *Ain't nobody here but me and Lady. It'd do her and the house good to have kids in it for a while.*

Probably do me good, too.

The sandwiches were not quite ready to flip when Meg returned with the foil and Ginnie was struck at how fragile she looked, maybe only ten or eleven years old, with that lanky innocence girls on the cusp of puberty had. Not a baby, yet not a teen, and she had no mama to watch out for her.

"Thank you for helping us," Meg said.

"You're welcome, honey. Can you put that back for me? Second drawer, right there by the fridge."

Meg put the foil away and asked, "Can I have a drink of water?"

"Of course you can. I've got milk and juice. Pepsi, too. Even coffee. You can eat and drink whatever you want. Ain't no one here to tell us different." Ginnie pointed toward the sink. "There's a step stool. Can you reach that top cupboard?"

"Yes, ma'am. And water's fine."

She heard Meg fetch a glass and fill it at the sink then sigh as she sat at the kitchen table.

Ginnie grabbed two soup bowls from the cupboard and she wondered how long it had been since she'd fed someone besides herself in her own kitchen. A year? Longer? Cooking for Joyce wasn't quite the same.

She set a bowl in front of the grieving child, the other at her usual spot, then fetched spoons, a hot-pad, and a plate for the sandwiches.

Meg looked at the food, then Ginnie, then lowered her head again. "Thank you for helping us."

"Honey, you don't have to keep thanking me," Ginnie said as she filled Meg's bowl. "Anyone would've helped you."

"I don't think that's true," Meg sighed, her head shaking ever so slightly. Lady trotted in from the living room and nudged Meg's hand for attention.

Ginnie slid the plate of sandwiches closer to Meg. "Well, you're safe here. Eat all you want, okay? I've got plenty."

"Thank you, Ma'am." Meg stroked Lady's head a few times before she ate a spoonful of soup.

"Just call me Ginnie." She reached for a sandwich. "In

case you're wondering, you're on my farm, out here in Madison County."

"This is a farm?" Meg asked, glancing up while slurping another spoonful of soup.

"Yep. My great, great, I lose track how many greats, grandparents homesteaded here. I live on part of the original land, and rent out another hundred-fifty-some acres more my grandparents bought during the depression. Some of it's pasture, but most is tillable."

Meg watched her, hopeful. "Do you have horses and lambs and stuff?"

Ginnie grinned. "Sort of. I have one milk cow, fourteen hens, a hutch of rabbits, and three milk goats. Every spring I buy a couple of piglets and a steer for slaughter. No lambs, though. Never got a taste for mutton. I used to have a horse, but it's been a long time. There's some cats in the barn, though."

Meg's eyes grew wide. "Wow. Never met anyone with so many animals before."

Ginnie laughed. "Well, now you have. You can meet them tomorrow if you'd like."

"Can I pet them?"

"You can pet Maude and the goats all you want. They love attention. No telling with the cats. The chickens... they're not too easy to catch, let alone pet, but you sure can feed 'em."

"For real?" Meg grinned.

"For real."

They talked about livestock while Ginnie watched the girl devour her soup and sandwich. "What'd you need foil for?" she asked, keeping her attention on her own late supper.

"To wrap Jake's head so he won't hear everyone's thoughts so much. It's why his nose is bleeding, why that man was chasing us. Why he almost never left his room." She shrugged. "Can I have another sandwich?"

Ginnie pushed away from the table and walked toward the stove. "Of course you can. And you can finish off the rest of that soup, if you want."

While Ginnie cooked, she wondered how that boy convinced his sister of such hearing-thoughts nonsense.

Meg ate her soup and chattered, excited over meeting a real cow, then she paused, silent and blinking, before crying over her lost mother again.

Ginnie turned off the stove then sat beside the girl and held her while she cried.

SEVENTEEN

HUEY WOKE AT 5:46 AM TO EMPTINESS ON THE BED BESIDE him and Warren banging around the kitchen downstairs, probably making some sugar-crusted concoction for the Christmas party at his mother's.

He rolled over to press his face into Warren's pillow, and his full weight onto the scorched and bandaged wound on his side. He sucked in a startled breath and returned to his back and tried to wish the throb away. *So much for getting a little more sleep.*

"Goddammit," he muttered three minutes later as he climbed out of bed and stumbled to the bathroom.

"Oh good, you're up!" Warren called from downstairs. "How are you feeling?"

"Shitty," Huey replied. He pissed, brushed his teeth, and touch-tested his wound. Hurt like a sunuvabitch, not as bad as being peppered with shrapnel but still awful. He sighed again as Warren bounded up the stairs.

"Lemme look at it," Warren said, entering the bathroom.

Huey stood still and focused at a corner of the ceiling

over the shower while Warren exposed and examined the wound.

"No blood, and no open sores, at least not yet, so it's probably not third-degree. Some of these blisters are pretty bad, though. Hold on."

Huey held, staring at the same spot on the ceiling while Warren rummaged in the medicine cabinet. He looked over, concerned, at the scent of isopropyl alcohol.

Warren poured the alcohol into a cough-medicine-dosage-cup then dunked the business end of a shimmering scalpel into it.

"When did we get a scalpel?" Huey asked, glancing from the alcohol-soaked scalpel to Warren to the scalpel again.

"Picked it up last night. Figured sooner or later I'd need to open some blisters. And I do." He swished the scalpel around then pulled it from the alcohol. "This actually shouldn't hurt much."

"Oh, really?"

Warren knelt beside him with the scalpel in one hand and a wad of gauze in the other. "Yep. Was an Athletic Trainer in High School and I used to drain blisters all the time. Only they were on basketball players' feet, not my husband's right torso. You're gonna have to hold still."

"Trust me, I'm not moving," Huey said, returning his stare to the corner over the shower. He felt a faint pin-prick, nothing more, then warm wetness. Warren wiped it up, Huey heard the scalpel swish around the alcohol again, then another pinprick and warm wetness, and another, and another. Then Warren smeared on ointment, which made it all hurt again.

Huey turned back when Warren stood. "That should

help some with the tenderness. Not much, it *is* still a bad burn, but some. I'll drain them again before the party if they need it." He gathered up his supplies. "You might want to take a sponge bath. I'd suggest you just skip it but..."

"Yeah. We're supposed to be at your folks' place at noon and you won't want me stinking up the place. I remember."

"Exactly." Warren leaned over for a kiss then left Huey to wash up.

GINNIE SAT in her kitchen with a half-eaten plate of eggs-and-toast and a half-empty cup of coffee when she heard male-muttering from the living room.

It's about time, she thought, taking another sip. *Been hearing him toss and turn since I got up.*

"I hear you in there," Jake muttered. "Where's your bathroom?"

"Over—" she started, but he'd already headed to the back hall with Lady's clacking nails following. Ginnie chewed another bite of egg and toast and waited. She heard the flush, water in the sink, then sock-feet and a dog walking down her hallway, so she turned her chair to face the hall instead of toward the living room.

Meg had said he was fifteen, but upright he looked a weird mish-mash of thirteen and thirty with her dog at his side—about her height with a slight build, baby-faced but with a world-weary frown, a furrowed brow, and the stoop of someone used to enduring great pain.

His eyes, though, were caramel brown and piercingly

intelligent. They stared at her, glimmering as if lit from inside his skull.

"That's ridiculous," he sighed, shuffling toward her table while Lady nuzzled at his hands. "It's just the lighting in here. You must pay a heckuv an electric bill."

He flumped into the chair across from her and released a heavy sigh. "Thank you for helping us, but we need to get going as soon as Meg wakes up. I have to get her to safety."

He contemplated her with his odd, knowing eyes as she wondered if he was hungry, or if she sat across the table from a murderer.

"Eggs and toast would be great, Thank you," he said.

She stood and had taken a single step toward her stove when he sighed, "And no, I'm not a murderer. Not yet, anyway."

She turned back. "What?"

He rubbed his forehead then lowered his hand and met her gaze. "You were wondering if I was hungry *or* a murderer, which, frankly, is an odd pair of thoughts about someone you'd just met. So. I *am* hungry. The granola bar I had yesterday seems like a lifetime ago, so I'd *love* some eggs and toast. However, if I get the chance to kill the man who murdered my mother, I intend to settle that score. As of right now, I promise I've never killed anyone. Him, I'm hopeful, but I haven't done it yet. Does that help?"

She staggered to her chair and fell onto it. "This isn't possible. How can you know—"

"I really don't think you want, or need, to know the whole story of how we are how we are," he sighed. "Meg shouldn't have mentioned it at all. This thing I do, though," he said, twirling his fingers beside his forehead, "is absolutely poss..."

She held his gaze and thought, *Prove it.*

He sighed and scowled as she thought about bubble gum, MTv's moon landing promo, and her first kiss. "Okay. You want proof? *Fine.* Never heard of Bazooka bubble gum before, but it's a block of crappy pink gum with a red-white-and-blue wrapper, then you thought of the moon landing, but it isn't the *real* moon landing, is it? It's an ad for some vintage TV music thing, and I *really* don't want to know about Jeffrey Thomlin feeling you up behind the bleachers at homecoming, okay?" He tapped his forehead. "I have waaaay too much bad crap in here already."

"Holy shit," she muttered.

"Yeah. Holy shit. Woohoo! Let's make the genetically-damaged freak perform for your enjoyment!" He sighed again. "So now that that's out of the way, can I have some eggs, please? I'm really hungry. We have money if you need it. And can you maybe tell me where we are and why I can only hear you and Meg? I'll even wait for you to speak, if it'll make you feel better."

"It might," she admitted on her way to the stove. "Um, you're on my farm."

"Where's your farm?" he asked and she smiled at the weary politeness in his voice.

"Uh, rural Madison County." She turned on the stove and wondered if he'd like a drink while he waited for breakfast to cook. "We're south of Van Meter and just west of Badger Creek Park."

"How close is that to Patterson?" he asked. "And, yeah, right now I'll drink just about anything."

She laid four strips of bacon in the skillet then returned the package to the fridge. "Coffee? Milk? Orange juice?"

"All sound great."

She still had half a pot of hot coffee, so she poured him a cup and he wrapped his bandaged hands around it and sighed, smiling, before taking a sip.

Ginnie returned to cooking. "Patterson's... uh, twelve, fifteen miles? About? Ain't much down there, I never go that way unless I have to go to Winterset or Creston, and even then I usually take 169 down. Only reason I found you kids at all was 'cause I was on my way home from out by Orilla. I had to..." She shrugged.

"Had to take care of Joyce. Yeah," he said. "Glad it was you who found us and not him."

She adjusted the bacon. "Who is he?"

"A guy who does bad things for money," Jake replied. "It's just business to him."

"Killing people? Kidnapping?"

"Yeah, plus extortion, intimidation, corporate espionage... Whatever the client needs," Jake said. "Just a bad guy for hire."

"Meg said he wants to sell you."

"Sort of. He was hired to catch and deliver us." She heard him sip. "I don't think us running was part of his plan and he's getting desperate to find us."

"Desperate can be dangerous." Ginnie flipped the bacon and snuggled it against the edges of the pan before cracking three eggs into the middle. "You really think you can kill a guy like that?"

Jake paused. "Since I know what anyone's going to do

before they do it, I think I have a chance to avenge Mom. I have to try. But I need to get Meg to Patterson first."

Ginnie couldn't imagine anything important being in Patterson.

"Meg's dad lives there, so I'd say that's pretty important. He's the only family either of us has. If I can make sure she's safe with him, I can maybe track down the shit who murdered our mother."

Ginnie turned to glance at Jake and saw an exhausted teenage boy petting her dog. A boy who smiled and ruffled Lady's ears when she jumped up to lick his face.

A boy who heard her thoughts as if she'd spoken them aloud.

EIGHTEEN

Fourteen inches of snow fell on Des Moines overnight.

Fawkes left for work an hour early but arrived eleven minutes late despite his commute being only four miles, nearly all of it on major roads. He still beat Garrel to the office for the first time, ever.

Once he reached his desk, he shrugged off his coat and called her.

She picked up on the second ring. "You coming in today?" he asked.

"Hopefully. I'm currently stuck behind a clot of goddamn idiots trying to merge onto 80 at Altoona. Hate to think what 235's gonna look like."

Fawkes rubbed his aching bicep. "Are you willing to make a detour? I want to go back to the crime scene and take another look at it. Especially since most of our case's been stolen."

"All right," she sighed while someone in the background lay onto their car horn. "I can meet you there. Not sure how long it'll take me, but I'll get there. Just have to take off by one to make it to Noah's appointment."

"Absolutely. Drive careful," he said, then clicked off before dialing Becca.

She, too, was stuck in stop-and-go traffic just past Ankeny but agreed to meet up at the Adamson house, as long as Fawkes brought a collection kit and supplies from the lab. He agreed, then informed both supervisors before slogging out to the snow and loading supplies into the back of a DMPD Explorer.

AFTER A BREAKFAST of fresh-from-the-oven quiche and cinnamon rolls, Huey took a couple of Ibuprofen and drove through treacherous roads to Kate's house in the south side bottoms where a rusted-out Dodge Caravan sat snow-bound in the driveway. He drove past and paused around the corner about a block away.

"Someone's home," he said when Warren picked up. He recited the Caravan's plate number and Warren quickly confirmed it was registered to a Katherine McLean at that address. After adhering *Capitol Electric* decals to the side of his SUV and pulling on a matching blue cap, Huey drove around the block to park behind her minivan. He grabbed his tool bag and walked to the driveway-side door, even waved at a neighbor shoveling his porch steps.

A bleary, saggy, middle-aged woman in a grubby bathrobe opened the door. She reeked of cheap liquor, cigarettes, and cat piss. Matt apparently knew how to pick a winner.

"Ms. McLean?" Huey said, pretending to consult his phone.

She glanced at his SUV. "Yeah, but I don't need no electrician."

"I'm not here about your electric."

Huey shoved his way in and knocked her to the floor before locking the door behind him. He opened the cabinet beneath her kitchen sink then returned his attention to her.

She tried to scuttle away, but he stood with one booted foot on each side of her belly and stared down at her as switched his winter gloves for rubber ones. "You can make this easy, or you can make this hard."

"I... I won't put up a fight or cause trouble," she said, turning her head away. "I don't have any drugs, but I have a little money. Not much. Twenty, maybe thirty bucks. You can have it. My purse is by the couch. Just take it and go."

"I don't want your fucking money," Huey snarled, crouching over her. He grasped her chin and turned her head to the right, then the left, showing her he could do whatever he wanted.

She whimpered. "Please. Please don't rape me. Please. It's Christmas."

"You're not my type," he muttered. He pulled zip ties from his bag and strapped her wrists together. She struggled, but he was bigger, stronger, and held the superior position.

"Where's Matt?" he asked as he pulled her arms over her head and dragged her to the sink. He fastened her wrists to the sink's trap.

Confusion flowed across her fear as he stepped away to open her kitchen drawers. "M-m-matt? I... I don't know any—"

"Oh, yes you do," he said, pulling a rusty pair of tongs from a drawer and tossing them aside to clatter beside her. He dropped a wooden rolling pin on her, then a plastic pie server and a cracked wooden spoon, all while she watched with growing alarm. "You slipped through a wall with him just last night."

"A *what?* You're crazy. I was at the bar until closing. Ask anyone. And I don't know anybody named Matt!"

Huey found a jagged grapefruit knife in the drawer and smiled, letting it wink in morning light filtering through her frosted-over kitchen window. Crude weapon in his fist, he took two steps to straddle over her again. "Congratulations. You've picked the hard way."

A grubby kitchen towel helped keep her screaming volume to a reasonable level.

———

"OH MY GOD, I'm glad to be off these roads," Kate muttered as she climbed the steps to her apartment with two sacks of groceries, bought with money Matt had given her. Enough groceries to make them a nice holiday dinner with a little ham and those heat-and-serve rolls and everything!

Maybe we could eat it in bed, she thought, grinning as she unlocked her door.

She dropped off the food in the kitchen and found Matt cleaning the bathroom, which had to be just about the sexiest thing she'd ever seen a man do. She leaned against the doorframe for a moment, watching him with a smile teasing her lips as he kneeled over the tub and scrubbed, his reasonably-fine ass pointed at her. She breathed in the clear aroma of soft-scrub and toilet bowl cleaner.

"Nice view," she said and he turned, grinning, a soapy scrub-sponge in his hand.

"Thanks. Welcome home." He stood and reached for the tub faucet and turned it on to rinse away the bubbles. "Wanna share a nice, clean shower?"

She grinned. "Lemme put away the groceries and I'll be right back!"

———

FAWKES PULLED up in front of the Adamson Crime Scene to find Becca reading in her pickup. He called her over to wait with him in the SUV.

"Thank you, sir," she said as she slid into the passenger seat. "My heater's not the best."

Fawkes sighed at the house, its crime-scene tape fluttering in the breeze. "No problem. Did you take down the tape?"

"No sir. Was like that when I got here but I took three photos of it from different angles. I didn't see any footprints in the snow and didn't want to contaminate the scene."

She paused then handed her camera to him. "You need to see this. I've zoomed in."

The imaged showed the door slightly ajar and the jamb busted.

"So who broke in?" she asked. "Neighborhood kids? Someone looking for stuff to sell?"

He handed the camera back to her. "Someone involved with the murder?"

"Why would they come back?"

He sipped his coffee and smiled at Garrel's CRV coming around the corner. "Dunno. But we're gonna find out while we're looking for whatever we didn't see the first time we were here."

They exited the SUV and Becca pulled the tech kit from the back while they waited for Garrel to park. All three stood in the road for a moment before stepping into the yard.

"I'll carry that," Fawkes said to Becca as they approached the house. "You take better pics." He hoped he didn't wince at the pain in his bad arm.

The snow leading to the house was unmarred by footprints or divots, but Becca had them pause before climbing the stairs.

"The steps were shoveled off when we were here yesterday." She pulled a long-bristled brush from the kit and whisked off fresh snow while the detectives watched. She soon unearthed two icy sets of large boot prints, coming and going, on the concrete landing.

She took pics then said, "Let me cast them, then we can go in."

While she worked, Fawkes and Garrel walked the yard's perimeter through knee-deep snow and noted an open crank-out window that wasn't open before, and mud on the top of the gas meter right below a closed window near the dining area.

Garrel leaned over it and took a picture with her tablet. "Was that there yesterday?"

"I don't know," Fawkes admitted. "I don't remember seeing it when I walked the yard."

"I don't either, and..." She swiped her tablet a few times.

"It's not there in yesterday's photos." She took another, closer, pic.

Once they reached the back yard, which was smooth and flawless with fallen snow, Fawkes said, "Let's take a walk up the alley."

Each took a side and they found three likely places the kids could have hidden before Becca came looking for them.

NINETEEN

MEG WOKE TO THE SMELL OF BACON. SHE FOUND JAKE IN THE kitchen shoveling in breakfast while Ginnie sipped a cup of coffee and gazed out the kitchen window at a brilliant blue sky.

"Morning," Jake said without looking up from his plate of food.

"Morning," she replied around a yawn.

Ginnie turned toward the stove with her *SA/Feeds* coffee cup in hand. "Would you like some bacon and toast? I have frozen waffles, if you'd rather."

"Whatever's easy," Meg said. "Thank you, ma'am."

"She wants to offer you eggs, but I've eaten them all," Jake said, chewing. "She's also pretty sure there's more out in the coop, but there's a lot of snow to move fir—"

Meg stood between him and Ginnie. "Stop it. Mom always said it was rude for you to repeat people's thoughts like that. Ginnie's helping us. Quit being a jerk."

Jake fell silent for a moment then said, "I was just trying

to simplify things and avoid any confusion before we head to your dad's."

"Maybe I don't want to go to my dad's!"

"Maybe we have nowhere else to go! We sure can't stay here!"

"Why not?" Ginnie asked as she arranged bacon in the skillet. "We're surrounded by fields and surely no one knows you're here. It'd be better than you trudging through deep snow for what, twelve, fifteen miles or so, wouldn't it? It'd take you two days, at least, to walk that in this weather, and there's no telling when another storm'll blow through." She glanced over her shoulder at the kids. "You can surely wait until we're plowed out, anyway. Might be late today, might be tomorrow or the day after. I can manage the half-mile to the paved road north to Van Meter easily enough, but Patterson? Helluva lot farther and nothing south's plowed right-off or paved, not unless I go clear around to the in—"

"No interstates," Jake said. "Too many people."

Ginnie turned to face them. "It's your choice, hon. I ain't keeping anyone here against their will, but it's damn short-sighted and silly to head out on foot right after a blizzard like this. You'll freeze without survival gear, and I don't have it to give you. Heavy coats and gloves for a trudge out to the pasture and back, sure, but I have no tent, let alone any other supplies for a two-day trek. There's room here, and heat and food and quiet. You told me how you need the quiet."

She paused. "You know where her dad lives? Been there before?"

"I know the address on his child support notices," Jake snapped.

Meg took a step back. "Mom said he hadn't paid in like a year. He might not even be there anymore."

"What else am I supposed to do? I have to get you somewhere safe!"

"I *am* safe," Meg said and she stared at him. "And you'll freeze long before I will. Then what? Besides, what if someone sees us? What if Huey finds us in a field or something?"

"Fine," Jake said, bursting to his feet. "We can stay until the snowplow comes, but not one minute more. Then I'm taking you to your dad's. If he's not there, well, we'll figure it out then!"

He stomped off and slammed himself into the bathroom.

HUEY SEARCHED the one-bedroom house while the woman lay bound and whimpering on her kitchen floor. He saw no evidence a man lived there or had visited her at any point. And, as he stared at a fistful of late-notice bills in his hand, his gut clenched. All were addressed to a *Karen* McLean.

Fuck.

He returned to the kitchen and towered over her.

She cowered away.

"Who's Kate?"

She swallowed and scrunched her eyes closed, but he grabbed her by the chin and forced her to look at him. "Who. The *fuck*. Is Kate. McLean?"

"My daughter, you shit," she spat.

Sunnuvagoddamnbitchwhore! Fuck!

Huey paced across the cramped kitchen, his hands

clenching and unclenching. He wanted to call Warren, wanted to know where to go next, what to *do* next to find Meg, but Warren was at his mother's by now, elbow deep in oyster dressing and cream pies and fresh-made eggnog while singing *Little Drummer Boy* and playing Canasta, and all of that felt a world away from a cramped, roach-scuttling kitchen with a bleeding woman on a ragged vinyl floor zip-tied to her sink.

"Fuck!" he snarled aloud then turned to his hostage and pulled his knife from his tool-bag.

"Where," he said, crouching beside her while her attention locked onto the knife, "is Kate?"

"I don't know." She dragged her gaze from the knife to his face. "Ungrateful little bitch left weeks ago. I kicked her ass out. Might be at the homeless shelter. Might be fucking some guy for a roof over her head. Might be sleeping in the shitty car she bought. Might be dead at a truck stop. I have no fucking idea where she is. But when you see her, let her know I want the thirty-two bucks she stole from me."

Huey flipped the knife in his hand and leaned close enough to whisper, "I'll be sure to tell her."

———

FAWKES and Garrel returned to the front steps and, with Becca behind them, Fawkes pushed the door open.

The house's interior stank of death and melting snow, but looked mostly the same as the day before, other than fingerprint powder everywhere.

Becca took two pictures of a ruler beside muddy boot-prints on linoleum just inside the door. "Look similar to the prints on the steps to me."

"Yeah, me too." Garrel pointed toward the dining room. "Let's check there first."

All three stepped in and put on gloves and booties before walking across the living room to the window over the gas meter. The window was locked, but fingerprint powder on the sill and lock had been wiped away. Garrel put number markers on them then took a picture.

Fawkes knelt to touch the mud-smeared carpet beneath. "It's wet," he said to Garrel as Becca took a picture. "If someone broke in that way, why lock the window? Why are there entry and exit prints at the door?"

Garrel nodded, typing. "Two different break-ins?"

Fawkes stood. "Maybe."

"I'll dust for prints. Maybe they left something," Becca said.

"Dust the computer, too," Garrel said, gesturing to the old PC at a desk in the corner of the living room. "Especially where the hard drives were."

"Will do."

"Okay," Fawkes said, looking around. "Let's see if anything's been moved."

Crime-scene tape remained un-moved on Cheryl's doorway, but Matt's door had been kicked in. Both detectives paused, hands falling to their guns, before nudging it the rest of the way open.

The room appeared different than the relative-neatness Fawkes remembered, with clothes tossed about as if someone had packed in a hurry, as well as being searched by Becca yesterday. Snow had blown in through the opened crank-out window, but the gap was far too narrow for anyone to squeeze through.

"Think Matt Adamson came back?" Garrel asked.

"Probably. Let's find one of his shoes and see if their size matches the prints on the front stoop.

"Or the gas meter," Garrel said. She took a few pictures with her tablet and they separated to search for a shoe.

"Hey, Les," she said from near the open window. He heard her tablet take another pic. "I've got something."

Zipper teeth, jean buttons, coppery rivets, and a scattering of coins lay beside the wall. Two grapefruit-wide curves of narrow metal crowned Matt Adamson's sprawl of discards.

"Aluminum?" he asked, waiting for her third pic before lifting one of the curves.

Garrel stood, frowning. "Maybe. I've never wondered what underwires were made of."

Underwires? "So he brought a woman here?"

"Looks like it," she sighed, walking away.

"That's not all it looks like," he said, standing. "Looks like he and that woman went through that wall."

She turned. "No."

"Yes. What other explanation is there? They went through that wall and left metal behind, just like he left his underwear and elastic booties yesterday at the station."

"It's not possible."

"Then tell me what is. How else would those things," he said, pointing, "be laying on the floor in a pile like that? It's metal bits from clothing, stuff he couldn't drag through that wall."

Garrel crossed her arms over her chest. "It's *insane.*"

"What's insane?" Becca asked as she walked in. "I found a decent shoe print in the kitchen like the one on the gas meter, only for the other foot. Looks like a women's shoe, by the size."

"Take a look at this," Fawkes said, pointing. "What do you see?"

Becca crossed the room to the wall and took three pictures of the pile of stuff. "Metal clothing notions and some change." She looked up. "Why would anyone take the teeth out of a zipper like that? "

"Because zipper teeth won't go through that wall."

"Come on, Les," Garrel muttered.

"What? Nothing goes—" Becca paused, her eyes growing big. Then she clamped her mouth shut and looked down.

"This is why I asked you last night what the possibilities are," Fawkes said.

Garrel sighed. "What possibilities?"

Becca took a breath and explained about the oddities in the short arm of Chromosome 19, especially the calcium channel and missing NOTCH3, with Garrel shaking her head all the while.

Fawkes took a step toward Garrel. "The mutation might explain how Matt Adamson disappears through walls, how Meg—"

"No. I'm going to search Jake's closet. You two can keep this nonsense to yourselves."

Fawkes frowned and watched her leave.

Beside him, Becca said, "If what you think is true, either this woman can slip through stuff too, or he can take someone with him."

"What?"

"*Two* people went through that wall—two piles of zipper teeth, two buttons—and at least *one* of them was a woman. We have a shoe print and bra underwires, so a woman *was here*, right, and it doesn't look like she left through the front door. So, considering all of *that*, is the condition spreading, like along virus vector, or is it transferable on purpose? Like maybe by touch? Or by thought?"

A thought? Jesus.

"Goddammit," Garrel said from across the house.

Fawkes hurried to find her kneeling in Jake's closet, her flashlight pointing at a deflated lump of rubber that emerged from the scuffed hardwood floor.

"What's that?" Fawkes asked.

"Looks like the tip of a damned rubber glove coming through the floor." Garrel tugged on it with a heavy sigh. She looked up at Fawkes. "If I wasn't breastfeeding, I'd make you take me out to get drunk."

He helped her stand. "Can I take you to the basement instead? See where the rest of this glove is?" He assessed the overturned bed and strung about mess. "After we examine the rest of this room?"

"Goddammit," she muttered as Becca entered. "I'll be back. Just need some fresh air. Consider it my non-smoker cigarette break."

While Becca photographed the glove tip coming through the floor, Fawkes found rope hunks beneath the overturned bed, some flecked with blood, and five bloody craft-knife blades. The same kind of knife-blades a kid might use to help build a model, like the purple robot on the floor beside the desk.

Becca took pictures of it all and bagged every piece.

They righted the bedframe and Becca said, "Something glinted, there, at the left-side headboard."

Fawkes leaned over to examine the headboard and found three more craft-knife-blades taped to the headboard edge facing the wall so they could be peeled off.

"That's how he cut his hands," Fawkes muttered, straightening to look around the room again.

"Who cut what?" Becca asked, leaning over to take a photograph of the taped knife blades.

"Every surveillance photo we've seen of Jake and his sister, his left hand was bloody from little cuts, or bandaged."

"So, there's all these rope pieces... And rub marks on the headboard frame. He was tied here," Becca said. "But why'd he put X-acto blades in the headboard to cut himself loose? He'd have to know it was going to happen, right? Like precognition? Seeing the future?"

Just like Jake knew the cop-killer was approaching in the mall and ran for his sister before he saw the guy, Fawkes thought. "I don't know yet. But it's probably because of the chromosome mutation."

Fawkes examined the flaps cut into the wall foils. All seven were on the same wall, the wall over Jake's desk, the span of wall facing directly across the house to Matthew's room.

His phone rang. "Fawkes," he said, picking the robot off of the floor.

"Got an ID on the shit who killed Joel. Hubert Rawlins, ex-Army Intel Collection, ex DoD Counter Intelligence, now working freelance. And we have an Urbandale address for the fucker."

"We're on our way," Fawkes said, trotting toward the front door.

Becca followed. "What do you need me to do here?"

"Keep processing. I'll call for another tech, plus a patrol cop to secure the house in case someone comes back again."

"See if you can get Kameshia to assist me. If she can't, then Brendan's good, too. They're both scheduled to work today."

"Will do!"

Garrel looked up from texting, startled, and pocketed her phone. "What happened?"

"Joel's killer lives in Urbandale. You want to ride with me or follow?"

"I'll follow," she said, rushing to her SUV. "Noah's appointment's on the west side."

TWENTY

MEG WIPED THE LAST OF THE BREAKFAST CRUMBS OFF THE table while Ginnie washed dishes. Washrag in hand, Meg turned toward the sink and realized Jake stood in the archway to the hall. He'd washed the slickery-soap out of his hair and looked more like himself again.

He glanced at Meg, then said to Ginnie, "I apologize for being rude, Ma'am. You've been incredibly kind and I've..."

Meg glared back. "Been a jerk."

"Right. A jerk," he repeated, then took a breath. "Ginnie... I've had, *we've* had, a hard couple of days, I know, but I shouldn't've—"

"It's all over now," Ginnie said, returning to her dishes. "No harm done."

He nodded. "Thank you." Jake took a step toward the kitchen table and paused. "You don't need to worry about shoveling. I can shovel. And feed the animals. You're right. I can help out while we're here, same as Meg."

"You're responding to thoughts again," Meg sighed,

rolling her eyes. "And you've never shoveled or fed farm animals."

"What?" Jake said, his brow furrowing. "I've shoveled."

Not really, Meg thought, then made kissy noises. "Just a path to the back gate so you can visit your girlfriend!"

"Meg," Ginnie said, turning to frown at her.

"Trinity's not really my girlfriend." He shrugged on his coat. "She's a neighbor and a solid bubble of quiet. I think she likes me, but that doesn't make her my girlfriend. We mostly just talk, like *regular people* talk. It's great because I don't know what she's thinking. Everything's a surprise and it's... It's *amazing.*"

"But I've seen you kissing! That means she's—"

"Meg! Leave him alone. There's nothing wrong with your brother kissing a girl."

"Actually, she kissed me. The first time, at least," he said with a grin. "Had no idea it was gonna happen, but then it *was.*" He cleared his throat and turned toward the back door. "I'm gonna go shovel."

"Why'd you tease him like that?" Ginnie asked after Jake went outside.

"I dunno. Just..." Meg stared at the floor for a moment then said, "He really hasn't shoveled much. We had too many neighbors so being outside hurt his head. And we've never had any pets, let alone a cow and chickens."

Ginnie handed her a plate to dry. "A young man needs to work. To feel useful. He had to be frustrated, being stuck in his room most of the time, like you'd said."

Meg dried the plate. "I guess so. He mostly read and built anime models, when Mom could afford them."

"That sounds sad and lonely." Ginnie nudged her and

winked. "Honey, there's no reason to tease him over kissing a girl. As long as he's not forcing her to kiss him, it's *just fine*, okay?"

"What?" Meg's belly felt twisty as she set the dried plate on the counter. "Jake wouldn't make her... Make her do something like that. Trinity's super nice and they've been friends as long as I can remember."

"Good. So try to remember he's old enough. And who he kisses is none of your business. Even siblings need their own space."

"Yes, Ma'am."

They washed and dried dishes in silence for a few moments, until Ginnie said, "So. What do you think about baking Christmas cookies after we're done washing the breakfast dishes?"

Meg nearly dropped the coffee cup in her hand. "Can we? Can we really?!"

"Yeah. See that red cookbook ever there?" Ginnie said, pointing. "There's a whole section on cookies. Pick out a couple of kinds and we'll get 'em made. Maybe we'll make a pie, too."

"Even with sprinkles?"

Ginnie smiled and patted Meg's shoulder. "Even with sprinkles!"

FAWKES REACHED HUBERT RAWLINS' high-end home on Oakbrook Drive with Garrel right behind him and apparently the entire Urbandale Police Force on site, along with several vehicles from Des Moines and West Des Moines PD.

Fawkes and Garrel hurried up the heated walkway to their Chief pacing on the split foyer's front porch.

"Yeah, they just got here," he said into his phone. "I'll relay the info."

"What info?" Garrel asked as she pulled out her tablet.

"First of all, the murderous shit isn't here," Chief said. "Urbandale served a no-knock warrant, via SWAT, but nobody was home. All the evidence stolen from your crime scene is here, in totes we've already confiscated, and we've put out a state-wide APB for Rawlins as well as his boyfriend. There's a lot in there to search and clear. Urbandale PD's gonna be here a while. They've requested we stay out, for now at least."

"You got a picture of the boyfriend?" Fawkes asked.

"Yeah. It should be on your phones within minutes. None of this is on the radio, okay? Phones only. But the boyfriend's some kind of hacker. They found a bank of computer monitors showing camera feeds, texts, I don't know what it all is, but he's hacked into our radio system, the busses, mall security footage... Everything electronic related to this case. It's all right there on his screens." He pointed at Garrel's tablet. "Take that thing to cyber crimes and get it checked for breaches."

"It's not breached," she said, "I run Sopho—"

"Detective, it's not a suggestion."

"Fine," she muttered and handed him the tablet. "You do it."

Urbandale's police chief walked to the porch with an opened Christmas card envelope in hand. "Maybe they went home for Christmas," he said, handing the envelope to the

Chief. "It's from the hacker's mother, and we've already called Ankeny PD. They're en route."

The card was sent to Warren and Huey at that address, but the return was from Mom, at an address in Ankeny. Fawkes noted the info and had to run to catch up with Garrel.

"Oh, my God, Traci! That's so awesome!" Warren said while arranging a cookie assortment on a tray. "Yale?! For real?"

His lanky, freckle-faced cousin beamed. "Just applying. It's really competitive."

"Oh, you'll do it," he insisted. "Top of your class, TAG, Debate Club, basketball, track..." She lowered her eyes, blushing, then he added, "Amazing SAT scores, *and* you've been published in the local paper. They'd be crazy not to accept you!"

"She's gonna be a Senator," her father said, stealing a cookie. "First one in the family."

Traci blushed again. "Dad!"

Mom walked by with a basket of hot rolls and dropped her eleventy-billionth, "Where's Huey?"

"He'll be here," Warren assured her again, but he stole another glance at the big clock beyond the ornament-packed Christmas Tree. *We're eating in eight minutes. Where are you?*

Those eight minutes flew with final food preparations and moving over-loaded serving dishes to the big table in Mom's sunny dining room. Its curved bank of windows looked out toward the housing development's pond and the towering fir tree in her back yard, a tree fully decorated and sparkling in the snow. Hip-high wooden elves frolicked on her deck festooned with holly and shimmering garland that matched the twinkling holly-garland she'd hung throughout the house.

Christmas was Mom's holiday, complete with a mountain of presents and enough food to feed the entire neighborhood. Woe to anyone who messed it up.

Everyone sat precisely on time, Huey's seat still empty to Warren's right, and they said grace. Uncle Bert had just passed Warren the ham when the doorbell rang.

Oh thank God he's here, Warren thought, smiling as he stood, but Mom burst out of her chair and bolted for the door while he followed, hoping to defuse the coming flurries before they had a chance to turn into a full-blown Mom-Blizzard.

"Well! It's about time!" Mom said as she flung the door open. "I suppo—"

She took a sudden step back, and a pair of police officers stepped in, one holding a piece of paper. Maybe a dozen more waited behind them. "We have a warrant, Ma'am," he said, holding the paper out to her. "We're looking for a Hubert Rawlins."

Aw, shit, aw shit, Warren thought and he glanced over his shoulder to see four more officers walking onto his mother's holiday-crusted back deck. Most of the family stood and stepped away from the table, looking at Warren, then the cops, then Warren again.

Mom glanced back at Warren then took a breath and accepted the paper from the policeman. "He's... Huey's he's not here," she said, a meekness in her voice Warren hadn't heard before. "He's late for Christmas Dinner."

"Sorry to hear that, Ma'am. May we take a look around?"

"Of... of course," she said, stepping back. "Yes. But he's not here. He's late. As usual. We were just starting dinner."

The second policeman held a smaller piece of paper in his hand and his gaze locked on Warren as the other cops on the front steps poured in, two standing between Warren and the rest of the house.

"Warren Redman?" the cop with the small paper asked.

"Yes," Mom said, glancing at Warren, "but my son's not responsible for Huey's—"

"You're under arrest," one of the cops behind him said. He slapped a handcuff on Warren's wrist and pulled it behind him before cuffing the other one. Warren did not resist.

"*Arrested?* For what?" his mother snapped, her voice rising as she turned to glare at the cop cuffing her son. "We were just starting dinner!"

"You don't want to know, Mom," Warren said as the cops escorted him out his mother's front door. "Sorry to ruin Christmas."

"OKAY," Becca said as Kameshia lugged in her collection kit. "This is going to be kind of weird."

"Every crime scene's weird," Kameshia said, glancing at Officer Daniels moping around the living room.

Becca led Kameshia to Jake's room. "Nearly everything I collected yesterday was stolen—"

"Yeah, I heard about that. Tim got his ass fired."

"Yeah, I know, but this house was broken into last night.

Twice," she said as she walked to Jake's closet. She pointed to the glove-fingertip sticking out of the floor. "And we have this."

"The hell?" Kameshia said, kneeling to touch the glove with her gloved hand.

"Yeah. So along with re-processing pretty much the whole house, we need to remove this part of the floor and figure out how this happened. No telling what else we'll find. And we'll have to note anything that looks disturbed or taken."

Kameshia gave her a *gurl-you-have-got-to-be-shitting-me* expression then shrugged. "Let's do it. I can definitely use the overtime."

"Me, too," Becca said as she reached into her kit for her cordless 4.5-inch circular saw. "I'm glad Brian's got the next three days off so we don't need to pay babysitter holiday rates." She flicked on the saw and started removing the floor while Kameshia held onto the glove tip to keep it from falling.

"I WILL DELIVER one of the Adamsons," Huey said to the ever-crankier SynAg contact. "I've never failed a job. They're somewhere, and I *will* find them."

He threw his blood-flecked jacket into the river and contemplated tossing his phone in after it, but instead, he pocketed it and drove north, wondering how he'd fulfill his contract this time, with utterly no sightings of any of the Adamsons anywhere.

He stopped at HyVee in Ankeny to pick up a massive

poinsettia and three pricy bottles of wine before driving to Warren's mom's, but had to stop a couple of blocks away as a line of police cars left the neighborhood, lights and sirens blaring.

"Aw, fuck me," Huey muttered, watching the cruisers pass. He drove forward, past the turn to Warren's mother's cul-de-sac, and glanced toward her house. Four police cars parked in front of it, along with a crime scene van and more cops than he could count in the moment he took to look.

"SHIT!" he said, pounding his steering wheel as he worked his way out of the executive housing development. He drove toward home, confident it'd be a clusterfuck too, but he needed to be sure.

From the next block over, he paused long enough to see cops carrying computers and totes out of his house. He drove through to the next intersection then directly to their rented storage facility. He hoped the cops hadn't found it, too.

It started sleeting a couple of minutes later. It was just that kind of day.

TWENTY ONE

GINNIE LEFT MEG TO DECORATE SNOWMAN COOKIES AND strode down Jake's freshly-shoveled path. For a kid who'd never really shoveled, he did all right. Ragged-edged and too narrow, but perfectly passable and cleared all the way to the barn.

Her shovel leaned beside the barn door awaiting his return, but the wooden shaft was smeared with blood.

Aw, shit, she thought, shoving the door open. She rushed in then stopped, dead still as Jake looked up, startled. He sat in an open stall with Maude, petting her while she munched on handfuls of *SA/Feeds MilkMakerNuggets* out of his palm he'd scooped from a bucket by his feet.

He'd been crying, his tears leaving shiny tracks on his face.

"I didn't hear you," he said, scrambling to his feet. He wiped at his eyes with the back of his blood-smeared hand, then held her gaze. "I didn't *hear* you. I didn't *feel* you. Nothing. Not until you came through the door. How is it possible?"

"I don't know," she said. "None of this makes sense to me. But are you all right? You've been gone a while, and I saw blood on the shovel."

He glanced at his hand then tucked it behind him and lowered his gaze. "I cut myself yesterday getting us out of the house. The other..." He shrugged. "It's an electrical burn. The bandages came off."

"Aw, hell," she muttered, trotting to him. "Why didn't you say something? Let me see it." She eased his fists open. His right palm and fingers were over-heated red and oozing from opened blisters, and a web of thin, intersecting cuts had sliced through the fingertips of his left hand, most superficial, but a couple were deep enough to make her flinch. A rough abrasion had broken the skin of that wrist almost all of the way around. Rope burn, it looked like, and she wondered who'd tied this kid up.

She looked into his eyes. "How the hell'd you shovel like this? *Why'd* you shovel like this?"

"Because I needed to thank you, and I didn't know how else to do it. You saved Meg, saved me, and you don't even know us. But you're right. We're *safe* here. We've been here since last night and *nobody* knows." He sat beside Maude again and sighed before looking up at Ginnie. "Why'd you do that? How could you do that? We're strangers to you."

She huffed out a breath and knelt before him. "You needed help. That's all that mattered."

"I'll have to trust what you say," he said, running the back of his fingers over Maude's head. "Because your and Meg's thoughts faded about halfway here, to this barn, and if I'm near this wonderful, amazing cow, for the very first time in my *life* I can't hear a danged thing except with my ears."

Ginnie smiled and scratched Maude's shoulder. "I don't know why. She's nothing special, just a plain ol' Jersey. Had her since she was a heifer, just like I'd had her mother before her."

"She's wonderful," Jake insisted.

Ginnie stood. "She also needs milked. Want to learn how to do that?"

"Yeah. Absolutely!"

"First we have to take care of those hands. Come on back to the house, and we'll get you fixed up, then I'll show you how to take care of Maude."

———

BECCA AND KAMESHIA cut out a square foot or so of flooring around the glove-tip and Kameshia lifted it out while Becca put the saw away.

"This is *whack*," Kameshia said, flipping over the square. The remainder of the glove slumped against spiderweb-covered subfloor and she held it still while Becca took photos from three angles, plus two more showing the fingertip above, and the rest dangling below.

Kameshia bagged the evidence and Becca shone a flashlight into the hole.

"There's stuff down there," she said, moving the light over the dirty crawlspace. "Money, I think. Over toward the hallway."

Kameshia leaned over to look. "Wow. Seriously? That looks like a hundred dollar bill. How did it end up beneath a floor?"

Becca took a breath and leaned over to put her head and

the flashlight in the hole. "There's more money down there. Other stuff, too." She pulled out, clicked off the light, and stood. "Let's go see if there's better access downstairs.

Kameshia followed her to the basement door with the collection kit and, after flipping on the light, Becca started down then paused about halfway.

How is this possible? She thought, then chided herself. *How is any of this possible?*

"Hand me the camera."

"Why?"

"Because the floor's all cruddy, but the footprints in it only come *this way*."

After the series of photographs, they continued into the basement and Becca took photos of footprints leaving from beneath a newish cinderblock wall, past the water heater and on to the stairs, as well as part of a black handle-grip sticking out of a different cinderblock wall about hip level.

"How are we gonna get *that* out of there?" Kameshia asked.

"I have no idea." Becca called their supervisor and asked for the ground-penetrating radar, along with someone who could take down part of a cinderblock wall.

When he questioned her request, she forwarded him the photos.

"They're on the way. Stay put," he said, then ended the call.

AT THE STORAGE CENTER, Huey exchanged the Caddy for an F150 King Cab, then loaded the back with clothes, weapons, camping gear, and non-perishable food. He grabbed the duffel pre-packed with toiletries, cash, a burner phone, two sets of false drivers licenses for each of them plus matching passports, pre-loaded credit cards for all four identities, more phones, and Warren's emergency laptop. He assessed the remaining stored gear, decided he didn't need anything else, then pulled his working bag from the Caddy, locked up the stall, and drove away.

Entering the secured facility to departing took him less than seven minutes, most of that moving vehicles. He saw no police when he turned onto Douglas and drove toward the interstate. He wiped down and tossed the phone dedicated to Warren out of the window before turning at the onramp.

MID-AFTERNOON, Garrel returned pale and visibly shaken after Noah's appointment. Fawkes asked once how the baby was, but she only shook her head and walked away to get coffee. She returned to focus on tweaking her newly-assigned tablet's settings while he reviewed what little intel they had on Hubert Rawlins and his husband, federally-indicted corporate-cyber-hacker, Warren 'Red' Redman.

Ankeny PD delivered Warren in an orange jumpsuit and prisoner restraints. While they waited for Warren to complete his official processing into their custody, Fawkes searched through his bag of clothing and belongings in interview Room 2. Garrel took pictures of the contents and noted the details, none of which were very interesting beyond the high-end quality. Designer wool slacks, sweater, shoes, socks, and boxer briefs, a Baume and

Mercier watch, gold Cartier wedding band with tiny diamonds, new iPhone, platinum keyring with Jeep and house keys, and a leather wallet with a hundred-eighty-seven dollars, driver's license, four platinum cards, two debit cards, and a frequent customer punch-card to an auto detailing shop.

"Must be nice to be a criminal and afford expensive stuff," Garrel muttered as she finished the pics. "The watch alone could make my house payment for months." She picked up the iPhone and clicked a few moments before bypassing its passcode and opening Warren's contact list.

"Nothing here for Hugh or any similar name," she said, flicking to another screen. "And the activity log... Here we go. Several calls a day to an un-labeled local number."

She switched to her tablet and put a trace on the cell associated with the number, then frowned. "It's sitting still on Douglas around the 80/35 bridge. He might be waiting for the light."

Fawkes checked every pocket in Warren's clothes, every seam, every fold. "That's what, maybe a couple of miles from their house? He might have tossed the phone. Call Urbandale. Have them send someone to pick it up."

"Yeah, it's not moving," she said before dialing Urbandale PD.

She was still talking with them when the door opened and a pair of officers escorted Warren into the room.

"Mr. Redman," Fawkes said, gesturing to a chair. "Have a seat."

"Hey, Les," Warren said with a slight smirk. "How they hanging?"

"Just fine." Fawkes pulled the chair out. "Sit. Let's talk."

"Sure," he said, sitting. "How's the baby, Jennifer? I hear he's been sick."

Garrel turned, her eyes narrowing.

"I wouldn't do that if I were you," Fawkes said.

Warren smirked. "Yeah, you probably wouldn't. She carries the balls of this partnership, doesn't she?" He picked at his pile of clothes with his fingertips, then clasped his hands together and leaned back in his chair. "I don't know why you pulled me away from my family's Christmas, but I'd like to get back to it. Had a big pile of presents under the tree."

"Who's Hubert Rawlins?" Fawkes asked.

Warren pushed his sweater away. "Oh, come on. You're gonna have to do better than that."

"How do you know about me?" Garrel asked.

"Oh honey, I've heavily researched every tech specialist in the Midwest. I keep an eye on you because you're local law enforcement." He turned his gaze to Fawkes. "But I stopped hacking years ago. Scout's honor. Can I go now?"

"No."

Fawkes read Warren his rights, and Warren yawned then said, "Yeah, whatever. Heard it all before."

Fawkes began his list of statements and questions, all of which Warren deflected or ignored. He checked his fingernails when Fawkes informed him his assets and passport were frozen, sucked something out of his impeccably-bright teeth when told his home had been raided and his computers confiscated, and he leaned forward, one cheek on his fist and his eyes closed when Fawkes suggested he was implicated in the murder of Cheryl Adamson. He sighed and appeared to doze off when Fawkes asked about what happened to Hubert Rawlins after the events at Valley West Mall the night before.

"Are you even listening, Warren?"

"Blah, blah, blah, how can I not?" he sighed. "I'm not hearing any charges in there. You did this, you think that, none of which warrants yanking me from my mom's Christmas dinner, confiscating my shit, or dragging me in here in cuffs. So why am I here? You need me to do a table dance for your cops-and-gay-boyz holiday party? Sure, but you could've just asked."

"We need to find Hugh," Garrel said.

Warren laughed and settled in for a nap. "Yerp, not my problem. Marital privilege and all. Can I go now?"

"No. You can explain how you have video—"

The door opened and Malcolm Grant, yesterday's swanky Ag Company lawyer from Hunters, Grant, and Stanhope, strode in. "This interrogation is finished until I get a chance to talk with my client," Grant said. "Thankfully, you haven't misplaced this one, too."

"Who are you?" Warren asked, his eyes narrowing. "I haven't requested—"

"Keep your mouth shut," Grant said, handing papers to Fawkes. "I've filed a motion to get these ridiculous charges—"

Fawkes watched Warren lean away from Grant, his voice steely. "Who the hell are you? My mother'd send Jeffrey, and you're not him, nor anyone on his staff."

"I'm your *lawyer*," Grant said, still glaring at Fawkes. "I'd like to get to the courthouse before the holiday recess—"

Warren stood. "I'm not doing shit until I know who the goddamn fuck you are!"

"Malcolm Grant, from Hunters, Grant, and Stanhope," Garrel said. "Your attorney."

"The fuck you are."

Grant laid a hand on Warren's shoulder but he scrambled away and backed against the wall. "Do not fucking touch me."

"We have to go, Warren," Grant said. "Your arraignment is in less than an hour, and, with luck, I can get you released before—"

Warren stared at Fawkes and Garrel. "This corporate shit is *not* my lawyer, and do not let me be alone with him, especially like this," he said, shaking his restraints. "He'll kill me."

Fawkes turned his gaze from Warren to Grant. *Flat-broke Matt Adamson walked through a wall to get away from this guy. Now he's spooked this witness too, and he can afford him.*

"I'm your lawyer," Grant said. "And these officers need to leave so we can discuss these ridiculous charges."

Warren scuttled closer to Fawkes and Garrel. "No. I want Jeffrey Levin, my mother's attorney. He handled a civil case for me a couple of years ago. If he's out of town for the holidays, get me a public defender. Shit, get a bankruptcy lawyer or a kid fresh outta school who hasn't passed the bar yet if you want, I don't care, but *this ghoul* is *not my lawyer* and I refuse—"

"Warren, you need to calm down," Grant said, pulling a prescription bottle from his blazer pocket. "Your mother said you'd be upset so she sent your pills. Why don't you take a couple?"

Warren reached for Garrel but didn't quite touch her. "Check my records. I know you can if you haven't downloaded them already. I'm on a prescription for allergies. *Clarinex*. That's *it*. I use CVS on Hickman. I don't have anxiety. I don't have *anything*, except tree-pollen allergies!"

Garrel shook her head and took a step back. "I can't do that."

"Warren, you're being ridiculous." Grant gave Fawkes a *see-what-I-have-to-deal-with* smile.

"He's refused your services," Fawkes said. "You need to leave."

"He's my client."

"No, I'm not!" Warren said, watching Grant, his spine pressed against the wall.

"I've seen enough. Goodbye, Mr. Grant," Fawkes said. He strode to the door and tapped for the officer to open it. "Please escort this man from the building. Immediately."

Grant gathered his coat and briefcase. "You will hear from our offices, Detective."

"Looking forward to it," Fawkes said.

Once Grant had left the room, Fawkes closed the door again and Warren sagged, bending at the waist with his hands on his knees while taking deep, shuddering breaths.

"Thank you," he said. "I..." He took another breath then stood straighter. "Thank you."

"Who is he?" Fawkes asked.

"Shit," Warren muttered, shuffling to his chair again. He sat, holding his head high, and met Fawkes's gaze. "Corporate fixer. Yeah, he's a lawyer, but he mostly makes problems disappear."

"What sort of problems?" Fawkes asked, sitting across from Warren.

"Like a hacker who knows what his company's done." He

glanced at Garrel, still standing, then back to Fawkes. "Or a couple of special kids."

Garrel sat and opened her note app.

Warren nodded at her then smiled. "A few things up front. I won't talk about my husband, and you can't compel me to, but I'll tell you anything you want to know about the shits at SynAg. Can I get a glass of water, though? Maybe a snack? This is gonna take a while."

TWENTY TWO

A POLICE COURIER DELIVERED THE GROUND-PENETRATING radar unit and a handheld hammer drill to Becca and she signed for them at 2:48 pm. After several minutes of setup, she pressed the GPR against the basement wall while Kameshia and Officer Daniel peered over her shoulder at the viewscreen.

The screen showed, mostly, gray static and a black gap. One slender arc indicated a narrow line of metal, probably wire since no plumbing ran through that area.

"Do you know how to use that thing?" Officer Daniel asked.

"I attended a seminar," Becca said, shifting the unit low on the wall. *There we go.* "There's metal back there. Something besides the wire."

"How can you tell?" Kameshia asked.

"See that big arc in the static? That's metal. Let's open the wall and see what it is."

AFTER TWO UNIFORMED officers escorted Warren to the court-house, Fawkes and Garrel walked to the break room to freshen their coffee and await news from the coroner.

Garrel stirred in her double-sugars. "Redman can't really believe SynAg is behind Cheryl Adamson's murder instead of her son."

"Why else would that pompous corporate shit show up for both him and Matt Adamson?" Fawkes peered at her from over his cup. "SynAg is the only thing he and Adamson might have in common."

"Even if you discount that he's probably covering for *his husband* who shot you and tried to steal the kids, Redman's got no proof of what he's telling us," she reminded him. "No industry reports of the genetic manipulation after grain and insecticide ingestion, no documentation of pigs floating because they mutated after eating hog-kibbles made with SynAg corn. C'mon, Les. It's all hearsay *and* crazy."

"Adamson walked through that wall," Fawkes said, pointing toward the witness bathroom, "And Meg Adamson blew up almost half of a mall. Two people in the same house didn't get that way playing checkers in the park."

"Valley West had a shorted-out feedback loop in the electrical system," Garrel muttered, "Not a kid—"

"You saw the video," he snapped, his voice low. "You saw lightning come out of her, same as I did. Hell, you sent it to me."

She took a step toward him and lowered her voice. "It's simply not possible, Les. No jury—"

"They would if they saw that video. And what about the boy?"

"You mean our primary suspect, the 'person of interest'

we've spent *two days* trying to catch, the kid we both know killed his mother and kidnapped his sister?"

"No, he didn't." Fawkes flipped back through his notebook. "All the foil in his room, that special... what was it... Here we go. Lead, nickel, and tin. He'd been tied to the bed, Jenn. He's obviously prone to doing something too, something his own family tried to contain in that metal-lined cell."

"Yeah. Like wanting to kill his mother and kidnap his sister. It seems pretty straightforward to me."

"But Warren said Jake hears what people are thin—"

She sipped her coffee. "A convicted corporate hacker who's done hard time and married an assassin-for-hire who we're *still* looking for. Warren Redman is not the most reliable witness to ever sit in that chair."

"But what he says makes sense, if you just look—"

"It makes more sense that Jake Adamson has some mental problem the state wouldn't help with, so the family managed as best they could by locking him in that room, sometimes with restraints. He got loose yesterday morning, shot and killed his mother, then kidnapped his sister. That's where the physical evidence leads."

"What about the gun in his closet? How many suspects hide—"

"You've got to be kidding me," she said, rolling her eyes. "At least a third of them put the weapon in their trunk or kitchen drawer or leave it sitting in plain sight on their coffee table, and you know it as well as I do. Disorganized killers are not very good at covering their tracks, and teenage boys with mental issues are *definitely* disorganized."

A clerk came in for coffee, so the detectives moved to the far corner of the break room.

Fawkes whispered, "What evidence says Jake Adamson was disorganized, let alone a killer?"

"He had motive—being stuck in a foil room with nothing to do would drive anyone insane, let alone a fifteen-year-old boy with emotional issues and an apparent need to show dominance over *at least* the man of the house, maybe everyone. Cheryl had a handgun registered to her and we have no idea why, so we have to assume it was for self-defense. Becca found its box empty and some ammunition missing, that gives him means." Garrel took a sip of coffee. "He lived there and was obviously up and moving around the house the morning of the murder, so that gives him opportunity. This whole case isn't following any normal patterns. We haven't been able to predict Jake at all. He's aware of cameras but doesn't do anything to avoid them, in fact, he stares at them and *blinks*? He hides under moldy furniture and beneath bridges? That's surely disorganized thinking and reacting on his part."

Or we're missing something. Fawkes watched the clerk finish making his coffee and walk out. "So you're trusting Matt Adamson's testimony?"

"At least it makes sense. Who else in that house would want Cheryl dead and Meg for their own? Matt came in willingly, told us about everyone in the family, how Jake was trouble, how his sister was the primary breadwinner."

"What if Matt lied? He certainly never mentioned Meg..." Fawkes lowered his voice again when an aid walked in and rooted in the fridge, "...being able to make ball lightning in front of her! I'd think that'd be worth mentioning."

"Electrical feedback power surge. You've seen the official statement."

"Jesus." Fawkes paced in a tight loop. "*Again,* I've also seen the actual footage, as have you."

"Fine. Even if, *if* the green ball wasn't a relic of footage being actively compromised by the power surge, that doesn't absolve Jake from any of it. He still killed his mother and kidnapped his little sister. He's a disturbed teenage boy, and it happens."

"But why'd the lawyer, a *SynAg lawyer*, show up, twice, to advise two otherwise unrelated suspects during their—"

Garrel's phone chirped. "It's Dan," she said, sighing, and gave Fawkes a hopeful smile. "I know it's fun tilting at windmills, Les, but I gotta take this. Be back in a minute." Then she walked away, the phone crushed to her ear.

Fawkes finished his coffee then bought a bag of cookies out of the vending machine to munch while he wondered what was up with Garrel. He'd never known her to hold onto a theory after video evidence obliterated it.

His phone rang and he stood, expecting it to be the coroner's report or a heads up that Warren had been arraigned, but Becca's name crossed his screen.

"Did you find something?" he asked when he clicked on the call.

"You might say that."

He heard animated chattering in the background so he pulled his notebook out of his pocket then sat again to better balance the phone on his shoulder. "What'cha got?"

"Well, there's a big hole beneath the kids' rooms, right behind the foundation wall, and we found six guns of different types hidden in there, two sets of really expensive golf clubs with the price tags still on them—"

"How expensive?"

"Ah, one's about fourteen hundred, the other about seventeen."

"Dollars?" Fawkes said, noting the info.

She laughed. "Certainly not Yen. Okay, there are also three mint-in-box iPads, a literal tote of cash that looks like it's been dug through recently—Kameshia's dusting everything for prints, by the way—, some other small electronics like Galaxy phones, iPhones, a couple of LGs, and two Dell laptops, all unopened in their boxes, some new and used power tools, a push lawnmower, some disgustingly skanky porn, large plastic garbage bags, and you're gonna love this last one."

Fawkes continued to write. "Hit me. I need a laugh."

"Three *cases* and a partial of Thin Mints."

"As in Girl Scout cookies?"

"As in. All of it in a hole beneath the kids' rooms. They're where the garage used to be, right?"

"I think so, yeah. Haven't pulled up the property records yet."

"Might be something to look at," she suggested. "There were some other odds and ends, too," she said, "and I dunno how many rubber and silicone gloves. It'll all be in the report, complete with photographs, but the only other thing you might be interested in was one of the gloves, the same kind and color as the one partway through the closet floor, had blood on it. I'll send you those pics right now. Hold on."

A few seconds later his phone pinged and he pulled it

from his shoulder to examine the rubber glove, blood smeared on the fingertips of a right hand.

"Dunno if you can see this or not," she said as he put the phone back to his ear. "But on the thumb and every finger but the index, the blood's in a grid pattern. Zoom in, you'll see."

Sure enough, every fingertip had a smear of blood, but all except the index had been imprinted with a grid pattern, some of it smeared but much clearly marked.

"I can't say for sure what it is, Sir, but," she said, "but it looks a lot like handgun grip texture."

That it does. "Does it match Cheryl's gun?"

"I don't know, Sir. I don't have it to compare."

"Jake had cuts on his left hand. Could he have made these?"

"Not unless he turned the glove inside out before putting it on, turned it right-side-out again after taking it off, then pressed the fingertips against whatever made the grid marks. But there'd probably be more blood, and it'd be really smeared. I think. Looks more like a right-handed user grabbed the blood-smeared gun to me."

"Can you prove it, one way or the other?"

She laughed a little. "Absolutely, if I have enough time in a lab."

Fawkes checked the time. *After four and still nothing from the coroner. Shit.* "It's about time for you to go home, isn't it?"

"Actually, I shoulda clocked out more than an hour ago. But, Sir, I have a kid at home and a husband whose job has iffy hours, so I am always up for overtime. If you want to sign off on some, anyway."

"It's not going to cut into your holiday?"

"Nah, Gabrielle's two. She doesn't care when Santa comes. I'll get all this evidence cataloged and taken in, and I'll get you a definitive answer on that glove tonight. Promise."

———————

IT WAS GETTING on toward evening when Ginnie walked down the path to find Jake. He'd remained in the barn all afternoon tending the animals and mucking stalls.

"Hey!" he said, glancing over from washing milk pails when she walked in. "I think I'm getting the hang of this."

The stalls and pens looked all right, well-scrubbed and reasonably-tidy, the food bins filled, and the livestock all happily settling in for the night.

"Found nine eggs and got a little over two-and-a-half gallons from the goats, but Maude gave five gallons today, total. I put it all in bags in the fridge like you said. Marked and everything."

Ginnie smiled. "Yep, we'll be making cheese tomorrow."

"Well, you will." Jake sighed and finished rinsing the milk pail. "I heard the plow go by. We'll need to head out in the morning."

She fetched her chainsaw then leaned against a post and scratched a goat between the horns. "How're your hands?"

"Hurt, but they're feeling better. I'm just taking my time." He smiled and turned off the water before facing her and pulling off his elbow-length rubber gloves. "It's nice to have the quiet. Thinking I might sleep out here tonight. Maybe. See what it's like to have my own dreams."

"That'd be just fine. Got plenty of blankets you can

borrow, and lots of hay to snuggle into. But I need to ask you a little favor, first."

He set the gloves aside. "Sure. Whatcha got?"

"Can you stick around the house while I run into VanMeter for gas? I don't know if I have enough to get to Patterson and back in the morning. Thought it best to get the gas outta the way and I don't want to leave Meg all alone. I'll only be gone twenty minutes or so, then you can head right back down here with your blankets."

"Yeah. Lemme grab my coat."

They were about halfway back to the house when Jake chuckled. "Gas? Really?"

"Can't keep secrets from you," she said, giving him a wry smirk.

He sighed happily and looked up at the first stars twinkling in the sky. "It is Christmas. I won't say anything."

Almost to the porch, she paused, and he did too, his brow creasing. "You're thinking about the shotgun on the living room wall."

"Can you?" she asked. "Just in case? I put fresh shells in it while Meg built that snowman. Lady'll start barking if someone else comes onto the property. That'll give you a little warning, at least, a little time to be ready."

"I dunno. I've never..."

She thought through all of the specific steps on removing it from the bracket, to flipping off the safety, pumping it, and firing. "No one knows you're here. Hell, almost no one knows *I'm* here, but I don't want to leave you kids unprotected for the little while I'll be gone."

"I can do all of that. If I have to, I will," he said.

"Fair enough."

They reached the porch and he opened the door for her. Meg sat on the rug in front of the TV with Lady and giggled at *Rudolph the Red-Nosed Reindeer* who was about to lose his fake nose. "Jake! Come watch it with me! Mom loved this show!" she said, motioning for him to sit beside her. Lady looked over and thumped her tail but didn't leave Meg.

Ginnie lingered near the door. "Meggy, I need to run to the gas station, so Jake's gonna stay in here with you for a while. You want me to pick up some pizza while I'm there?"

"Pizza!!" she squealed, bouncing on her butt. "Pepperoni! Pepperoni!"

Ginnie chuckled. "I love pepperoni, too. What kind of pop do you like?"

"Dr. Pepper." Meg returned her attention to the TV and Jake crossed the room to flump onto the couch, a sad smile on his face.

Ginnie looked at Jake. "You?"

He snagged one of Meg's Christmas cookies from the tray on the coffee table. "Any kind of pizza's great, but I like Mountain Dew the best."

He met Ginnie's gaze and smiled, then nodded toward the door.

"Be back in a few." Ginnie closed the door behind her and walked down to her Willys with the chainsaw. She knew just the tree to cut down before heading into VanMeter.

Her dirt road had indeed been plowed, more or less, but the highway into VanMeter was cleared of snow down to the concrete. She drove through town to Casey's and wondered for a moment if she should bring Meg into town to look at the holiday lights, then decided it wasn't worth the risk.

She pulled up at the pump and filled her tank before walking into the store.

"Hey, Miss Ginnie!" Francie at the cash register said.

Ginnie grinned and waved as she walked past. "Kids excited for Christmas?"

"God, yes," Francie rang up Phil Hintermann's cigarettes and beer. "About to drive me crazy!"

Ginnie winked at her. "Then they're doing their jobs!"

They shared a laugh. In the kitchen, Danielle pulled something out of the air fryer then turned around. "Hey, Miss Ginnie! Orderin' your usual toasted ham-and-cheese with peppers tonight?" she said as she dumped a sizzling batch of popcorn chicken onto the sheet-pan and scooped it into paper cups.

"Actually, no," Ginnie said. "Can you make me a large pepperoni, and, um..." she looked up at a menu she hadn't paid attention to in years, "...a large supreme combo?"

Danielle finished scooping popcorn chicken. "Party at your place?"

"Just me and Lady. We got a hankerin' for some old movies and pizza. Just gonna stay bundled up at home for a few days."

"Got room for me?" Danielle laughed. "I am so sick of holiday stress."

"Aren't we all?" Ginnie said, then walked to the pop coolers.

She'd put her beverage selections on the corner of the checkout counter while her pizza cooked then wandered the aisles gathering anything she thought the kids might like. Cheetos and Starburst and light-up-fuzzy-gloves and Santa-shaped chocolate and Travel Yahtzee and a jigsaw puzzle of

Santa's Workshop. Gift selections would be vastly better at any big-box retailer in the city, but she didn't want to spend that much time on the road or lose even more time fighting holiday shoppers. Slim pickings or not, Casey's in VanMeter was her only option.

Ginnie bent over the shelf of kid toys to dig through a box of plastic video game characters when someone on their way to the bathrooms stopped behind her.

A guy checking out my fat ass, the thought, then sighed and stood. She turned, ready to tell him to buzz off but sucked in a breath instead.

Rachel Glaxney, high-school classmate and nosy bitch around town, raised an eyebrow at her. "What are you buying besides two large pizzas?"

Aw shit. Ginnie gathered up her eclectic selections and turned away. "Nothing. Just collectibles."

Rachel followed. "Well, you can throw your money away on anything you want. Have to fill that big old house with something, I suppose."

"Great to have your approval," Ginnie muttered. Francie at the cash register gave her an understanding grimace as she deposited the armload of gift items on the counter to be rung up.

"Yes, well, regardless of your affection for whatever that yellow bunny with a long, jagged tail is, I should probably remind you about tonight's midnight service. We haven't seen you in the pews for—"

"It's been twenty-two years." Ginnie glanced at the clock. *Pizza should be about done.*

"I knew it had been a long time, but not that long,"

Rachel said with her disapproving smile. "Pastor was asking about you the other day, in fact."

"I doubt that." Ginnie slid the bottles of pop over to add to her pile, and reminded Francie she'd ordered two pizzas. "He's only been pastor for three years."

"Well, he saw you in town."

"You know I don't go to Winterset unless I have no choice. He's never met me."

She turned her back on Rachel and approached the kitchen. "How're those pizzas doing, Dani?"

"About to come out. Another minute or two!"

Rachel had followed Ginnie but looked over her shoulder to frown at the collection of stuff Francie still rang up. "I know what happened," she said, turning back. "Everyone knows. But you have to let it go and come back to—"

"I don't have to do shit," Ginnie replied, brushing past Rachel to Francie. "And I'm not setting foot in that church."

"Ginnie..."

She pulled out her debit card and swiped it through the keypad. "Fuck off."

"Ginnie, honey," Rachel said, rubbing Ginnie's shoulder. "We were good friends once. I know how you've suffered, but isn't it time to come back—"

"I am *not* your honey, and I will *never* come back," she snapped, turning.

"The Pastor can help you. *We* can help—"

Ginnie took a step toward Rachel, who backed up. "Will the Pastor bring back Craig and the kids?"

"Of course not, but he can help you manage your grief."

"My grief is just fine," she muttered, glaring.

"God is here to help."

"Bullshit," she snapped. "My family died because some idiot old man with a heart condition decided he should drive on ice. God didn't do a damn thing to stop him. Didn't do a damn thing to have Craig drive a miniscule amount faster or slower or take a different route or anything at all to avoid being hit. God didn't do a damn thing to make a single passersby stop to help while Craig and Kevin were still savable." She took a step toward Rachel. "I know Todd died on impact, but Kev and Craig *suffered* and God did nothing. Nothing!"

"You can't possibly blame God—"

"How about Jessi? What about her? She didn't die from the accident, she died from freezing to death in the churned-up snow. She was unconscious and none of the rescuers found her until she was too cold." She thought of the little girl the night before, the same size as her Jessi, stumbling into a snow-covered road, and how it would have been so easy, so damned easy to just drive right by.

Ginnie wiped her eyes, sucked in a harsh breath, and stared at Rachel. "God did nothing until Jessi was too cold. She would have been just fine if your damned God would have had *one* of them look that direction. Just *one* of them! And I would still have my daughter. She'd be thirty-one this Christmas. THIRTY-ONE. I might have grandkids if your God told one damned fireman to look in a fucking snowdrift instead of fussing over my already-dead baby for twenty minutes."

"It's not..."

Dani watched wide-eyed, pizzas in hand, then set the boxes on the warmer.

"And after it all, when I asked Pastor VanMuer to officiate the funeral for my family, he said at the service that it was God's will to test me and we should pray. *God's will*, Rachel, he fucking said it was *God's will* with my husband and three kids—my whole fucking *life*—right there behind him."

"He has a plan for all of us, you just have to beli—"

"Fuck that, and fuck your filthy God. I will never, ever, set foot in any church again. *Ever.* And you can fuck off, too."

Ginnie turned away and wiped at her nose as she stomped to the kitchen window.

Dani rushed to get the pizzas. "Just finished cutting them. Only been on the warmer a few moments."

"That's fine," Ginnie said, pulling out her wallet. She accepted the pizzas and handed Dani a twenty. "Merry Christmas."

Before Dani could say anything, Ginnie turned away, glaring at Rachel who backed up and let her pass.

Francie had the purchases bagged up, but Ginnie paused long enough to hand her a twenty, too, then took a breath and gave her one more. "Give that one to Hazel when she comes in at six. Enjoy your kids. Make memories. And have a Merry Christmas."

Then she walked out the door into sputtering snow.

TWENTY THREE

HUEY PAID CASH FOR A CRAPPY MOTEL ROOM THAT STANK OF old cigarettes and stale semen, picked up Chinese take-out, then settled in for a long night listening to the trunked radio and watching the local news.

He'd received no intel on the kids since the explosion the evening before, had no intel on Warren's status or whereabouts, and his SynAg phone had remained silent far too long for comfort. For all he knew, the kids had burrowed into someone's garage, Warren had resisted arrest and suffered death by cop, and SynAg had brought in another acquisitions specialist.

Not that he, or she, would have any luck picking up the ice-cold trail of a kid who heard thoughts and his electro-explosive sister. Especially without someone to watch all the surveillance feeds and slip into computer systems and find the digital threads to follow in the real world.

He'd had no contact with Warren since confirming the owner of the minivan at Karen McLean's house. No texts, no phone calls, no hot coffee concoction, no kisses or quick gropes in the kitchen.

So he watched the early local news, cleaned his arsenal, and ate sinus-clearing Kung Pao alone in a cruddy motel room.

CBS Evening News opened with a story about the current gasbag in the White House in the midst of tense discussions with China over the same damn National Security back-and-forth hacking bullshit the US and China had bitched about for decades.

All talk, no action, he thought, standing to take a piss. Two steps later, while a reporter in Beijing prattled *they-said/we-said/here's-what-we-know* ersatz nonsense, his SynAg phone rang.

He scrambled to pick it up before the next ring. "Yes?" he said, trying to sound bored.

"We have your husband with us."

Huey sat, relieved. "Let me talk to him."

"Alas, he is unconscious," the voice on the phone said. "And he will remain so until shortly before noon tomorrow."

They can't be this stupid, Huey thought, leaning forward, but said nothing.

"If we do not have possession of our property by noon, we will raise your husband from anesthesia and begin conducting a methodical dissection of him."

"You're not doing this."

"Yes, we are. Our... physician is en-route as we speak. How long do you think your sweet little ginger will survive without narcotics, Mr. Rawlins? Hours? Minutes? How much pain will he endure before he loses consciousness or expires?"

Huey stood. "You tell him to walk out of there and call me, and we'll forget this phone call happened."

"We had a contract, Mr. Rawlins, a contract you have neglected to fulfill despite our generous deposit, and there are consequences for such failures."

"I am happy to return your deposit in exchange for Warren. I suggest you accept the offer."

"You failed us, Mr. Rawlins, and perhaps we will remove his freckles first. A man can live quite a long time without skin. Do you like his freckles, Mr. Rawlins?"

"This is your last chance to do the right thing, I swear to God—"

"Pray all you want, but be assured if you arrive without our property, we'll dismember him before you enter the building. Freckle-removal begins at 12:01 pm, Mr. Rawlins. I suggest you complete our agreement before then."

The call ended, leaving only empty air.

Huey opened Warren's back-up laptop and ran a location search for the client's cell number. The call came from SynAg's local executive housing near the center of a gated community for magnates in West Des Moines with high walls, security guards, dogs, and constantly monitored video-and-heat-signature surveillance, along with more security measures on the home itself. He could get in, sure, and most likely get out again, but collateral damage would be high and several residents of the community were well-paying clients.

Not only would a rescue attempt likely get Warren killed, it'd also close several revenue streams.

Mind churning, Huey took a piss then stood at the sink, staring at his reflection, at the electrical marks Meg

Adamson had burned onto his face. No one knew about them, no one but Warren, and they rambled, like roots, toward a possible solution.

He pulled a razor from his grooming kit and began shaving his head, his dark hair falling to the sink like iron filings, and stared at himself in the mirror as each pass of the razor exposed electrical lines across his scalp.

Perhaps there was an upside to being disfigured.

GINNIE PULLED up in front of the house and left everything but the pizza and pop in the truck while doing her best to think only about the tree in the back and supper in her hands.

Jake opened the door right before she reached it, and he wore his coat and the boots she'd loaned him. "Go on in," he said. "I can carry the tree."

He headed down the steps to the Willys so Ginnie went inside to find Meg still sitting with Lady and watching Christmas shows.

Meg turned, grinning, and announced, "Pizza!" while hopping to her feet. "Smells *sooooo good!*"

"We can eat right here in the living room," Ginnie said. "I might even find some Christmas movies we can watch." She set the pizzas and pop on the coffee table then turned and smiled at Jake carrying in a spruce tree taller than he was.

"A tree!" Meg squealed, running to it. "Oh, wow! We've never had a real tree!"

Jake leaned it against the wall then closed the front door. "Do you want me to get the decorations?"

"Nah, I've got it," Ginnie said, smiling at Meg's enthusiasm. "Why don't you kids fetch some plates and get started on the pizza. I'll be right back with stuff to put on that tree."

She hurried upstairs and to the drop-down steps to the attic. *At least the light still works,* she thought after flicking the switch at the top. Boxes and totes sat tucked between rafters, but she tried not to look at them, at the bits and pieces of lives that no longer were. Three totes of Christmas stuff stood stacked to the right, and she worked the first one down the ladder only to find Jake waiting for her.

"Let me help," he said, scooting up the steps and back for the second tote, then up again for the last one.

"Maybe not that one." Her voice caught as she called after him. "I... I don't..."

"Sure," he said. "I'm sorry."

The attic light flicked off. "Yeah. Me too." She watched him descend the steps and lift them to the ceiling again.

He sighed as he picked up the heavier tote and carried it toward the stairs. She followed with the smaller one.

"I feel what you feel," he said, his voice soft. "And I'm so sorry. You didn't deserve any of that."

"Nobody does," she said. "And neither did you kids, or your mom."

They said nothing as they descended to the main floor, but she saw Jake wipe at his eyes after setting his tote beside the tree.

It took her a few minutes to find Elf playing on TNT and they all piled together on the couch watching the movie, eating pizza, and putting out decorations during the commercials as if it was how they celebrated Christmas every year.

THE CORONER'S office called Fawkes three minutes before five PM.

"Hey, Les," the coroner's assistant said when he picked up and put it on speaker so Garrel could hear. "You ready for this?"

"Absolutely."

He heard papers rustling. "Okay, T.O.D. remains at 6:40 AM, give or take five minutes. The victim was thirty-two years old, blonde hair, hazel eyes, five foot seven inches, one-hundred-thirty-eight pounds. Physical examination found a bruise on her left hip, a few random scars of no importance, and a pre-cancerous mole low on her back she was likely unaware of. She had no evidence of recent sexual activity, alcohol intoxication, or recreational drug use, however, the tox screen came back positive for midazolam at a high enough level to keep her unconscious. There were still traces of it in her gut."

"So she was drugged?" Fawkes asked while Garrel clicked away on her tablet.

"Yes. We could not determine if a large dose was added to her food or if someone injected her too, but she likely lost consciousness within minutes."

"Do you have any idea when that might have been?" Garrel asked.

"Sometime the evening before. At least six hours before she was killed, but may have been twelve. Examination of her digestive tract indicates she ate supper around twelve hours before her death. It's possible she ingested the drug then, but highly unlikely she did so before eating."

"So sometime at or after supper?" Garrel asked.

"That's our best guess since we don't know how much was ingested. With the dosage she received, she would have, at minimum, been incapacitated if not completely unconscious within ten to fifteen minutes and remained that way for several hours. High dosages can cause death, but she was alive when the first shot was fired into her skull."

Fawkes asked, "So she was drugged, then shot?"

"Yes. There is no way Cheryl Adamson could have been aware of, let alone heard or fought off, her killer." The coroner's assistant paused and Fawkes heard another shuffle of paper.

"Okay, C.O.D. was a single shot through the frontal bone, 4.8 centimeters superior of her left eye socket, then passed through the skull, brain, throat, and chest to embed in the fifth right rib beside her spine. She died instantly. We pulled the fatal bullet, a standard low-cost 9MM, and have sent it to ballistics. GSR indicates the shot came from approximately nine inches away. The remaining three bullets matched and were fired shortly afterward from almost three feet away. They passed through her chest—"

"Wait," Fawkes said, glancing at the phone. "The fatal shot went through the *top* of her head?"

"Yes. Well, roughly halfway up her forehead, between her left eye and her hairline, at an angle that sent the bullet into her chest."

"From her head?"

"Yes. And she felt nothing, heard nothing, due to the medicat—"

"Was the body moved at any time after the first shot? Rearranged or something?"

"No," the coroner's assistant said. "All four bullets had standard trajectories and all four were recovered. Crime scene photographs show she was not moved or rearranged prior to our arrival—you'll have to check with the ballistics lab to confirm—but our assessment of blood-spatter on the headboard and wall matches a sleeping victim killed with a single shot through their forehead toward the chest."

Fawkes watched Garrel who tapped on her tablet, "So you're telling me someone held the gun near the top of her head and shot her, while she was in bed, as we found her?"

"Yes."

"And, from that gun, held near the top of her head, the bullet traveled through her, until it rested in her chest?"

"Yes."

"How is that possible if she was unconscious in bed, with her head near the headboard?"

"I don't know," the coroner's assistant admitted, "but that's what the autopsy showed. I'm sorry, Les, but I have another call to make before I get to go home for our holiday dinner. I'll email you the full report."

Fawkes wished her a happy holiday then ended the call before turning his attention to Garrel. "Let's look at the crime scene," he said.

Garrel pulled up the images and they examined Cheryl, curled on her right side, under blankets, in bed. Garrel zoomed in to examine the hole in her forehead above her left eye and the splatter the shot had left on the headboard and wall. Other bullets had penetrated her upper chest, left shoulder, and her throat near her left jaw.

Garrel clicked over to pull up the email from the coroner's office. Two drawings of a body—one the standard standing-with-hands-splayed illustration, the other drawn as she had lain—showed each bullet's trajectory. The coroner had marked three shots from in front of Cheryl, and one, very clearly, from beyond the top of her head.

"Matt Adamson killed his sister," Fawkes said, leaning back. "He passed through the wall between his room and hers, then shot her. Then he came into her room and shot her three more times to potentially confuse the crime scene."

Garrel stood and reached for her coat. "People do not walk through walls. Or shoot through walls. They *don't*."

"Well, he does. And he murdered Cheryl Adamson. The conclusive evidence is *right here*."

"You know who killed your victim?" the Chief said, entering their cubicle.

"Yes," Fawkes said, standing.

Garrel shrugged on her coat and said, "No."

"Glad we cleared that up," Chief said. "Wanted to give you both a heads up. Jordan Creek Town Center sent us footage of your missing kids."

Fawkes stood and grabbed his coat. "They're at the mall?"

"No, it's from last night. While looking for footage of a rear-end-collision at the parking lot entrance on Jordan Creek, the city of West Des Moines noticed your kids crossing at that light, heading west, less than three minutes before the fender bender."

"What time was this?" Fawkes asked.

Chief checked his notepad. "Approximately 8:32 PM."

Fawkes tapped his hand on his desk. "They must have taken another bus. Valley West to Jordan Creek. Shit. Why didn't DART send us the footage?"

"Maybe they didn't notice." Garrel took a step toward the hall. "I need to get home."

"I need the footage," Fawkes said. "Whatever busses run westbound between the malls before 8:30, and whatever the stoplight cams picked up."

"Goodnight!" Garrel said, waving, then she walked away while dialing her phone.

Fawkes and the chief followed a few yards behind.

"We'll get it to you," the Chief said, "but the West Des Moines PD told me the city's already released the traffic cam footage to local news stations."

"Then let's hope we find those kids before Hubert Rawlins or SynAg does."

TWENTY FOUR

FAWKES' PHONE RANG BEFORE HE GOT OUT OF DOWNTOWN DES Moines traffic. He wanted to get home and take a pain pill.

"It's Becca," she said when he picked up. "Got your bloody glove processed."

"Let me guess. It's Jake's blood."

"How'd you know?"

"Just an educated guess. Do the marks match the gun?"

"Yep, plus it's covered with GSR and everything, but the weird thing on the outside is the marks indicate the blood came from a left hand, but the weapon was fired by a right hand. Like someone with a bloody left hand held the gun, but it was fired by someone in gloves, with their right hand. The glove picked the blood off of the gun, not the original blood source."

Fawkes managed to not rear-end the idiot in front of him. "Makes sense to me. Thanks, Becca."

"I'm not done, Sir."

"What else did you find?"

"There were several slivers of wood inside the glove. All

kiln-dried pine, like they use in construction studs. I'm still waiting for its FISH analysis for DNA comparison to Jake. Sorry, Sir, but it won't be ready until sometime tomorrow morning, at the earliest."

"That's fine. Put a note on the blood sample for the tech to call me as soon as the test is done and send Garrel and me the report on the glove. Then go on home, and have a nice holiday with your family."

KATE HEARD a knock on the door and put the cushions back on her sofa. She'd looked for her phone most of the day but couldn't find hide nor hair of it, anywhere. Not in the couch or under the bed or even in the fridge. It wasn't anywhere.

She peeked through the peephole and grinned when she saw Matt.

"That was quick," she said, opening the door. "I figured it'd take you a lot more than an hour for a grocery run on Christmas Eve."

"I'm an efficient shopper." He carried in a small sack from the grocery store and a massive, taped-closed bag from Target. He handed the massive bag to Kate. "This is for being so awesome, for taking me in and helping me out, for not griping when I left us no leftovers from that amazing lunch you made, and, well, for being a good friend. Sorry I didn't have a chance to wrap everything."

Kate sat, stunned, and opened the bag. Matt left the grocery sack on the counter and pulled a kitchen chair over to watch her.

An HDR TV filled the bag and Kate looked from Matt to the TV to Matt again. "How could you afford..."

"Told you I had money," he said smiling. "And I thought you'd like a nice TV. I got streaming cards for everything they had. Spotify, Hulu, HBO, Netflix, Disney Plus..."

"Really?" she said, boggling at the opportunity to watch *The Queen's Gambit* and *The Mandalorian*.

"Yeah, everything. I... I didn't know what service you might like."

"Wow." She pulled the TV from the bag and set it aside, expecting to see a handful of gift cards in the bottom, which she did, but boxes for an iPad, iPhone, chocolates, and mints sat amongst the cards. She lifted the small electronics from the sack.

"I paid for two years unlimited service for both," he said, standing. "The activation info's in the sack with the cards."

She looked up at him. "This is too much."

"No, it's not. It's not even close to enough for all you've done for me. Let me know when you're ready to set up the TV or if you need help with the other two."

She watched him walk to the kitchen and unpack steak and salad from the grocery sack, then she took a cleansing breath, opened her new iPhone, and wondered how she got so lucky.

FAWKES SAT at his kitchen table eating a HungryMan frozen dinner while he watched the footages of the kids on the bus from Valley West and crossing Jordan Creek Parkway, on his phone. Jake did not stare at the bus camera, nor blink his odd blinks. He looked ill, weak, and still suffering the effects of whatever Rawlins injected him with. Fawkes wrote on his notepad to re-check if any injectors had been found near the blast site.

Meg helped Jake off the bus and, several minutes later, helped him cross the street and disappear from camera view. *Where are they going?* Fawkes thought. He switched to the map app on his phone and put in the locations for their house, the McDonald's they'd bought breakfast from, Walmart, both malls, and the intersection where they were last seen.

McDonald's was almost straight south of their house, but the other three spots nearly lined up in a west/southwest trajectory and, as he checked the local bus route maps, Jordan Creek Town Center was the farthest southwest point on the bus routes.

"They have a destination in mind," he mumbled, zooming out on his map app. "And wherever it is, it's southwest."

Booneville was a few miles southwest of their last known location, then a whole lot of nothing but snowy cornfields until Winterset. Twenty miles, or so. Assuming they maintained a southwesterly trek.

He sighed and munched some of his dinner. They could have walked south or west or turned north and crossed the interstate again at DeSoto or, well, anything. Even if they found shelter, they had no gear, no food or water, and no one had reported finding two lost kids within the past twenty-four hours or so. At best, they'd soon turn up hungry and cold. But if they stayed on foot, kept pressing to wherever they were headed, they likely had become overwhelmed by last night's storm were lost in the snow somewhere in hundreds of square miles of fields and wouldn't be found until spring. Definitely not the result anyone wanted in a missing children investigation.

"Shit," he muttered, standing, then dropped the rest of his frozen dinner in the trash. After muttering to himself for a few moments, he shrugged on his coat and bundled up for a trek across the tundra to Claire's place and hoped she was in the mood for some toast.

KATE WASHED up the supper dishes while Matt channel-surfed on her new TV, finally settling on local news. There had been robberies and fistfights over the latest gadgets, more snow was in the forecast, an unnamed woman on the south side had been found bound and horribly beaten in her home, and new footage showed two missing kids in West Des Moines the night before.

"That's them!" Matt said.

Kate turned, soapy plate in her hand to see Matt standing and pointing at the TV.

"Oh my, God, it's them!" He grinned and turned to her. "We've got to go!"

"What? Where? Didn't it just say they were spotted *yesterday?*"

He trotted the few steps to her. "I know where they're going! Don't you see? They're heading to where my sister's ex lives. My niece's dad's place!"

She tilted her head and squinted at him. "What?"

"They're going to Patterson!"

"What?" she said, still confused. "Where's Patterson?"

"I dunno, somewhere near Winterset, my sister said." He turned and pulled his coat from the back of the chair. "We've gotta go find them!"

"Do you know his address? Can we Google it? I'm not even sure where Winterset is, and it all looks the same out in the country anyway. I don't want to drive endlessly around snow-drifted cornfields, especially at night."

"I've got to go get them! Let's go!"

He grabbed her hand and tried to pull her toward the door, but she held her ground. "I'm not driving around rural Iowa in the dark in a snowstorm, especially without a destination in mind. That's crazy!"

He shoved her hand away and snapped, "I am not crazy, and we'll find them!"

"How? How the hell can we find two kids, walking, in the dark, *maybe* somewhere near Winterset, in a snowstorm? HOW?"

He stomped to the door. "Fuck you. I treat you nice, get you nice things, and when I ask you to help me find my family, you—"

"Look, I'm sorry," she said, following, "but take a minute and think about it. "You don't know where he lives, Winterset is a long way away, and there's a freaking snowstorm!"

He turned his head to face her. "Goddammit! I know all that!"

"Use my new phone and track him down. Get his actual address. We can leave first thing in the morning because then, at least, we can *see*, okay?"

She watched his hand squeeze the doorknob, then release, then squeeze again. He huffed out a breath and his shoulders sagged before he turned back to her. "Okay," he said, yanking off his coat. "First thing."

"First thing," she assured him and touched his face. "It's just a few more hours, baby."

"Yeah," he muttered, meeting her gaze. "I need to find them. They're all I have, except for you."

"I know," she soothed, drawing him into her arms. "I know. We'll find them. We'll save them."

She kissed him, tasting his fear and fury, then led the beast back to her bed.

HUEY HAD PREPARED for his plan to rescue Warren but didn't need to leave until two-thirty in the morning, so he munched cold eggrolls and watched the ten o'clock news after they teased about the *Metro Mommy Murder/Kidnapping Update!* Most of the piece was bullshit, but a snippet of traffic cam footage showed the kids crossing Jordan Creek Road on foot, along with the warning that Jake was a person of interest in the case. The kid was exhausted and weak in the four or so seconds of film, not a threat to anyone. His sister, however, was bright, alert, and focused. Huey leaned forward to watch her, the fingers of his left hand tracing along the twisted scarring of his right arm. So small, but so powerful. Surely SynAg knew about her. Surely she was why they'd placed such a high bounty on the pair, not physically weak and mentally compromi—

The burner phone rang and Huey sprung to his feet and snatched it from the dresser, his heart slamming. Only one other person knew the number of the phone they kept in the storage bay. Only one person paid cash for the damn reload cards and reloaded them every month on schedule, just in case.

Did the fuckers torture Warren to get this number? So much for an efficient death for them, then. I'll give them the slow and painful package instead.

Teeth clenched, he flipped open the phone and made himself say, "Hello?"

The robotic voice on the other end asked if he wanted to accept the charges of a collect call from Polk County Jail, and that the call was being recorded.

"God, yes!" Huey said, sitting on the edge of the bed, then nearly wept as he heard Warren's precious voice.

"You okay?" Warren asked. "Took me forever to get a line since apparently everyone here wanted to call home for Christmas. Glad I caught you at work."

"I'm fine. Great," Huey assured him. "And, yeah, I'm working." He reclined back onto the bed and grinned at the ceiling as relief flooded over him. "So you're in jail?"

"Yeah. There's a whole pile of mocked-up charges and bail's set at a hundred-grand, cash only. God knows why."

Because they know you're a flight risk, Huey thought, grinning. "I'm sure someone will bail you out in the morning as a Christmas present."

"Sounds great to me. Any luck finding your puppies?"

Huey glanced at the TV. "No, but someone saw them running. Maybe."

Warren chuckled and his voice lowered. "Where were they running?"

"Over by Jordan Creek. Not sure if I should go look for them there, since it's a ways from where I last had them."

"Jordan Creek? You're sure?"

"Yep. Heading West. Why?"

"Well, I thought it was nothing..."

Huey sat again. "What was nothing?"

"Pretty sure one of our pups was sired out near Patterson, Iowa. Check her papers. It's been over a year, but maybe she's running home."

"Is the sire still there?" Huey asked, reaching for Warren's laptop. "Just in case we need to look for a pup or two."

"Yeah. Should be in her papers. Might need to pay 'em a visit, see what they have available for adoption."

Huey grinned and found Meg's primary file. All of Warren's notes were set up in separate sub-menu file folders, all labeled, including one for Biological Father. One click later, Huey saw everything he needed. "Found it. Looks like he's in a good breeding kennel. Looks nice, and it's easy to get to. Thanks. I'll check 'em out. Might make a good Christmas present for somebody."

"Awesome," Warren said, then chuckled. "Well, I'd better sign off before the dude behind me loses his shit."

"Love you, Babe."

"Love you, too. See you tomorrow."

GINNIE GOT the kids to bed then took a couple of minutes to smile at the tree, its eclectic collection of ornaments illuminated by blinky lights. She saw glass ornaments that had been her mother's, and a paper rocking horse Kevin had made in kindergarten. The funky primitive Santas she'd bought on a whim while pregnant with Jessi, the dancing elf

Craig had received on a package from his parents when they were still newlyweds, the plain, unbreakable plastic balls they'd used when the kids were little, and other ornaments she and Craig had acquired through the fourteen years they were together.

Jake and Meg had hung every one, covering their tree with her memories while they'd talked, and cried, about their mom and their Christmases. She hoped it had helped them grieve a little.

She took a quick jog out to the truck and back with the sack of gifts then spent a few minutes wrapping them in holiday paper she hadn't looked at in two decades. It was brittle in places, and the bows didn't stick very well, but she managed to make them look nice then put them under the tree.

After one more smile at the tree, she climbed the stairs to bed. Morning came early and Jake wanted to head to Patterson right after breakfast.

FAWKES' phone rang at 2:17 AM and he groaned, grabbing it off of the nightstand beside Claire's bed. He didn't recognize the number.

"Yeah, what?" he mumbled. Beside him, Claire rolled over.

"Yo, Detect-tive?" a woman's voice said.

He sat and rubbed his face awake. "Who is this?"

"It's Jacqui! Just wanted to tell you the wedding was awesome, and the party..." she giggled a little then lowered her voice, "it's still going on."

"Good, I'm glad," he muttered. "Why don't you call me tomorrow when you've sobered up."

"I can't," she said before he hung up. "Because then I couldn't tell you what I needed to tell you."

"What did you need to tell me?"

"I keep thinking about those kids. They're special. You gotta remember that, detect-tive. Remember they're special."

He stood and stumbled to the bathroom to piss. "Yeah. We figured that out."

"Oh, good!" she said. "Did Jake show you his trick?"

"Jake has a trick?"

"Uh-huh." He heard a thump in the background and she giggled then let out a whooshy breath. "He knows *everything*. Always. Pick a card? He knows what it is, even if you've written something on it. Think of a fruit, he knows it's an orange-colored blackberry. He knows what you ate for breakfast three days ago and what you named your dog when you were six and he *really* knows if you're lying to him. So never, ever lie to Jake, okay? Never, never, *never*."

Fawkes finished pissing. "I'll remember that."

"Awesome. Because that chemical company that made them special wants him *really* bad. Cheryl told me last week, she'd been getting calls. They tried to buy her son from her. Offered her a million bucks."

Fawkes sat on the edge of the tub and wished he'd brought pain pills and his note pad to Claire's. "What?!"

"Yeah. They wanted him for some big corporate mess. Hostile takeover of a competitor, maybe, I don't remember for sure what, just they need him in Washington the first part of January for some meeting, but Cheryl told them he wasn't for sale. She asked me to get her emergency housing, but with the holidays, there wasn't nothing. So it's partly my fault she died. My fault because I failed." She sniffled. "Are you gonna arrest me? Maybe I should."

Fawkes took a breath and pointed her back to the task at hand. "The chemical company needed Jake for meeting in Washington?"

"Yeah. Senators or something, I dunno. They need Jake to tell them how they can keep their company from being shut down."

"Holy shit," Fawkes muttered. "How's Jake supposed to do that?"

"I told you," she whined. "He knows *everything*. Even what Senators are thinking. No, that's not what Cheryl said. It was something else. What they... Fudge, what *was* it?"

"Take your time. Try to remember."

"What they believe? What they feel... No. Maybe what they want? Yeah! What they *want*. He can tell them what the Senators want so they can give it to them! That's it!"

"Jake will know how to pay-off the Senators?"

"There ya go! You understand!"

"What about Meg?"

"Meggy? Shhp. She's just a sweet kid. Don't let her play with your phone, though, because it'll short out and croak."

"How'd the chemical company make them special, Jacqui?"

"Oh, that? Ha! I'm not supposed to talk about that. That's... That's waaaay secret in their file."

He smiled and lowered his voice. "But I thought we were friends."

"We are," she said then muttered, "Crap, I stepped out of my shoe. Where'd it go?"

"How'd they become special, Jacqui?"

She grunted. "Dangit! It's not under that chair. Can you help me find it, Detect-tive? You're good at finding things, right?"

"What'd the company do to them, Jacqui?"

"Chemically-modified grain experiments messed up their great-grandpa. He changed, became *special*. And when he had kids... They were spec—There it is! There's my shoe! Yay! My shoe!"

Fawkes stood and stared into the dark, his eyes wide. *SynAg accidentally mutated their great-grandfather's Chromosome 19 and when he had kids, he passed down the mutated chromosome. Warren said SynAg's mutating hogs and who-knows-what-else. No wonder the Senate wants to talk to them.*

He heard a couple of grunts then a crash, like a vase or a plant falling off of a table.

"I can't get my shoe back on with one hand, Detect-tive. Better let you go."

"Thank you for your—" he started, but the call had clicked off.

TWENTY FIVE

"WHO THE HELL'S CALLING ME AT FIVE IN THE GODDAMN morning?" Warren's mother said when she picked up the call.

"Just me," Huey replied. He'd gotten five hours sleep, and had developed a new, hopefully more profitable, plan. No one threatened Warren and survived. No one. Not even a client. "I need you to—"

"I don't need to do shit, you fucking criminal!" she screeched.

He winced and pulled the phone away from his ear, but he still heard footsteps thumping in the background.

"It's your fucking fault my baby's been arrested, and it ruined Christmas! Your goddamn fault, Hubert."

Huey sighed, "You're right, Brenda."

"Damn straight I'm right! And now my sweet Warren's in prison! Again! Because you fucking fucked it all up, Hubert!"

"Just jail, not prison," Huey said.

"They're the same goddamn thing! I don't know where

he is or if he's even okay and if you were here, I'd kick you in the goddamn balls."

"I'd probably deserve that. But I need you to—"

"I ain't doing shit for you, Hubert!"

"Then do it for Warren," he said. "I have his bail money."

She graced him with a few moments of silence. "Bail's been set? Goddamn it, Hubert! I can't get to the bank until tomorrow."

"I have it in cash right now and I will give it to you. Meet me at Northcreek Park in one hour."

Then he closed the burner phone and grabbed his coat.

———

Ginnie woke early and started bacon before she mixed pancake batter. She laid the third slice in the pan and heard a thud in the living room. Lady walked into the kitchen, stretching.

"What were you doing in there?" she asked. "Thought you went to the barn with Jake."

Ginnie hurried to the living room to check and found Jake asleep on the couch, barefooted and wrapped in her old afghan and the quilt she'd sent with him.

Chuckling, she covered his feet, then returned to cooking bacon.

She'd cooked most of the package when Meg thumped down the stairs.

"Bacon? I smell bacon," the girl mumbled and she walked, groggy, into the kitchen and flumped into a chair beside the table while Lady nudged at her hand to get petted.

"Merry Christmas, sweetie," Ginnie said. "I'll make you some pancakes and eggs. Get our morning going."

Meg yawned and stretched. "Want me to go get Jake?"

"That's up to you. He's asleep in the living room." She flipped the last four slices of bacon and turned on the flame beneath her griddle.

"Jake!" Meg hollered as she stood and walked to the living room, Lady following. "It's time to wake up! Ginnie's making break—"

Ginnie smiled at the moment of silence then Meg squealed, "Presents!!"

"Whaa?" Jake said, blearily. "How'd she..."

Ginnie poured pancake batter and heard him rush to the tree, heard them laugh and shake presents and chatter like most kids did Christmas morning. Then Jake grabbed her hand from behind and barely gave her time to turn off the stove before he dragged her to the living room where Meg squealed over her fluffy mittens and reindeer headband. Ginnie sat and watched Jake settle down beside his sister and laugh over a handheld video game and ear-muffs and candy. Meg sucked happily on her candy cane and opened her next gas-station gift. For a moment, they were regular kids and all was right with the world.

"WISH MY MOM WOULD PICK UP," Kate mumbled, setting aside her new phone. She drove south down I-80 past the Cumming exit in heavy traffic, unable to avoid the morning sunshine pouring through the gap between her visor and the edge of her windshield. Matt sat beside her, foot tapping as he stared straight ahead.

"We still have like twenty miles to go," he muttered. "Can't this car go any faster?"

"On fresh snow and ice? Are you crazy?"

He turned his head and snarled, "Don't call me crazy!"

She fell silent and drove, following an SUV with kids in the backseat while her heart seemed to thud low in her belly yet high in her throat, and her hands stayed clenched on the steering wheel. *Stay calm. It's okay. You've been through a lot worse than this. He's just eager to find his family.*

"We have to get there before they do," Matt said for surely the eightieth time. "Shit, we're probably too late."

"If they're already there, it's okay," she soothed.

"No, it's not," he muttered. "I need to surprise them."

Oh, I think us showing up unexpected on Christmas morning looking for kids this guy doesn't want would be a pretty big surprise, she thought but said nothing.

"There!" Matt said, pointing to the left lane. "There's a gap! Get around that damned SUV!!"

"It's icy and we're fine right—"

He flung his hand through her right arm and it felt like a slap on the inside instead of her skin. "Get in the mother-fucking left lane and get around that slow fucking SUV!"

She sucked in a startled whine and steered into the other lane, fishtailing and nearly skidding into the center ditch before regaining control. "Aw, crap," she gasped, but Matt didn't seem to notice.

"Now go! GO!"

I never should have let him stick around, she thought, her grip white-knuckled on the steering wheel. *Never should have slept with him, great sex or not. I'm so damned stupid! Why can't I ever learn not to trust men? They're shits, they're all shits. Maybe I should drive this damned car into the ditch. Make him walk. Let him freeze.*

She took a breath and blinked back tears. *Maybe it's all my fault. It's always my fault.*

"Hey, baby," Matt said, his voice soft. "I'm sorry. I just need to see my niece and nephew. I've been so, so worried and scared. I've lost my sister and they've lost their mom, and all I have is you and you're so incredible. I don't know what else to do."

He touched her right hand, ran his fingers over hers. "I'm just worried they're lost in the snow or her deadbeat dad will turn them away, so, if we get their quick enough, maybe they'll be okay. You can understand that, can't you, baby? But we'll find them, right? We will. Won't we?"

"We'll find them." She gave him a comforting smile then returned her attention to the road.

She wondered which Matt was the real one.

FAWKES and Garrel climbed another set of steps to yet another cookie-cutter house in a housing development just southwest of Jordan Creek Town Center while, across the street, a pair of West Des Moines cops did the same.

Fawkes knocked while Garrel looked up something on her phone, and a very pregnant thirty-ish woman in a holiday bathrobe and a messy bun opened the door, bringing a vanilla-scented blast of warm air with her.

"Yes?" the woman said, glancing at the police car idling a couple of doors down the block. "Can I help you?"

Fawkes held up his badge. "I'm Detective Fawkes with the Des Moines Police Department," he said, exchanging the badge for a pair of photographs of Jake and Meg, one from the latest bus footage, the other from the traffic cam. "We believe this pair of missing children may have walked past your house night before last. Can you take a look, please?"

"Um," she said, accepting the pictures. "I saw these kids on the news."

"Glad you watch the news, Ma'am," he said while Garrel continued to text. "But did you see them in your neighborhood around eight-forty to nine PM, night before last?"

"Hey, Jeff!" she called back into the house. "The cops are here. Didn't you say you saw some odd kids the other night?"

"Yeah." A tall slender man with a bushy beard walked up carrying a toddler who bapped him on the head with an Elf on a Shelf. "Some girl in blue and a Goth-looking boy. Never seen them around here before."

He handed his wife the baby and examined the pictures. "Yeah, that's them, I think. I only saw them as I was coming into the house. Was dark." He shrugged and handed the photos back to Fawkes. "Didn't get a good look at them."

Garrel looked up from her phone.

"What direction were they heading?" she asked, nearly the first words she'd said all morning. "Did either appear injured?"

"The boy stumbled and looked sick. Thought maybe he had too much Christmas cheer, ya know? They were going that way," he said, pointing south.

"Thank you. If you think of anything else, give us a call," Garrel said, handing him her card."

They descended the steps and Fawkes said, "South. I still think they're heading to Winterset."

"Maybe they're heading to Creston or Osceola or Kansas City," Garrel muttered. "We need proof."

They turned at the sidewalk and continued to the next house.

HUEY CIRCLED Northcreek Park three times and cruised through nearby neighborhoods twice but saw no cops, only a Lincoln parked near the slides. He pulled in beside Warren's mother and completed another visual scan before exiting his pickup.

She unrolled her passenger-side window and her eyes grew wide as he approached.

"My God, Hubert, what happened—"

"Listen. Don't talk," he said, handing her the envelope. "Full bond's there, plus a little extra. He'll know where to go. If I haven't arrived by dark, you tell him I said Gamma. He'll know what to do."

She accepted the envelope and he said, "See you on the other side, Brenda."

Then he slid back into his truck and drove to the interstate, tossing the wiped, factory-reset burner phone onto the middle lane between East 14th and Second Avenue.

Smiling, he cranked up Slipknot and headed South.

ONCE THEY'D LEFT the interstate and headed west on Highway 92 toward Patterson, it didn't take Kate long to realize Matt had no real idea where they were going. He muttered, "Shit. Is that the road?" at every dirt-road intersection they passed.

Oh my God, she thought. *We're driving around bum-butt Iowa and he has no freaking clue.*

Highway 92 had been cleared nearly down to concrete, but the side roads were covered with snow and tire tracks. Maybe they were passable, but she wasn't in a hurry to find out.

"Do you want to stop in Patterson?" she asked. "Looks like it's nestled in that curve up ahead and maybe they have somewhere we can ask for direc—"

"We're not asking for directions," he snapped. "He's on Quail Ridge, south of Patterson. That's what my sister said. But I don't remember the house number."

Good Lord, she thought, wanting to bang her head on the steering wheel. *What if Quail Ridge runs parallel to this highway? What if his memory's faulty? Are we gonna be stuck out here forever?*

He stared, glowering at the microscopic town as they passed. "Turn around at the next road. It's here somewhere."

She slowed down to turn right onto gravel, but he said, "Are you a fucking idiot? Not north! *South!* Turn the next road south!"

"Sorry," she said, the back end of her car skidding as she accelerated again. A road south lay about a quarter of a mile ahead, and she took it, grinding her teeth when it doubled back and took them right into Patterson.

He growled low in his throat, and Kate didn't know what

to do. So she drove, slowly. The road he'd directed her to take led them through Patterson and back to the highway east of town, as did the next road south. He had her stop midway through Patterson and take a side-street south, but it ran two blocks in town then ended at the river, so she doubled back again while Matt pounded his fists through the passenger seat.

She paused at the intersection of Fourth and Long streets, then sighed and turned south again without much hope. Seemed like the little loop of a town had a highway on one side and a river on the other. She saw another street running east/west, just like before but, as she continued south toward the river, this time the road ahead went down-hill, to a bridge instead of dead-ending.

"Here we go," Matt said.

They crossed a frozen river on a skinny little bridge and the street signs said they drove on Terrace Avenue, which, Kate noted to herself, was not Quail anything. South they went, her car struggling through barely-plowed snow, past another gravel road, then Terrace swung west.

The roads seemed to get worse with every farm they passed. Far, far ahead, Terrace looked like it curved north again, and probably went back to Patterson or the highway, but another street T'd off of Terrace and headed south. "Do you want me to take that southbound road?" she asked, hoping they didn't get stuck.

"Yes!" he snapped and she was partway through the turn when he screamed, "Stop!"

She stopped, her heart slamming as she held her breath and blinked at him.

"Why are you turning here?" he said, pointing at the

street sign at the intersection. Terrace apparently became Quail Ridge Trail after it curved west. He pointed west, the way they had been traveling. "Look at that sign! Go that way."

She managed to back up without getting stuck or sliding into a ditch, and eased her car west on Quail Ridge Trail.

GINNIE SAT on the couch with her coat on, ready to go, and wished she could just wait in the truck. Maybe her heartbreak would be easier there.

Meg played by the tree with her My Little Pony playset and had reluctantly put on shoes, but not her coat or mittens. "I don't want to go."

"I know," Jake said, glancing over at Ginnie. "But we have to. We can't stay here."

"Why not? I like it here. She's nice, and we're like *normal* here."

"We're not normal anywhere," he said. "We need to go. You need to be with your dad."

Meg made the little pink horse hop toward the orange one while Lady watched, her tail wagging. "I don't want to be with my dad! I want to be with Ginnie!"

"We can't."

"Why not?" Meg turned to Ginnie. "Can we stay here with you?"

"It's not up to me, honey. There's laws, and there's nothing I can do."

"She's probably already in a lot of trouble for letting us

stay as long as we have," Jake said. "Do you want her to go to jail?"

Oh, damn, don't tell her that, Ginnie thought, but Meg shook her head and Jake gently took the horse toys out of her hands and put them in a faded little suitcase that had been Jessi's, back when.

"Let's go. Get it over with."

Meg stood, crying, then ran out the door with Lady right behind her.

"It's okay," Jake said, watching her go. "She's heading to the truck."

Ginnie stood. "You sure you want to do this? Leave your sister with a stranger, even if he is her dad?"

"No. But I don't know what choice I have. Not if I want to avenge our mother."

Ginnie doubted more killing would solve anything, but thinking it all morning long was surely good enough. No need to tell him, too. She sighed. "You'd be welcome to stay here, both of you, if we could square it with whoever decides such things. I'd be happy to have you."

"I know." He hefted the backpack she'd given him and stuffed Meg's coat and mittens inside. "Maybe someday we can, but don't bet on it. Can you check in on her sometimes for me? If... if he'll let you?"

"Of course I will."

He wiped at his eyes with the back of his hand, and Ginnie put her arm around him. "Shh. It's gonna be okay."

He turned and hugged her. "Thank you. Thank you for, well, everything."

She hugged him back, then he stepped away, held his head high, and walked out to the snow.

She followed and closed the door behind her. Meg sat in the middle of the Willys' bench seat, staring straight ahead with Lady beside her doing the same thing.

Jake shooed Lady out of the truck then climbed in beside his sister and closed the door. Both kids were buckled in by the time Ginnie slid behind the wheel.

No one talked as she drove south to Cumming Road then west. They'd just rounded the big s-curve when Ginnie saw Rachel Glaxney and her damn fool husband at the end of their driveway waiting to turn west onto the highway, same as them.

"Shit, shit, shit," Ginnie mumbled, forcing herself to stare straight ahead.

"Aw, crap," Jake muttered, looking back as the big car turned to follow them. "She saw us and is wondering why you have two kids in your truck."

"Don't look at her," Ginnie said, but both kids looked back anyway.

"And now she's recognized us from the news!" Jake said. "Oh, no. Oh, no. She's telling her husband you've got the missing kids from the news, that I... And now she's dialing 911. What do we do?"

Shit. Where can I hide them? If we'd only been a minute faster or slower.

If only.

If only I had. If only Craig had. If only someone looked in a damned snowdrift.

God.

Why are the holes in my life full of if only?

Why does it still hurt so much?

Ginnie clenched the steering wheel so hard her fingers hurt. *Doesn't matter. I have to save these kids!*

"Will that man find us again?" Meg wailed. "Will he..."

"I don't know," Jake said, putting his arm around his sister and holding her close while watching Ginnie as if she were their only hope.

"I... Shit. There's lots of patches of woods around here. If I can get far enough ahead of them..."

"Yeah," Jake said. "We can hide in the trees."

"Unbuckle your seat belts and get down. Make sure she sees you hide."

"Got it," he said.

Ginnie heard the kids unbuckle then she slowed down to let the Glaxneys get a little closer.

"Hold on, hold on..." Jake said. "Duck, Meg!"

Both kids ducked, Meg onto the floor first and Jake bent over her right after, his head by the door.

Ginnie floored it and the Willys surged forward.

"I think I know a place. We'll be out of their sight for at least a few seconds."

She sped down Cumming Road, expanding the distance between her and the Glaxneys as much as she could, then turned south. "The road we're on is Quail Ridge. You got it, Jake?"

"Yes."

"Stay on it," she said, imagining their journey, but her memory was of summer, with clover and grazing sheep. "Cross the highway. It'll dogleg west, then south, then east and take you right to her dad's place. I'll drop you off at an S-curve on the far side of some woods and try to get them to follow me back home. You hide 'til it's clear."

"Got it."

Quail Ridge was low-maintenance but the Willys didn't care. She expanded the distance to a quarter-mile, a half, maybe more, before the S-curve near the Halvorsen farm.

"Hang on, kids, this is gonna be tricky. Hope we don't end up in the ditch."

She downshifted and slammed on the brakes, taking the first turn far too fast. The Willys back end skidded but the front drove true and she continued southeast to the big swath of trees, then slid through the lower end of the s-curve and to a sloppy stop.

The kids bolted for cover, and Jake gave her one last look before she slammed the truck into first gear and surged forward again.

She glanced in her rearview mirror and saw only trees, then, just coming to the start of the S-curve, the Glaxney's Buick. Far to her right down the highway, she heard police sirens.

"Godspeed, kids," she said, running the stop sign and crossing highway traffic while turning east, hard. The Willys' back end skidded onto highway 92 as she sped toward Patterson.

TWENTY SIX

"COME ON," MATT SAID AS HE GOT OUT OF THE CAR. "DON'T be shy."

Kate looked out at a newer mobile home. A shiny four-wheel-drive pickup with a tow winch waited between the deck and a big, ugly dog barking on a chain. "I think I'll stay right here," she said.

"Give me the keys and get out of the car, Kate," Matt said, then slammed his door.

Kate unclenched her hands from the wheel and did as she was told.

She followed Matt, her head down, as they crossed the yard to wooden steps leading to a deck and the trailer. He climbed up, but she hesitated until he gave her a silent glare. She took a breath and joined him on the deck.

"Here we go," Matt said, squaring his shoulders before knocking on the door.

A tiny woman in a Jason Aldean t-shirt and baggy sweatpants opened it and stood there rubbing her bleary eyes. "Yeah?" she said, blinking in the morning. "Somebody slide off 92 again? Chad's been up all night, but gimme a minute. I'll go get—"

Matt grabbed her by the wrist and flung her toward the deck railing. She squawked, hands in front of her to catch herself, but the rail slipped through her throat, arms, chest, and belly until Matt let go, leaving her impaled from the back of her shoulders to the front of her hips.

Kate covered her mouth as the woman's legs and neck shuddered then fell limp. *Oh, God! Oh, God! He killed her!* She squawked her surprise when Matt grabbed her wrist, dragged her into the trailer, and closed the door.

She took a breath to scream, but he clamped his hand over her mouth and snarled, "Keep your fucking trap shut or I'll put your head in the goddamn wall."

She nodded then sagged, sucking in desperate breaths. Helpless, she watched Matt cross the living room to the hallway.

"Hey, Chad!" he hollered as he stomped down the hall. "Been a long time, buddy!"

Kate heard a squawk and a tussle. *How am I gonna get away from him?* she thought, inching toward the door, then held back a scream as a good-looking man wearing only underwear staggered backward into the living room. He held a handgun in one hand and clutched at a book embedded sideways beneath his collarbones with his other. Matt followed, glaring. Chad's face turned red and he gurgled nonsense, then he fell onto his ass, splay-legged, and blinked at Matt as he raised his gun and tried to fire, but the trigger didn't move.

"Forgot to release the safety, you idiot." Matt grabbed the

gun and flung it aside then leaned over Chad. "Seen your kid, idiot? The one you never pay for?"

Chad shook his head and his mouth moved as if saying no, but nothing came out. Then he fell over sideways, staring at Kate, his mouth gasping like a fish out of water, but his chest remained unmoving, his air blocked by the book. He reached for her, but she was too far away, even if she could help.

Matt muttered, "Fuck," then stomped down the hall again.

Chad's mouth ceased moving and he fell limp, but his lovely blue-gray eyes kept staring. And staring.

Kate sidled closer to the door. *What if his niece and nephew never come? What if he's imagined this whole thing? What if,* she thought, meeting Chad's dead gaze again, *what if he kills me too?*

"They aren't here yet," Matt snarled, returning to the living room. "But they're coming. I know they're coming."

He knelt beside the body and pulled the gun through the dead man's clenched hand. He slid the clip from the gun, checked it, and pushed it back in. "How about a blow job while we wait?"

Kate shook her head. "I... I don't think so."

"You're no use to me, then," he said, then shot her.

FAWKES HAD JUST RUNG another doorbell when his, and Garrel's, cell phones rang. He clicked on the call. "Fawkes. Whatcha got?"

"Hit on your kids," Wanda from the radio room said.

"Madison County, heading southwest on Cumming road toward Highway 92. Local Sheriff en route to intercept."

Fawkes turned and trotted down the icy steps, Garrel following. "They on foot?"

"No. A blue Willys Jeep Pickup. Owned and driven by a Genevieve Waters of rural Madison County. We've texted your partner her ID info and plate number, but—"

Shit, it's slick. Fawkes slowed to keep his balance. "But I doubt many blue Willys Jeeps are evading the Madison County Sheriff. We're on our way."

"She's fifty-two. Widowed. Lives on a farm near Badger Creek State Park," Garrel said, trotting past Fawkes. "No warrants, no priors." She climbed in their DMPD SUV and slammed her door before reaching for the radio.

Fawkes slid behind the wheel, flipped on his lights and siren, then dropped the SUV into gear while Garrel said into the radio mic, "Unit 462, Code 3 to last location of missing juveniles."

"Copy, G," dispatch replied as they screamed out of the neighborhood. "Pursuit in progress for blue Jeep. Host county's been notified of your approach and will update you directly. Shift to—"

"I know the channel," Garrel said and they barreled toward the interstate listening to updates on the pursuit of Ms. Waters' Jeep on Highway 92.

———

"No one's seen us." Jake huddled low with Meg in the drifts behind a mass of bushes.

Meg heard police sirens to the right. "Are they coming after Ginnie? Is she gonna be okay?"

"Yeah, she's trying to draw them off, and I don't know what'll happen. She's smart. It'll be okay."

He shoved Meg downward as the car following them approached from the north. She and her brother held still until the car turned onto the highway and followed Ginnie.

The sirens came closer, growing louder, then Sheriff and Winterset Police SUVs flew past, sirens screaming and lights flashing.

"Stay down, stay still," Jake whispered in her ear. "Folks at the farm over there are looking to see what's going on."

So they waited while time stretched and the sirens grew softer and turned north again.

"I don't hear Ginnie anymore," Jake sighed, his head turning toward the fading sirens, "and the neighbors have gone inside. It's okay to get up now."

Will they arrest her? Meg thought.

Jake looked to the southeast, toward where her father lived, and he sighed. "Probably."

It's not fair.

"Maybe not," he said, "but she knew taking us in was risky." He turned to Meg and wiped her tears away with his un-bandaged fingers. "And she knew helping us today was riskier still. She wanted to do it, Meg. Maybe to make up for losing her kids." He took her hand and clambered back to the road. "I dunno. It's complicated."

"Ginnie had kids?" Meg asked.

"Yeah, husband too, but they all died in an accident a long time ago. She's still angry, but I think we helped. I hope we did."

The highway was clear, so they trotted across and said little as they walked south down Quail Ridge Trail.

FAWKES DROVE in the far left lane of I-35, listening to the Madison County dispatcher update the northbound pursuit of Genevieve Waters on dirt roads, followed by an announcement of a pileup on Interstate 35, both directions, at the North River bridge.

"We'd better take the Cumming exit," Garrel said, examining the GPS map on her phone. "Between the pileup and her northerly track, we'll miss her if we take 92."

Fawkes muttered, "Shit," and moved right. Thankfully other drivers made room. He pulled off the interstate and sped west, lights and sirens blazing.

The road turned south about two miles later, then west again while dispatch updated the pursuit to northbound Cumming Road and reminded them the suspect was a fifty-two-year-old woman with no warrants, no priors, and only one registered firearm—a shotgun.

Fawkes nodded when Garrel glanced his way. They were heading toward the pursuit and, with luck, they'd intercept and block her escape.

"They certainly plow a lot better out here," Garrel said as they flew down the county highway.

Fawkes eased into a slightly southward curve. "Less traffic to compact it all down."

About half a mile ahead, a bright baby-blue pickup fishtailed off of the highway onto an unplowed road, creating a

plume of snow and barely slowing, with three law enforcement vehicles a hundred yards or so behind.

"There she goes!" Garrel said, pointing, and Fawkes
turned hard to follow the pack northbound onto Badger
Creek Road. A zig, a zag, the Willys gaining a little distance
from its pursuers, yet all four vehicles followed.

"Did you see?" Garrel asked. "She turned left again!"

"I see," he said, as the lead Sheriff SUV slowed then
followed her. "I think it's a driveway."

Garrel checked her tablet. "What the hell? She's taking
us home."

───────────

GINNIE SKIDDED to a stop in front of her porch and clambered out of the Willys, slamming its door and trotting to her
front steps as Sheriff Jackson pulled into her driveway with
his siren wailing and lights flashing.

She got to the porch and turned to sit on the top step, as
steady as she could considering her heart was beating
roughly three-million beats a minute, and she placed her
hands on her head as Sheriff Jackson stopped behind her
truck and the rest of the posse flowed into her property like
squawking chickens heading to the food pan. Lady trotted
up to her and snuggled, thumping her tail.

"Hey, Paul," Ginnie said, her voice more out-of-breath
than she wanted, when he stepped out of his SUV. "I know
it's Christmas, but you didn't need to come all the way out
here."

"What the hell you up to, Ginnie?" he asked. The three

other cars parked, two flanking his, and the DMPD in front of her Willys. "You've about scared the shit outta all of us."

"Didn't mean to. And you didn't need to chase me."

"You didn't need to run!"

Guess you have me there, she thought, shrugging.

The remaining deputies and police stepped out of their vehicles, and she knew every one of them by name except for the skinny middle-aged guy and the thirty-something dark-haired gal from Des Moines. The young deputy in the back of the posse pulled his gun but didn't point it at her. Yet. Lady trotted down the steps and over to Deputy Lassert, looking to get petted. He brought his family out to pick apples in her pasture every fall, and Lady loved playing with his kids.

Newbie Deputy's hands twitched and Ginnie sucked in a breath. *He'd better not shoot my dog. That'd evaporate every ounce of my neighborliness.*

She nodded hello to everyone. "Look, I know I was driving too fast, and probably too reckless, so if you all wanna give me a ticket or three, you can get back to chasing meth dealers and wife beaters."

"Where's your shotgun?" the Sheriff asked.

"On the wall in the living room, same as always," Ginnie said, shrugging her head toward her front door. "But I know my rights and you're gonna need a warrant to go in there, or in any of my property, including my truck. I'll stay right here until you get it, if it's all the same to you."

"You got any more guns on you or in the house?" Deputy Lassert asked, kneeling slightly to pet Lady who licked his face.

"No, I do not, Steve. Just the one I use on coyotes,

weasels, and coons who wanna get at my chickens. How's Mary and the kids?"

"They're good, Miss Ginnie. But we're here for—"

"Is my tail light out again?" she asked him, trying not to look over at the two from Des Moines approaching her truck, kind-eyed skinny guy with his hand on his gun and fussbudget gal tapping on her tablet computer. "Just got it fixed last month."

Lassert said, "It's not—"

"We got a call saying you had two kids in your truck, two kids whose mother got murdered a couple of days ago," Sheriff Jackson said, standing in front of her.

"Ain't no kids in my truck," Ginnie said, "and I got nothing to do with any murder."

"I notice you neglected to mention you had nothing to do with missing kids," the guy from Des Moines said. He glanced at the woman with the tablet, then turned his gaze to the Sheriff. "There's a new My Little Pony toy on the passenger side floor."

The Sheriff took the two steps to the truck and peered inside. "Yep, there it is. Save us all some time and open the truck, Ginnie."

She sighed, but kept her hands on her head and tried not to look at the deputy with his gun out. "Oh, it's unlocked, Paul. I broke the door lock button on that side back in, shit, '98?" She shrugged. "I dunno for sure."

"You giving us permission to search your vehicle?" Sheriff Jackson asked.

"Nope. We'll just wait for that warrant." She turned her attention to the twitchy-handed Deputy watching Lady sniff the men in her yard. "So help me, Josh, I know you're scared of dogs, but if you shoot my Lady, I'll talk to your mama myself. No one here is causing any trouble, so put that damned thing away before you hurt somebody."

"She's a nice dog," Lassert said. "Aren't you, Lady?" He tapped his fingers and she trotted right back to him.

"So, about those traffic tickets," Ginnie said. "I'm figuring one for speeding, one failure to yield, and at least one bullshit fine for, I dunno, improper driving in adverse road conditions or something. That sound about right to you, Sheriff?"

"Rachel saw you with the kids, Ginnie, and you ran. Where are they?"

"I don't know where any kids are," she said, staring into his eyes.

The statement is technically true, she told herself. *I know where they were, and I know where they're going. Where they are, though... I have no idea. Not specifically, at least.*

"Got a property search warrant from the State of Iowa," all-business-with-a-tablet said. She gave Ginnie a hard smile and handed her tablet to Sheriff Jackson. "Murder and kidnapping cases tend to bring out some urgency and we'd already interrupted the Magistrate's Christmas breakfast while we were still on the interstate."

She gave Ginnie a bright smile. "So. You want to unlock your front door, or do we need to kick it in?"

Honey, I'd eat my shoes if you could kick in my door, Ginnie thought staring at the detective, but said, "This ain't the big city. The door's unlocked."

The sheriff entered first, followed by the two out-of-town detectives while Deputy Lassert waited with Ginnie and Lady on the porch.

"What'd you do, Miss Ginnie?" he asked.

"Only thing I could." She sighed and looked up at him. "I haven't hurt anybody, and I'm not resisting anything. Y'all take your time and do whatever needs doing. However your chips fall, I'm good. Honest. And I hope you and your family have a good Christmas."

She smiled and resumed looking out at her yard, then lifted one hand from her head to wave at the Glaxneys coming up her driveway.

TWENTY SEVEN

FAWKES LEFT GARREL TO TAKE PHOTOS OF THE EVIDENCE AND walked out to the front porch where the Deputy who'd been watching the suspect had his back to her while dealing with an irate woman in the driveway. A middle-aged man—Fawkes assumed him to be the woman's husband—stood beside the Buick's driver's-side door, shaking his head.

Genevieve "Ginnie" Waters could have wandered off or caused trouble, yet she sat in the same spot, with her hands still on her head. She turned to see Fawkes and she smiled. "Welcome, Detective, and it's nice to meet you. There's hot coffee in the pot, and clean cups in the cupboard just left of it. Help yourself."

"Who's she?" Fawkes asked, nodding toward the driveway.

"Snoopy pain in my ass," Ginnie said. "She chased me. I got scared, so I came back home. I'm guessing she called you guys."

"How does that explain the three sets of dirty breakfast dishes, Christmas wrapping paper with tags marked Meg and Jake, packaging from a variety of gifts and candy, a twin-sized bed and a couch that've been recently slept in, and the toy in your truck? One that just happens to match plastic packaging in your kitchen garbage?"

"You're the detective. You tell me."

He settled onto the step beside her and sighed, clasping his gloved hands together between his knees. "I think you found them, kept them warm and fed them, and I think you helped them do whatever it was they'd decided to do."

She moved one hand from her head and wiped her eyes. "I gather you're good at your job."

She cared about them. Bought them presents. Kept them safe.

"Usually," he admitted.

"Am I under arrest?"

That's the key with her, I think. Safety.

He hid his smile. "Depends. Did you take them somewhere safe?"

"No," she said, nodding her head toward the woman arguing with the deputy. "Was going to, but I had to leave them in a ditch, to keep them the hell away from that nosy-ass bitch. They've had enough troubles without her making it worse."

Fawkes turned his gaze to the argument and stood. "Do you know where Jake and Meg are going?"

Ginnie looked up at him. "What are you going to do with them if I tell you?"

He took two steps down toward the yard before turning back to her. "There are some bad people after them, so protective custody to keep them safe. Maybe witness protection, if I can swing it with the Feds."

Then he, too, walked away, leaving her to sit on the steps alone.

The husband told the wife to get in the car, but the woman continued trying to convince the deputy to tell her what had happened to those criminal kids Ginnie was hiding.

"Who are you?" Fawkes asked.

"Rachel Glaxney," the woman said, extending her hand.

Fawkes stared at her but did not accept the handshake offer. Instead, he pulled out his note pad.

Mrs. Glaxney pursed her lips and pulled back her hand before nodding toward Ginnie. "I saw her, last night, buying two large pizzas and a bunch of kid-junk at Casey's in VanMeter. She said they were collectibles, but I knew better." She glanced at her husband then added, "And I was right, wasn't I? She had those criminal kids from the news."

"Did you report all of this last night?"

"No," she said, "because Ginnie's half crazy, living out here all alone, taking in strays and..."

"And?" he asked.

"And tending a piece of trash out in Orilla."

"So, how'd you decide Ms. Waters was hiding the two juveniles?"

"Saw them in her truck," she said, head held high as she gazed past him to Ginnie. "Boy and a girl. Recognized them from TV. They looked right at me."

"Did either of these juveniles appear to be in danger?"

"Well, she was driving awful fast."

"Before or after you saw them, Mrs. Glaxney?"

"After," he husband called out. "Rachel made me chase them. She's had a toot for Ginnie ever since—"

"Brad!" Mrs. Glaxney barked at him. "You hush."

"Ever since what, Mr. Glaxney?"

Brad Glaxney swallowed. "Ever since Ginnie started dating Craig in high school." He glanced at his wife. "All the girls liked Craig. Even Rachel."

Mrs. Glaxney let out a huff of air. "Dangit, Brad."

Fawkes merely shook his head. "So, let me get this straight. You called us because a woman, what, thirty-some years ago, dated a boy you liked in high school and she—"

"*Dated?*" Brad Glaxney asked. "Ginnie *married* him. They had three kids." He looked at his wife. "I know I wasn't your first choice, Rachel, but Craig was sweet on Ginnie clear back in fifth grade. You were never—"

"I told you to hush," she hissed.

"Mr. Glaxney, did you see the juveniles leave Mrs. Waters' truck?"

"No, sir," he said. "I was too busy trying to keep the car on the road to pay too much attention to Ginnie. She was a good half mile or so ahead of us, maybe more, when we got to 92."

Half a mile lead would give her time to drop them somewhere out of sight, Fawkes noted.

"Thank you for your information. If we have any other questions, we'll contact you." Fawkes closed his notebook. "You're free to go."

Mrs. Glaxney protested, but the deputy herded her toward the car and ordered her to leave.

As they drove off, the deputy said, "There's been bad blood between those two as far back as I can remember, but it's been mostly one-sided. Ginnie'd never hurt anybody. She just wants to be left alone."

"Would she take in two lost kids?"

"Yep. Without a second thought, and she'd treat them like they were her own."

"Okay. Can you get her loaded into my truck? Tell her she's not under arrest, but we need to run some info by her. Have her look at some pictures and make an official statement, ask a few questions, then we'll bring her home. I'll square it with Sheriff Jackson."

"Sure thing," the deputy said, following.

"You go on with him. We just want to make sure Jake and Meg are okay," Fawkes said as he passed Ginnie and headed into the house.

He found the Sheriff easily enough and quickly explained the outside events. "I need to find those kids before a hired killer does. She's the only one who can help us, so we're gonna take a little drive, all right? See if we can figure out where she hid them. If you need to charge her with anything, I'll bring her back to your station, once we have the kids secured."

"All right," the Sheriff said. "She's right, you know. She had control of her vehicle and no one was hurt, so all I have on her is a fleeing pursuit charge—which likely won't stick since she stopped here and waited for us—and a few traffic tickets. She's all yours. Go find those kids."

Fawkes looked across the living room and into the kitchen. "Where's my partner?"

"She went out on the back porch to make a call."

Fawkes nodded his thanks and walked through the kitchen and laundry room to see Garrel texting a 312-area-code-number, her back to the door.

He didn't recognize the number. *Certainly isn't anyone in*

the office or her husband or close family, since they all live in the
Des Moines metro. Maybe a hospital? Maybe—
  He paused.
  I attended a forensic seminar in Chicago the summer before
last. The hotel... Shit.
  He flipped to the inside cover of his notebook and pulled
out Malcolm Grant's business card, offices in Chicago, Los
Angeles, Manhattan, and Washington.
  Malcolm Grant's cell number matched the one on
Garrel's phone.
  What the holy fuck?!
  Fawkes took a calming breath before pulling his phone
from his pocket, still wearing the gloves he's put on before
searching Ginnie's house. He took a picture through the
window of Garrel and her text messages as evidence in case
she had an opportunity to delete the conversation, then he
pocketed the phone, grabbed his cuffs, and shoved the back
door open, nearly knocking his partner of four years off her
feet.
  "What the hell?" she asked, shoving the phone in her
pocket. "Didn't you see me? What happened?"
  "I saw you," he said. He grabbed her, cuffed her wrist,
and spun her toward the wall.
  "Les! What are you doing?"
  Despite her struggles, he leaned against her and dragged
her hands behind her. "How much have you told him?" he
asked as he clicked the second cuff closed.
  She peered at him with her one eye not mashed against
the wall. "Told who what?"
  Still leaning against her, he removed her phone from her
coat pocket and clicked it on. He held the screen so she

could see her texts saying the kids had been left in a rural area between Badger Creek State Park and Patterson, Iowa, and they were traveling on foot. "SynAg's sleazy lawyer where our kids are."

"I can explain," she said as he pulled her away from the wall and guided her through the laundry room and into the kitchen.

"I'm sure you can. I bet the chief would like to hear why their damned assassin always seemed to get to the kids before we did, how no matter the evidence you always insisted Jake killed his mother, how—"

"How they promised to fix Noah after their ag chemicals in our water and maybe our food somehow screwed him up," Garrel said.

Fawkes led her into the living room. "You do that by suing the bastards, not going to bed with them."

The Sheriff and deputies turned to look at him. "I need an evidence bag," he said. "And someone to deliver her to our Chief. I'll fill him in before she gets there."

The Sheriff held open an evidence bag and Fawkes dropped Garrel's phone and tablet into it.

"Josh!" the Sheriff said, "Take this suspect and evidence to Des Moines PD's Homicide Chief."

The young deputy took Garrel by the arm and started toward the front door, but she struggled, looking back at Fawkes. "Les, please, don't! I did it to save my baby!"

He shook his head and turned back to the Sheriff while Garrel was taken away. "I'm going to try to find the Adamson kids, assuming that assassin isn't already out here looking for them, too." Then he walked out to the front porch and Ginnie, still sitting there, this time with her hands in her lap, ignoring the deputy who tried to convince her to leave with Fawkes.

Enough of this bullshit. "Come with me," Fawkes demanded on his way past her.

She stood but went no farther. "Why is Josh taking the other detective away?"

Fawkes paused and stared out to the snow before turning back to her. "Because she's been in contact with the company that... that made them like they are. Do you know how the kids are?"

She took one step down. "Yeah. They're cursed, because of some chemical accident."

"I need to find them before SynAg's hired assassin does. And I need *your* help to do it, or he'll kill them. I won't force you to help me, but the quicker we find them, the quicker we'll get them away from the assassin, the quicker they'll be safe."

Ginnie followed him to his SUV without saying another word.

HUEY IMMEDIATELY STARTED BRAKING when wind-shear, ice, and too many tired holiday drivers had sent a minivan and a sedan well ahead of him against a guardrail. The minivan crunched and remained, but the sedan bounced back into traffic and hit the front end of a carload of college kids who spun out of control and side-swiped a hatchback, then a semi avoiding the whole mess swerved to miss them surged across the median, flipping onto its side just past the bridge into oncoming traffic, causing more chaos over there. He lost count of how many other crunched vehicles lay scattered on either side. He stopped without much trouble as most everyone ahead of him eased to a halt, then was rear-ended by a family on their way to Grandma's in Kansas City. Like a domino, he plowed right into the middle-aged couple in front of him who had also managed to stop on time, and they bashed a Nissan, someone ahead of them tried to pull sideways to avoid the car-dominoes but ended up sending the destruction in another direction, and so on.

He'd exchanged total-counterfeit-bullshit insurance information with everyone his truck had touched, then, completely blocked in, watched law enforcement and rescue personnel attend the injured and stuck. Nothing except ambulances and a few cars near the front left the area for more than half an hour as time—and his plan—slipped away.

Once freed from the vehicle quagmire, he ground his teeth and sped down the off-ramp, trying to make up lost time.

Four miles to Patterson then through town and south, following the instructions he'd jotted down the night before. When he made the turn west as Terrace became Quail Ridge Trail, he thought he saw a flash of brilliant green far ahead, moving south. Then it was gone to drifts and hills and gently falling snow.

Huey slowed, checking the address markers at the end of every driveway; it'd be a shame to kill the wrong people, after all. He saw a bright flash half a mile to the west and flinched at the brilliant green-white fire, then managed to stay on the road when the snow-and-debris-filled shockwave threatened to shove him and his pickup into the ditch.

TWENTY EIGHT

MEG LOOKED UP AS JAKE PAUSED AT THE END OF A DRIVEWAY. "This is the address," he said, his breath pluming as he looked at a trailer house and a couple of vehicles. "Nobody's home, though."

"Then let's go back to Ginnie's."

"No. Please stop whining about it." He turned into the driveway and started walking toward the trailer house and a barking dog, somewhere ahead.

She fell in behind him and tried to keep her thoughts to herself.

"Maybe he went to town," Jake said as they walked up rows of tire tracks to where a truck that said *Chad's Towing Service* and a dented Kia were parked. "Or a Christmas party or something."

He reached a deck missing a full section of railing then glanced back and her and motioned for her to follow.

"If nobody's home, what are we gonna do?" she asked. "What if they went on vacation or—"

"The tire tracks are fresh," he said as he climbed the deck's steps.

She stood before the bottom of the steps. "We can't just sit here in the snow. You'll freeze."

"Then maybe we can wait inside," he said, using his hands to make a tunnel around his eyes so he could see through the front door window. "Surely it'll be okay if we don't touch—"

He squawked, scrambling back, but the door burst open and Matt stood in the doorway with a gun in his hand, his head covered in foil and a big black pot with ragged holes drilled in it for his eyes.

"Hold still so I don't miss," he said, but, a moment before the shot rang out, Jake tripped over his own feet and flipped backward off the deck where the railing used to be.

Meg covered her mouth with her hands as her brother landed hard on his back in the snow. He groaned but barely moved, and Meg took a step toward him, halting when Matt turned the gun toward her.

"It's us!" she cried, holding her hands out in front of her. "Uncle Matty, it's us!"

"Of course it's you," he said, "been waiting for you and your brother to show up. This is either gonna go easy, or it's gonna go hard. But you are gonna make me a *lot* of money."

"No," she said, taking a step back, but paused as he pointed the gun at her.

"They only want your brother," he said. "They're offering a million bucks, Meggy! Your mother wouldn't listen to reason, so she had to go. Don't make me do the same to you."

Oh, Mom!

"How could you?! She was your sister!" Meg screamed, looking up at her uncle in the doorway of her father's trailer.

"A million reasons, Meggy," Matt said, drawing her attention to his face again. "I just want to shoot him in the leg so he can't run. Just his leg. Won't hardly hurt at all"

"A brother's supposed to protect his little sister!" she yelled back.

"Not when there's money on the—"

Meg saw his trigger finger twitch and she scrambled away, away from Jake and past the barking dog tied to the shed toward the back of the house. She heard Matt holler, "You goddamned bitch!" and stumble down the stairs after her, but she kept running.

"Get your ass back here!"

She rounded the corner of the house as a shot rang out, and heard a metallic ping off the siding behind her. Still, she ran, hearing him follow, and she rounded the next corner and skidded to a halt when she saw three bodies in the snow, a woman impaled with deck railing, another shot in the head, and a nearly-nude man with a book in his chest. His eyes stared straight at her. Even cloudy and dead, his dusty-blue eyes looked like hers. "Daddy?" she gasped, feeling fresh tears, then she screamed as a bullet grazed through the side of her butt and speckled her father's dead face with her blood.

Hurts hurts hurts! She stumbled forward and tripped, falling face-first onto the bodies, but she grabbed the deck rail and shoved herself up again. Beside her knee, she saw a cell phone half out of the woman's sweatpants pocket.

She grabbed the phone, clutched it to her chest, and *pushed* her pain and anger and terror into it until it glowed white-hot, then turned to see her uncle only a few feet behind her, his gun pointed at her head.

"Goodbye, Meggy," he said, but she thrust the phone toward him and *pushed* again.

The screen exploded to shower him with green sparks and lightning. He fell backward in the snow, jerking and screaming at the lightning sizzling over him.

Meg dropped the phone and scrambled to the back steps and up into the house, limped across the blood-splattered living room and out again to Jake who lay dazed and struggling with blood on the side of his head and on the snow

"He's still coming," Jake said, then pointed toward the front door.

Meg turned.

Matt sagged against the doorframe, the gun in his hand and smoke rising from his hair. "He's mine," he said, pointing the gun at Meg. "Mine."

Meg screamed, her vision glowing and covered in electrical sparks, before the shot rang out. The bullet deflected, then another, both flying somewhere far to her left, away from her, away from Jake. She took a step toward her uncle, still screaming, then leaned forward, shoving the sparkling green at him, shoving and shoving and shoving while the world around her felt like it *heaved.*

When she sucked in a breath and blinked the green away, the trailer was gone, everything had flung against the fence except for a pipe spewing water out of the ground and a broken hunk of conduit and wire.

Matt sprawled mid-way up the rubble, unmoving, his clothes partly ripped off and his body covered in scorched lightning tracks.

Meg huffed out her fury and turned to Jake who lay flat on his back in the snow then rolled to his side. "Ah, dangit," Meg said, limping to him. "I'm sorry, I—" She heard a vehicle approach and, snarling, spun on her heel.

A pickup truck pulled into the driveway. She recognized the driver and green sparks slid over her vision again. "It's *him*."

TWENTY NINE

"Holy fucking shit."

Huey paused at the end of the drive, engine idling.

Meg stood about thirty feet away beside a mobile-home foundation, her sparking hands balled at her sides and green-white lightning flickering from her eyes despite what looked like tears coursing down her cheeks. Jake managed to sit behind her in the snow, holding his head. Past Jake, a garage had been flattened, part of it wrapped around a tree, and a chained dog cowered, looking at the mashed garage. Fifty, maybe seventy feet to Huey's left, shreds of a mobile home had crumpled against a fence, some of it flung into the snowy field beyond.

Matt lay in the rumpled rubble, barely moving but alive.

Only need one, Huey thought, watching Meg as he hopped out of the truck.

"I'm unarmed! I just want to talk!" he called out, his palms up before him.

She leaned forward and screamed, "No!!" Sparking current crackled toward him like lightning across the surface of the snow. He jumped away from the snow-lightning as his pickup flipped over, front-end over tailgate, and landed somewhere in the field across the street.

Huey pushed himself to his feet, helpless to gaze upon Meg's brilliant fury, the beauty of her, the impossible perfection of looking at a blazing star, a green dwarf, so close before him. "I want *him!*" he yelled, pointing toward her uncle, but Meg never shifted her sparking gaze.

"Get out!" she snarled.

"I will take *him*, take the man who killed your mother, and you will never see me or him again! I swear!"

Her head lowered and her breath plumed green-white and electric.

Huey took a step toward her, helpless, his boots crunching through the snow's wet-ice top layer, his hands out and open. "I will take *him* to the men who made you, and I will kill them *for you*. Avenge your mother *for you!* I swear! I only want *him*."

"You wanted Jake," she snarled.

"Not anymore." He dropped to his knees before her. "They've wronged me too. Threatened to kill the one I love, just like they did to you, so let me do this, this *one thing*. I will make them pay for what they've done, and you will never see me again."

She took a step toward him, then another. She snarled, growing ever brighter. He felt static electricity crawl over him and every hair on his body stood up.

Meg drew her hands back. Electrical fire erupted there like twin suns. "You lie!"

"He's telling the truth," Jake said. "Don't murder him. Please, Meg. That's not who we are."

A vicious tingle burned through Huey and dragged him to his feet, then higher, his toes not-quite-touching anything but air. Then the tingle disappeared, leaving an empty ache behind as he dropped and stumbled to keep his footing on ice-coated snow.

"Please, Meg," Jake said. "Matt harmed us, not him. He wants money, yeah, but he also wants revenge. Like us."

Meg Adamson stared at Huey, her furious gaze lit afire, while her brother begged her for his life.

"Take my uncle," she said at last. "Take him and never come back."

Huey walked across the snow to Matt and pulled him from the wreckage then pressed an injector of Propofol against his neck. He grabbed one of Matt's wrists and dragged him across the snow while Meg watched and, behind her, Jake managed to stand.

Huey looked across the street at his upside-down truck. "I need a car."

"Fine," Meg snarled, flicking her gaze to the Kia. Its ignition turned, then caught. Sounded like a cylinder was missing, but beggars couldn't be choosers.

Huey dragged Matt to the car, watching Meg step backward while remaining between him and her brother. She appeared dimmer, diminished, when he reached the car. He shoved Matt into the back seat and slammed the door.

Far away, he heard a police siren.

"Thank you," he said to her before sliding behind the wheel. He put the car in reverse and, with one final glance, backed to the road. It took him a few moments to pull his duffle from the truck then he sped away, heading toward West Des Moines.

FAWKES PULLED into the driveway Ginnie had directed him to then stopped. Meg slumped to her knees in the snow, weeping and her hair steaming, while, beyond her, Jake staggered forward. A garage looked bulldozed, and a mobile home lay broken and smashed against a fence far to his left.

"Stay here," Fawkes said before exiting the vehicle and taking a few steps toward Jake. The side of the boy's head was bloody.

Fawkes pulled his phone and dialed Sheriff Jackson. "Ted, we found the kids and need an ambulance at Chad Lyton's place. The boy's injured. Not sure about the girl yet." He glanced over at Meg as she slumped face-first to the ground. "Yeah, she's hurt too."

Sheriff Jackson promised the ambulance was on the way, so Fawkes clicked off the call and looked up to see Jake watching him.

"What took you so long to figure this out?" the boy asked. "I left messages."

"What messages?"

The boy began blinking erratically. "Matt," he said, the blinks pausing then starting again, "killed," another pause then more blinks, "her. I told you while we were at QuikTrip, but you still let him go?"

Fuck. Morse Code. How'd we miss that?

"You don't know Morse Code."

"No," Fawkes said, "but..." He shook his head.

"But your partner did. Didn't she?" Jake paused. "And she worked for *them*. Shit. No wonder..." He looked past Fawkes and smiled.

Fawkes turned around to see Ginnie cradling Meg in the driveway, cooing at her and smoothing her hair while the girl clutched at her and bawled.

So much for her staying in the car.

"You've never harmed anyone, have you?" Fawkes asked Jake.

"No. I witness far too much pain, anger, and suffering every moment of every day. I won't add to it. Not unless I have to save someone I love. I... I tried to save my mom, but..."

"It's okay. I know."

Jake nodded and Fawkes asked, "Where's your uncle?"

"On his way to SynAg," the boy said. "Huey's going to kill them. They threatened his family, so he's going to kill them all because they threatened to skin Warren alive." Then he staggered to Ginnie who drew him down and into her embrace.

Fawkes watched them a few moments then called Jacqui.

HUEY DROVE down the interstate toward SynAg's gated community in West Des Moines but instead of heading west on Grand, he turned east and found an empty parking lot off of Grand Ridge and parked with the Kia's trunk facing nothing but fields and snow.

The car running, he popped the trunk then hauled Matt, unconscious, from the back seat, then flung him, face-down, into the trunk, and unfastened his jeans. Huey pulled them down to below Matt's ass, then returned to the back seat for the duffle bag. He pulled out two 3/4 pound tubes of bisoxadiazole, wired each to blasting caps and remote detona-tors, then molded the whole mess against Matt's ass and balls. He returned Matt's tidy-whities and jeans to their orig-inal location, slapped some cuffs on him, slammed him in the trunk, and crammed the duffle beneath the passenger seat.

Fourteen minutes and three hand-washes at a gas station later, Huey stopped at the gated community's guard shack and told the guard, "Package for Malcolm Grant."

The guard squinted at him and the crappy old car he drove, but Huey merely smiled. "Call him, if you don't believe me. Tell him I'm completing my contract and I want my money."

The guard picked up the landline phone and, a minute or so later, the gate opened.

Huey drove through, still smiling, and nodded hello to the well-dressed, middle-aged fellow on the stoop with a goon standing on either side of him and probably a couple more in the house.

"Had a few complications," Huey said as he climbed out of Kate's car, "but a contract is a contract." He opened the trunk to show Matt laying there, cuffed, battered, bloody, and unconscious.

"The cuffs are lead," Huey lied. "Makes it harder for him to slip free. I suggest, though, you give him a shot of narcotics whenever he starts to come around. Just to be sure."

"We requested Jake—"

"Jake died trying to protect his sister. But Matt here can sneak into anyplace and steal anything you want. Observe *anything* you want. Can't you, Matty?" he said, patting Matt's leg. "He can put in hidden cameras or recording devices or, well, pretty much handle whatever corporate espionage your little black hearts desire."

"We're not paying three million for Matt Adamson."

"That's too bad."

He paused and stared at Grant. "I know you don't have Warren. And you probably know I know, because that's how this shit works, right? It's just like I know you're less worried about the Senate hearing next week than you are your billion-dollar transaction with China. But that slippery shit," he said, pointing at the trunk, "is the last Adamson with the chromosome you need to sell to the Chinese for whatever fucking reason they want to mutate their own people. So you can pay me the agreed price, or I'll find someone who will. Russians. Saudis. Kim Jung what's-his-nut in North Korea. Money's all the same to me."

He slammed the trunk and walked to the driver's side door and opened it.

"Wait," Grant said. He nodded to the goon on his right who tapped his ear and spoke quietly into his watch. The big man waited, scowling at his watch, then nodded.

"Three million. Sent to your account in the Caymans."

"Let me confirm," Huey said, checking his account on the iPhone Warren had set up for their new identities. The money had indeed arrived.

"I'd like to say it's been a pleasure doing business with you," Huey said as he unlocked the trunk again and flung it open, "but I'd be lying. And lying to customers is bad business."

He dragged Matt from the trunk and dropped him onto frosty concrete then tossed a zip-up pouch of filled syringes.

"He's all yours. Inject him with one of those every two hours until you have him in a secure facility," he said, closing the trunk. "Thank you for using Rawlins Security Specialists and give me a call if you need any more exterminations or acquisitions."

Then he got in the car and drove off, glancing in the rearview mirror to see the goons carry Matt and his hidden surprise into the house. Grant followed them in.

He waved goodbye to the gate guard and drove just past the front gate to a swanky gas station. Once he had the nozzle in the tank and the gas flowing, he checked his phone and smiled at Warren's message that he was just fine and waiting. Huey replied he was on his way.

He then swiped left and whispered, "Slip this, asshole," then tapped the screen twice. A fireball rose from the executive compound, then another, and, far away, sirens wailed. He felt a slight tremor beneath his feet and smiled.

Huey watched the fireball with quiet glee. *That should take care of it.*

Still smiling, he finished filling his tank and drove to Warren.

Bright and early on the morning of January second, Ginnie sat on her porch, waiting, Lady by her side. A Des Moines PD SUV pulled in her driveway on time, that nice Detective Fawkes driving and a pretty redhead beside him.

Lady woofed and trotted down the steps. Ginnie followed as the vehicle eased to a stop and the redhead stepped out.

"So nice to see you again," Jacqui Glees said, offering her hand.

Ginnie accepted it with a grin. "My pleasure, Ma'am."

Detective Fawkes opened the back doors of his vehicle and the kids clambered over each other to get out. Jacqui stepped back, laughing, as both ran to Ginnie, nearly knocking her over.

She hugged them and held them and laughed at Lady jumping at them, her tail wagging like mad.

She looked over Jake's head to Detective Fawkes who watched them with a slight smile in his warm eyes.

"What else do you need from us, Detective?" she asked. "Did the paperwork all go through?"

"Yeah," he said as Jacqui dug in her purse. "It's all done."

"Our cards are in here," Jacqui said as she handed over an envelope. "You call if you need *anything*."

Ginnie hugged the kids, *her* kids again, kissed their heads, then let them go. "I think we'll be just fine."

"I'm sure you will," Detective Fawkes said, and he nodded goodbye.

Jake pulled away from her and turned. "How can we thank you?" he asked.

Fawkes paused, his head down for a moment, then smiled at Jake. "Mind your mom."